Mr Landen

Raised by wolves, Steph[...] [...]
Pennine Shangri-la, Sheffield. Like all the town's
inhabitants, he is immortal.

Over the years, he's unearthed numerous people
stupid enough to employ him as a graphic artist and
mural designer. But his first love is unemployment, to
which he one day hopes to return.

The power of invisibility is his to use as he sees fit.
Semi-retired, he spends his days entertaining visitors by
playing piano in the style of Mrs Mills while pondering
the mysteries of this and other worlds.

BY STEPHEN WALKER

Danny Yates Must Die
Mr Landen Has No Brain

Voyager

mr landen
has no brain

Stephen Walker

HarperCollins*Publishers*

Voyager
An Imprint of HarperCollins*Publishers*
77–85 Fulham Palace Road,
Hammersmith, London W6 8JB

www.voyager-books.com

A Paperback Original 2001

1 3 5 7 9 8 6 4 2

A catalogue record for this book
is available from the British Library

ISBN 0 00 648381 X

Typeset in Meridien by
Palimpsest Book Production Limited,
Polmont, Stirlingshire
Printed and bound in Great Britain by
Omnia Books Limited, Glasgow

Acknowledgements

The author would like to express his appreciation of the following:

Lorraine Walker, Harry Walker, Nellie Walker, Ma'amselle Tufty, Battling Dave Murdoch, Sue Farmer, Bendylegs Calhoun, Liz Callaghan, Claire Fielding, Sam Witcherlow, Chris Smith, Lucas LoBlack and Susan Ford.

Dedication

For bunny rabbits.

THE LOVLEY DR RARMA RYDEZ
TO FREEDUM ON HER
BUFFERLOW. R. McDoddy
2006

one

'Quiver, female, for I am Lepus, master of the night, and soon you shall be my rumpy-pumpy boing-boing toy. Carrots. Carrots. Must have carrots.' And the 'master of the night' crashed out of Teena Rama's mobile home, leaving behind a huge, rabbit-shaped hole in the wall.

From where Sally Cooper stood, just inside the front doorway, she could hear him knocking wheelie bins over in his quest for carrots.

Across the room from her, Teena gazed out through the hole and watched his rampage. Still holding the shroud she'd had him hidden under before his grand unveiling, she enthused, 'Is *he* the best boyfriend you've ever seen or what?'

Mobile home? Sally'd been in smaller mansions. 'Teena, he's a rabbit. He's a seven foot, talking rabbit.'

'A super-evolved talking rabbit,' Teena corrected her.

'He referred to me as "female", called me his rumpy-pumpy boing-boing toy—'

1

'Which some would find flattering.'

'–and is more interested in carrots than in me. And you think that's a great boyfriend?'

Teena rolled up the shroud and cast it aside. 'His attitude leaves a little to be desired but whose boyfriend's doesn't?'

'Yours, according to you.'

Teena raised a suggestive eyebrow. 'Sadly not every woman can have a Man Who Does.'

'Just how desperate do you think I am that I'd go out with a giant rabbit?'

'At the risk of sounding insensitive, Sally, you must face facts.'

'What facts?'

'You're not an attractive woman and can't afford to be choosy.'

'Piss off,'

Knuckles on hips, Teena gazed at the floor and smiled bitterly to herself. She was five foot ten, nineteen years old and – according to her – sex on legs. She was wearing cut-off-at-the-knee jeans, and a red vest cut just high enough to bare her pierced navel. If she had hair, Sally'd never seen it. It was hidden beneath the mass of starched polka dot rags that now hung half-obscuring her oh-so-lovely face. Teena said, 'Well, how's *that* for gratitude.'

'Gratitude?' Sally's mind boggled.

Teena looked across at her. Her perfect left hand dragged the polka dot rags away from her perfect face and tucked them behind a perfect ear. 'I slave away during my holiday, super-evolving life forms for you–'

'Life form*s*? Plural?'

'I also have a cockroach and a rubber plant I'd like you to meet.'

'Good God.'

2

'But you throw it all back in my face. Yes, as men go, they're not that great, and in the rubber plant's case it's not all that male, but you have to appreciate that my techniques are not yet perfect. I'd love to create a Brad Pitt for you but I'm no goddess, I have my limitations. I did my best for you and that's all that matters.'

'Teena, for the last time, I'm happy as I am. I don't want you trying to make me boyfriends.'

Teena rolled her eyes in a way that suggested disbelief.

'You really want to help me?' said Sally.

'I only do these things for your benefit.'

'Then repair that hole and recapture that rabbit. Then un-super-evolve it and its mates back to how they should be.'

'But–'

'And if you make one more attempt to find me a boyfriend . . .'

'Yes?'

'I'll kill you.'

Sally slammed the mobile home's front door behind her and stood on its top step, counting every conceivable way of killing Teena. There were a hundred and eighty seven. She looked at her surroundings; the caravans, mobile homes and wailing seagulls that made up Wyndham-on-Sea's largest caravan park. Just nineteen, she was its youngest ever manager. And, apart from one highly noisy resident, there wasn't a soul in sight.

Three days earlier there'd been souls in sight, two of them, when the world's biggest mobile home had pulled into camp, a gleaming white double decker the length of

3

a Eurostar, the sort of thing the Rolling Stones would refuse to take on tour because it was too ostentatious. In the passenger seat, all long limbs and gleaming shark grin, had sat Teena.

The driver was her assistant, Mr Landen, a small man who made *vroom vroom* noises as he drove.

He'd said Teena was the world's greatest scientific prodigy all grown up, engaged and determined to have one last week of dullness before settling down to a life of marital excitement. And this particular stretch of North Yorkshire coastline had struck her as being as dull as they come.

Teena had said she was a total babe. The last four years running, she'd won the *New Scientist* Playmate of the Year Award. And while she didn't approve of such things – they demean women and trivialize their contribution to science – that didn't stop her pulling on her shortest, lowest-cut dress and turning up to collect them.

Now she was out to find Sally a boyfriend. It was to do with pity; it wasn't fair for other women not to share the pleasure she'd found. Teena never used the word love.

Resigned to another five days of the woman, Sally descended the mobile home's three metal steps, turned left and headed for her managerial offices, a low flat roofed building that incorporated her living quarters. On the way, she ignored that one resident in sight, the giant rabbit whose front-half was now trapped in a wheelie bin. For a master of the night it didn't seem too bright but few people in this place did.

She reached her offices and grabbed the door, ready to enter.

But then, reflected in the door's wire-glass, she saw them . . .

. . . the spinning moose heads of Bab's Steakhouse.

'Hello?' Sally stuck her head round the front door. 'Anyone here?'

No reply.

So she entered the dining area and took a look around. The moose heads of Bab's Steakhouse, a low, purple building directly facing Sally's offices, had only spun once before. She hadn't expected to see them spin again before the restaurant's grand opening, which wasn't for another five days.

According to her Uncle Al (the caravan park's owner), when those heads started spinning, the public would gasp in awe at their majesty. No one would be able to resist going in.

But at the try out, as soon as the heads had started up, the antlers had flown out with such force they'd decapitated the grinning shop window dummies meant to represent enthralled bystanders.

When she'd last talked with her uncle, he'd said that after a long and involved search he'd just hired the cook, a sterling woman with a wealth of experience – some of it involving cookery. And, though the steakhouse wasn't technically a part of the caravan park, despite being slap bang in the middle of it, Sally felt she should introduce herself.

But this was the most disturbingly decorated restaurant she'd ever been in. She tugged at one of the chains hanging from the violet ceiling. It rattled. She imagined its manacle around her wrist and pulled an appropriate face.

And what was that by the window? An iron maiden?

Sally pushed open the black, round windowed door

that linked the dining area to the kitchens. 'Hello? Anyone here?'

Still no reply.

She saw a small, white kitchen kept in a state of psychotic tidiness but she saw no cook.

She stepped into the kitchen.

Then someone hit her over the back of the head.

two

'Touch your toes, female, and you shall learn what it is to be brought to ecstasy by a supreme master of love making.'

'Thank you for your generous offer but since I'm an engaged woman and I forgot to give you any genitals, I don't think I'll bother.' Having finally got him back into her mobile home, and out of the wheelie bin, Teena stood Lepus before her. Mr Landen was hugging the rabbit's right leg. He was four foot tall, his flat head was as wide as his shoulders, and he had no neck. His one huge eye and one tiny eye gazed adoringly up at the rabbit as he stroked its leg a little too fondly for her liking. Still, she should have been grateful that someone was taken with the thing.

And perhaps Sally did have a point about Lepus but the situation might yet be saved. She said, 'If you're going to impress Sally into wanting you as a boyfriend–'

'Oh, no, I don't want to be her boyfriend,' said Mr Landen in a voice half Peter Lorre, half childlike, 'I'm happy with my bunny.' And he rubbed his cheek against its fur to prove it.

'I was talking to the "bunny",' she said.

'Oh.' He stroked on.

She told Lepus, 'If you're to be her boyfriend, you'll have to smarten up your act.'

'Smarten up–?'

'No more sexual boasting. And a little more style.'

'Style?'

'Young women like style. It shows a man's more than an animal. And to help you achieve that style, I bought you something to put on your head.'

'Is it a carrot?'

'Generally speaking, wearing a carrot on your head isn't stylish.'

'In rabbit circles, only the king rabbit gets to wear a carrot on the head. The rest of us must watch in envy as, once a week, he parades before us beneath his carrot.'

'How quaint. But I think you should settle for this.' From behind her back, she produced the black fedora she'd been hiding.

He studied it, nonplussed. 'And what is this?' He sniffed at it.

'It's a fedora.'

He nibbled its edges.

She said, 'If you want to be a master of the night, you could wear that and a monocle, and perhaps carry a silvertipped cane. Let's see how it fits.' She stepped forward, yanked it from him, made sure the nibbled side faced the back and, stretching on tiptoes, attempted to place it on his head at just the right tilt.

'Run, bunny, run!' Mr Landen urged. 'She's trying to strangle you!' And, half barging the startled rabbit over he pushed it toward the closet in the far wall.

Teena watched them flee. 'Mr Landen, you can't strangle someone with a hat.'

Half pushed, half running, Lepus said, 'Quiver, female, quiver, for I am heading for a cupboard.'

'Mr Landen?' she asked still holding the hat.

They ran into the closet.

They slammed the door.

And she heard them lock it from the inside.

Then there was silence.

She watched the closet door, baffled. If she hadn't known Landen was Britain's leading brain scientist – herself excluded – she'd think him a complete moron.

Lepus' door-muffled voice said, 'Quiver, female, quiver, for now I am in a cupboard.'

Some days weren't worth climbing out of bed for.

three

Why did her head hurt like a squashed melon?

Why could she smell cooking?

. . . And why could she hear a knife being sharpened?

Bleary eyed, Sally pulled her hair away from her face then checked her watch. Slowly, slowly it came into focus.

Two hours?

She'd been out cold for two hours?

And where was she?

She raised her head to look around. She recognized those white walls and that psychotic neatness, those gleaming utensils and polished cupboards. She was in the restaurant kitchen, lying face down on its table. Above the sizzle of simmering liquid a woman's voice trilled,

'♪Some day my prince will come.♪'

Then Sally noticed; each of her own fingers wore the tiny chef's hats that self-satisfied people put on chicken legs to make themselves look like real cooks. She looked down. Her shoes were gone and her toes had been decorated like petits fours.

And her face . . .

Her face had been basted?

She looked up again and winced, the movement making her head hurt even more.

Five feet away, in red PVC boots, a G-string and PVC corset, a woman stood over the cooker. Her back to Sally, she stirred the contents of a deep pot, her black hair hanging down to her waist. Finished stirring, she tapped the ladle three times on the pot's rim then placed it beside the biggest meat cleaver Sally'd ever seen. She took a box of salt, broke it open and emptied it into the pot. Her velvet voice told Sally, 'Don't mind me, naughty girl. I'm just here to cook you.'

That was what *she* thought.

Before the woman could react, Sally was off the table and out the door.

four

'Uncle Al?'

'Yes?'

'It's me; Sally.' The moment she got back to her offices, before she'd even got her breath back, she was on the phone to him.

And he'd better have a good explanation.

He said, 'Sally who?'

'Sally Cooper. Who do you think?'

'I may know numerous young ladies of that name.'

'Like who?'

'Sally Dunstable.'

'And who's Sally Dunstable?' she asked.

'It doesn't matter who she is.'

'Whoever she is you don't know her. You don't know any young ladies.'

'I know Miss Go-La-Go-Go,' he said.

'Cthulha's not famous, young nor a lady. And she works for you.'

'So?'

'So she doesn't count.'

'Then what about my beloved Catherine?' he asked. 'Does she work for me?'

'No.'

'And are you saying she's not a lady?'

'No.'

'Good. Because if you were–'

'She's a Japanese sniper.'

'I find your attitude wounding. And so would she if she were here.'

'She is there. And she'd find nothing. Speaking of wounding–'

'Yes?'

'Your new restaurant.'

'I have two; one in town and–'

'The one facing this building.' Now sat at her desk, she prised open the venetian blinds and peered out at it. It stood there in all its purple gory, no sign of a madwoman coming after her.

Her uncle said, 'Young lady, only three factors matter in business; location, location and location. That restaurant fails on all three counts.'

'Then why . . . ?'

'Mr Dunnett assures me its losses will lop substantial amounts off my next tax bill.'

'Your cook's just tried to eat me.'

'Nonsense.'

'She was about to stick me in the oven.'

'Were you on her table?'

'What's that got to do with it?'

'If it's on her table she cooks it. She was most insistent on that at the interview. For five years she was a school dinner lady.'

13

'So?'

'So that's how they do it in schools. With hundreds of mouths to feed there's no time for fussing over ingredients. Each year numerous school boys disappear in such a manner.'

Sally pressed the bump at the back of her head and winced at the pain it produced. 'Uncle Al, she knocked me out to get me on that table.'

'A woman of initiative.'

'She wears S+M gear.'

'That's right.'

'What kind of school *was* this?'

He said, 'I'm not at liberty to say but it produced half the British Cabinet.'

'You don't think you should sack her before she kills someone?'

'I'm counting on her killing someone.'

'What!?!'

'Oh, no one important, just one of your more socially challenged guests; old Mr Johnson perhaps, the one with the pervert dog.'

'Transsexualism's not a perversion. It's–'

'Dogs didn't do things like that in my day.'

'No one did anything in your day.'

'I did,' he said.

'I know you did. My God, you never stop regaling us with the full sordid details. But I was talking about real people.'

'Regardless, if Barbara kills someone, I won't have to pay her redundancy when I close the place down the day after my tax year ends.'

'And you're saying Charlie Dunnett suggested this?'

'Well no. He doesn't know about that part. And I suggest you don't tell him – or Barbara won't be the only one seeking a new job.'

14

'Uncle Al?'

'What?'

'You don't think she was involved in that scandal last year?'

'What scandal?'

'You know perfectly well what scandal.'

'Sally, I know how much that incident upset you. It upset us all but you mustn't go seeking scapegoats. Barbara's merely a woman who was attracted to the town by its subsequent reputation and should not be implicated.'

Then Sally realized; 'That's why you hired *me*.'

'I'm sorry?'

'You're hoping I'll kill someone!!'

'I don't know what you're talking about.'

'You don't think I can do the job!!! You're hoping I'll accidentally kill someone. Then you can sack me without paying compensation.'

'I may be planning to close the park at a similar time to the restaurant, yes.'

'I don't believe this!'

'Never mind that.'

'Never mind that!?! You don't want to pay your own niece compensation!?!'

'Well perhaps I'd want to pay her compensation if she hadn't been such a let down.'

'And what does that mean?'

'You know.'

'No, Uncle Al, I don't.'

'You want me to spell it out for you?'

'Why don't you?'

'C-H-I-E-F C-H-I-R-P-A.'

'Uncle Al, I won't apologize for not having grown up to be king of the Ewoks.'

'Some girls would.'

'No girls would.'

'Miss Go-La-Go-Go would.'

'She probably thinks she is king of the Ewoks.'

'And you could be, if you'd only meet those genetic scientists I told you about.'

'What kind of man adopts his niece in the hope she'll grow up to be a warrior teddy bear?'

'Chief Chirpa of the Ewoks happened to be the cutest character in all science fiction. Some girls would be proud to be him/her/it.'

'You don't even know what sex it was.'

'Sex isn't a factor in the magical world of George Lucas.'

'Do you *know* how sad you are?' she said.

'Do you know how disappointing you are?'

'Shut up,' she said.

'Getting back to the point,' he said.

'Which is?'

'The reason I wanted to know just who you were was because you might be Sally Dunstable pretending to be you.'

'And why would this Sally Dunstable want to be me?'

'To get her hands on what you've got.'

'What've I got? And if you say the love of a good uncle–'

'News.'

'What news?'

'The kind that'll make you think God loves dull people.'

'I'm not dull.'

'Don't be silly.'

'I have a busy and active social life.'

'Nonsense.'

'I have friends.'

'Piffle.'

'I have fun.'

'Never.'

'And, though I may currently be sans boyfriend, I've been known to have sex.'

'With a face like yours?'

'With a face like mine.'

'How can men sink so low?'

'Clearly some can.'

'This "fun" thing,' he said.

'What about it?'

'Stop it at once.'

'I'm not ruining my social life for you. I–'

'Ruin it for a million pounds.'

'What're you on about?'

'That's what's on offer to the safest caravan park in Wyndham.'

'That's us buggered,' she said.

'I'm not sure I like your attitude.'

'Uncle Al, half the people who stay at this camp are suicidal. That's why they come here, to sit alone in their caravans listening to Radiohead.'

'I prefer to call them characters.'

'And have you seen the latest two?'

'They had tea with me last week.'

'Who did?'

'A delightful young lady and her pet chimp.'

'The chimp was Britain's leading brain scientist,' she said.

'Then why did he eat my cushions?'

'Now do you see my point? They don't strike me as being the safest people to have around.'

'Nonetheless I have faith in you.'

She'd noticed. 'And if I win I get a million pounds?'

'The Council feels the huge death rate among tourists is damaging Wyndham's reputation as a fun place to be

– not to mention that scandal last year. So, as a publicity stunt, they're offering the reward. I'm offering you a one percent commission.'

'Offer me fifty.'

'Fifty?' he said.

'Sixty.'

'Sixty!?!' He sounded like he was about to have a seizure. Good!

She leaned forward in her chair. 'Uncle Al, without my help you get nothing. With my help you get four hundred grand.'

'I could easily hire someone else to do your job.'

'And have me spill the beans about "Barbara" and your little scheme? Or maybe I should tell her about it and she can come and get you. Have you seen the size of her meat cleaver?'

He slipped into a deep silence and considered the issue.

She waited, impatient, fiddling with the handset's coiled lead. She checked on the restaurant again. Still no sign of cooks. She released the blinds. 'Uncle Al?'

'Young lady?'

'Yes?'

'I suggest you set about stopping your guests from killing themselves, forthwith.'

five

'I'm going out now, Mr Landen, to collect materials for the Project X you were so excited about. Do you want to come along?'

No reply.

'I'll buy you an ice cream,' she said.

Still no reply.

Teena sighed. She stood on the front steps of her mobile home, one hand holding the door open, the other holding a camouflage jacket. Gazing in at the locked closet, she called, 'When I get back I expect to find you out of that closet, the rabbit wearing the hat and your attitude much improved. Remember, no one's irreplaceable, not even you.'

No reply.

'Mr Landen?' She frowned. 'Are you all right in there?'

No reply.

Resigned to getting no sense from him, she put on the camouflage jacket, closed the front door and left.

six

Incapable of doing this job? Useless? I'll show you, Mr Aloysius Bracewell, with your man-eating cooks, low-life whores and stitched up awards.

And you TV types with your smug grins, cameras and free cups of tea; *When Jobs Go Good*, let's see you do that one.

Sally slapped her paste-smothered brush up and down her living room wall with enough force to strip paint, all the while imagining it was her uncle's stupid face she was slapping. She dunked her brush in the bucket between her feet, stirred it round to collect a great thick dollop and slapped more paste on the wall.

The front door creaked open behind her. She ignored it. Unseen feet scuffed, not bothering to wipe on the Welcome mat. The door creaked shut and tea-leaf cigarette smoke announced Cthulha Gochllagochgoch's arrival before her footsteps had even entered the living room. The footsteps half crossed the room then stopped as though their owner

20

was stood looking around. The settee went flumpf and Cthulha said, 'So, what you up to?'

Sally pasted on, no intention of looking at her. 'We're redecorating.'

'We?'

'Me and Mr Bushy.' Mr Bushy was Sally's pet squirrel. She'd left him on her TV set with a paint brush for company.

Cthulha said, 'Sal.'

'What?'

'He's eating his paint brush. Interior designers don't eat their brushes – not even the ones in Changing Rooms.'

'So long as he's happy.' She grabbed a foam rubber square by her feet and stuck it to the wall, alongside the foam she'd already hung. She pressed it in place then prepared for more pasting.

Cthulha said, 'I take it this foaming's for the safety award?'

'It's called the Dullness Award. The council felt the word "Safety" might remind people of danger.'

'Whatever it's called you've no chance.'

Sally pasted on. 'Within days this'll be the safest caravan park on Earth.'

'Sal? How long have you been working here?'

'A week.'

'And in a whole week you've not noticed anything suicidal about the people who stay here?'

'Of course I have. I'm not blind.'

'I am,' Chulha said.

'What're you on about?' said Sally.

'I'm of the sightless.'

'Cthulha.' Sally pasted on, still not looking at her. 'You're not blind.'

'Shows how much *you* know.'

21

'I know you're not blind.'

'Twenty minutes ago, where was I?'

'No idea.'

'Outside Davey Farrel's.'

'You're always outside Davey Farrel's.'

'So?'

'Do you fancy him?'

'Don't be ridiculous.'

Sally asked, 'Why's it ridiculous?'

'He's my brother. Dr Steinbeck says all the other stuff's okay but close relatives are out of bounds.'

'Cthulha, Davey Farrel's not your brother.'

'Course he is. I used to shove him off his bike, as a kid, and ride off with it.'

'Maybe you did but he's not your brother. He's my cousin. He's no relation to you.'

'Then why was I shoving him off his bike?'

'I've no idea.'

'God, this town. You can't keep track of who's related to who in it.'

'I'd have thought you'd be able to keep track of who's related to you.'

'Sally, you must bear in mind that, due to a former hobby of mine, certain aspects of my past are a little vague to me.'

'Not to mention the flashbacks.'

'I don't get flashbacks.'

'What? Apart from you dropping everything to shout, "Aargh! Lobsters! Lobsters!"'

'I don't do that,' she chuckled. Then, after a lengthy pause; 'Do I?'

'Only three times a day.'

'Jesus.' Cthulha thought about this. 'Lobsters lobsters; I wonder what that means.'

'You don't know?'

'I've no idea.'

Sally said, 'Tell me about Davey Farrel's.'

'I was outside his shop. And what was the wind doing?'

Like Sally cared.

'It was slapping me from all sides,' Cthulha said, 'like I'd done something wrong.'

'You probably had.'

'So then what happens?' Cthulha asked.

'I don't know. I wasn't there.'

'My hat blows off.'

'You think it was a punishment from God?'

'Listen,' Cthulha said.

'What?'

'This is where it gets good.'

'Cthulha, your anecdotes never get good. They just stagger round till they fall into a ditch.'

Cthulha said, 'This bloke takes one look at my dark glasses, and my hat on the pavement, thinks I'm a blind beggar and chucks fifty pence in the hat. Can you believe that? From now on, when we're out in public together, I'm blind.'

'How dignified.'

'Every penny helps.'

Sally dipped her brush. 'Anyway, suicides don't count.'

'Who says?'

'Uncle Al faxed me the rules. They say, *Caravan park managers will not be held responsible for suicides. Suicides are committed at guests' own peril, unless death was initiated at the manager's request.* – like if I say, "Go kill yourself."'

'But you're always saying that to me.'

'Not for the next few days. Anyway you're not a guest, you're an intruder. You probably count as a burglar. Burglars are fair game.'

'Not that I'd kill myself. I wouldn't want to upset those who love me.'

'And who's that?' said Sally.

'My boyfriend, you, my mother–'

'Cthulha, your mother hits you with a stick.'

'But she must love me. She's a mother. Mothers love their daughters.'

Sally said, 'You don't love me.'

'Don't start that again.'

'You have to accept that when an eight year old loses her real mother, she'll look for a surrogate one. And you happened to be the one permanent female presence in my young life. When I had my first period, you told me I was dying. When I needed my first bra, you helped me buy it – not that you knew how to fasten it.'

'Those things are death traps. You can tell a man invented them.'

'Bras were invented by a woman.'

'Who says?'

'She knotted two hankies together then showed it to all her mates who were most impressed.'

'Were they used hankies?'

'Why would anyone want to wear used hankies?' Sally said.

'Why would they want to wear any sort of hankies? If you're sat in a restaurant on a date and, halfway through the evening, he declares that he makes his trolleys from knotted hankies, you're not going to be accepting any invitations into his home.'

'The point is that with you around ALL THE TIME you were bound to imprint on me. It's like ducklings that think a pair of wellies is their mother because it was the first thing they ever saw.'

'I don't believe this.'

'Believe what?'

'I bought you a bra, now you want me to buy you wellies.'

'I don't want you to buy me wellies. I want you to love me.'

'If you ever again sit in the pub on a Friday night, telling the men I'm trying to pull that I'm your mother . . .'

'But that's how I see you.'

'I'm only four years older than you.'

'Twelve.'

'Eleven and three quarters.'

'Twelve.' Holding the bucket steady between her feet, Sally dipped her brush in it, stirred it, then spread more paste on the wall. 'Is your mother still sending you death threats?'

'Yeah.'

'I'd go to the police if I were you; remember I've met your mother.'

'Yeah that's right,' Cthulha complained.

'What is?'

'If you worship a giant space octopus, people always want to think the worst of you.'

'Well it's hardly normal is it?'

'Loads of people must do it. They just don't admit it. Anyway, I'm sure she doesn't mean it. It's probably her idea of a joke.'

'Yeah. Right.' Sally hung the last foam rubber square and pressed it in place. She turned to face Cthulha.

Cthulha Gochllagochgoch, thirty one, gangled on Sally's settee, in an undertakers hat, little round sunglasses, black tuxedo, black jeans and black trainers. Beneath the open tuxedo, she wore a purple bikini top, with a rub-on transfer, IF I'M JUICY SQUEEZE ME, on her left breast. One lace-gloved palm held Mr Bushy while the other stroked him. Sat there she reminded Sally of the reptile aliens in *V*, the ones who could almost pass for human, till you caught them eating your pets.

Mr Bushy squeaked. Now sat up, Cthulha held him before her and chuckled. 'Look at this.'

'Look at what?'

'If you squeeze this it squeaks like one of those dogs' toys.' And she squeezed away, producing a string of random squeaks.

'Cthulha!'

'What?'

Sally snatched him from her and stroked him to calm his nerves. 'Dynamite Pete asked me – if anything ever happened to him – to look after his squirrel. It shouldn't take a genius to know that treating it as a rubber toy wasn't what he had in mind.'

'And as Dynamite Pete's intended profession involved swallowing a pint of nitro-glycerine then running round a stage till he exploded, it shouldn't have taken a genius to figure something was bound to happen to him.'

'I tried to warn him,' she insisted.

'Don't you always?' Cthulha settled back into the settee and took a drag on her cigarette.

Sally placed Mr Bushy back on the TV, with his paint brush, and continued stroking him. Dynamite Pete's demise; some experiences were best not remembered – especially when they were your fault.

Mr Bushy started nibbling his paint brush, which she took as a good sign, so she turned to face Cthulha. 'Do you actually have a reason to be here?'

'Uncle Al wants money.' Uncle Al was not Cthulha's uncle. Uncle Al was not the uncle of most people who called him Uncle.

'He always wants money.'

26

'Now he wants more money.'

'What's he want it for this time?'

'Fifty-six rolls of foil. Personally I think it's an excuse to get me out of the way. Though why anyone'd want a girl like me out of the way, I don't know.'

'Cthulha?'

'Yeah?'

'What kind of cooking needs fifty-six rolls of foil?'

She lowered her dark glasses to the tip of her nose and peered over them at Sally, eyebrows hoisted knowingly. 'Aloysius Bracewell doesn't do his own cooking – any more than he does his own eating. You know he has servants for that.'

'So what's he want tin foil for?'

She prodded her glasses back into place. 'To add to the roll he's just wrapped round his head.'

Sally squinted at her, baffled.

Cthulha said, 'Half an hour ago, some Texan turned up on satellite news. Seems he's broken the world record for wrapping his head in foil – except they called it "aloominum". The previous record holder was British. The moment Uncle Al hears that, he grabs a roll and starts wrapping it round his head, declaring his determination to reclaim the record for some place called "Blighty". He says someone has to restore the dignity it lost when it gave away some empire or other.'

'By wrapping his head in foil?'

'And Uncle Al won't be using "aloominum".'

'Then what'll he be using?'

'Lead.'

'Lead?'

'He says you can get lead foil from nuclear power plants, if you bribe the right women and sleep with the right men. That'll be my job. He will of course make sure the national

27

media knows all about his sterling act of patriotism and that he owns a chain of caravan parks – prices reasonable. I told him, "Uncle Al, you're a pillock. Lead foil must weigh a ton. You'll squash your head." He said that'd make his achievement all the greater – though guess who'll get to do all the wrapping? Still you've got to hand it to him; fifty-six rolls – no man's ever wrapped his head in so much lead.'

seven

'Excuse me?'

'Yeah, babe?'

'Where did you get that cow?'

'I didn't steal it.'

'I never said you had.'

'I found it down there.' His sucker tipped thumb pointed back guiltily over his shoulder. He said, 'It jumped out of a tree and landed on me.'

'And where are you taking it?'

'The obvious.'

'Which is?'

'To wallpaper it.'

In a country lane, fifteen minutes into her walk, Teena'd stopped to talk to a small grey man with a cow. His huge, black, almond shaped eyes blinked up at her from his too-large head. His spindly body wore a black turtleneck sweater and drainpipe jeans. He looked bruised, battered and bewildered, as though something had jumped out of

29

a tree and landed on him. Mouth no more than a slit, he said, 'It's my destiny.'

'What is?'

'To win the Turner Prize.' And a sucker tipped finger pointed to somewhere behind her.

A half turn brought her face to face with a field of cows wrapped in beige flock. It didn't suit them.

Behind her he said, 'It's an installation I call *Cattle Mootilation*.' She could feel his gaze on her buttocks.

'But why wallpaper cows?' she asked.

'Because gorillas always tried to tear my arms off.'

She returned her attention to him. 'Well, Mr . . . ?'

'McDoddy; Roddy McDoddy.'

'Is that your real name?'

'No.'

'Well, Roddy.' She grabbed his hand in hers and shook it vigorously. 'I'm Teena Rama. And if you're an artist, you may have heard of me.'

'Too right I have!' Now he was shaking her hand even more vigorously than she was shaking his. 'You've won the Turner Prize three years running.'

'And I'll be winning it again this year.' She yanked her hand free of his and gave it a sharp waggle to restore the blood supply.

'Wow,' he told her chest. '*The* Teena Rama. I can only dream of achieving your levels of artistic futility.'

'Why thank you.'

'And your bosoms are so pointy.'

'Thank you for that highly relevant observation.'

He gazed at them some more like he wanted to tell them something. Then he spotted her engagement ring. 'And you're a spoken-for woman?'

'I'm newly engaged, yes.' She couldn't resist gloating a little.

30

'Wow!' He told her chest. 'But I didn't know they'd even announced the Turner nominations.'

'They haven't but my victory's assured. And I have to tell you that these days it takes something more daring than wallpapering cows to impress the most demanding judges in British art.'

'It does?' He stroked his goatee, perplexed, still watching her chest.

'However.' She watched the cow beside him. It gazed back at her, chewing an Action Man. 'Is this beast for sale?'

'Make me an offer, babe.'

She had no intention of paying money for goods that might have been stolen. 'Would a kiss do?'

'Dr R,' he enthused, 'You're a crazy looking chick but get kissing that cow.'

'Roddy?'

'Yeah?'

'I did mean would you like me to kiss *you*?'

'Oh wow, man! *The* Dr Rama would rather snog me than my livestock.'

eight

Late that night, the doorbell dragged Sally away from foam rubbering yet more rooms. Entering the entrance hall, from the kitchen, she could see out through the wire-glass door. A figure stood in darkness, its back to the door, umbrella in hand.

The week's takings were in the safe in Sally's bedroom. Thanks to Cthulha, everyone in town knew it.

Or maybe . . .

. . . Maybe it was Cthulha's mother come looking for her daughter.

Sally stopped, and looked around for an escape route. She looked at the living room door and considered running into the room and hiding behind the settee like she and Cthulha had the first time her mother had shown up. They'd had to stay hidden as she prowled the living room, sniffing the air, sniffing objects, pushing over the lamp stand, trying to pick up their scent, before she got bored, decided they weren't there and left. The moment she'd heard the door slam, Sally'd tried to come out of hiding but Cthulha'd grabbed her wrist and stopped her. She stuck her hand over Sally's mouth and frantically whispered that her mother had a trick where she slammed the door to make it sound like she'd left but then stayed just inside the door hoping to lure you out into the open. But she always gave up after five minutes and left anyway because she had the brain of a donkey. Sally told her that whatever her problem was with her mother, maybe she should try talking to her about it instead of hiding. Hiding from your own mother seemed a pretty childish way to deal with a problem. Cthulha said you didn't deal with her mother when she was in a prowling mood.

And five minutes later they heard the door shut again.

Mrs Gochllagochgoch was a woman you could empty an ammo clip into and she'd still keep coming. You'd have to stop her by toppling heavy things onto her. Then, when you thought she was dead, you'd lean over her, seeking a pulse, and she'd come back to life and start strangling you.

Sally checked the Colt 45 she was carrying. Magic Keith had given her it and it weighed a ton because it was loaded. He'd insisted on a Colt 45 because the Shadow used them, and Magic Keith was as elusive as the Shadow – he'd claimed. She removed the safety catch, and stuck the gun down the back of her jeans' belt for easy access. She pulled the back of her sweater down to hide it, prayed that this wasn't Cthulha's mother, and readied herself.

She unfastened the door's top bolt.

She unfastened the door's bottom bolt.

She twisted the yale lock and opened the door.

The hissing sound of rain filled the entrance hall. Its back to her, the figure whistled a non-specific tune as the rain pummelled its umbrella.

'Hello?' Sally prepared to grab the gun but the figure turned and grinned at her, large droplets dripping from the tips of its umbrella spokes.

And frowning Sally said, 'Teena?'

Behind her 'winning' smile the scientist seemed embarrassed. 'Ah. Yes. We seem to have got ourselves locked out and were wondering if we could spend the night here?'

'We?' She glanced at the darkness surrounding Teena, relieved to see no giant rabbits or that creepy Mr Landen.

A sideways nod of Teena's head drew her attention to the string in Teena's right hand. The string's free end was high in the air, hidden by the top of the door. Sally leaned forward to see what was up there.

And her jaw dropped.

Floating at the end of that string was a cow.

'What sort of genius locks herself out of her mobile home?'

'When I said we'd got ourselves locked out, I should have said Mr Landen's locked us out. I didn't want to blame him outright because he doesn't seem to be himself lately.'

'And you don't have a key?'

'It's bolted from the inside. And, sadly, before I left, I repaired the hole Lepus left – an action taken at your insistence, I should point out.'

'Teena?'

'Uh huh?'

'What exactly is that?' Sally stood in the rain, holding the umbrella over herself as Teena tethered her flying cow to the offices' front door. Her mobile home was no more

34

than eight feet away to her left. What was it with her? She couldn't tie cows to her own front door?

As though to counterbalance the mobile home, a caravan stood at the offices' other flank. The sign hanging from its doorknob read, THE WYNDHAM FINISHING SCHOOL FOR DAINTY YOUNG LADIES but Sally wasn't interested in that. She'd seen its occupants.

Teena ignored the rain, tied off with a knot that only seamen should know, took three steps back and stood beside Sally. She smelled of strawberries. Not real strawberries but the strawberry-centre chocolate you always eat first from the box because it's your favourite. Anyone else wet smells like the Coffee Cream that sits ignored for weeks because you don't know anyone who likes them then has to be thrown away before it goes mouldy.

Polka dot rags plastered to her cheeks, Teena admired her own handiwork. 'Sally, meet my latest project.'

'It's flying.'

'Floating.'

'Big difference.'

'The moment I came across her I knew she'd be perfect for Experiment X.'

'Experiment X?' If this involved boyfriends.

'My venture into anti-gravity. You see, I've done what no one else has. I've proven not only that anti-gravity exists but that it's a force to equal gravity. I will of course be winning a Nobel Prize.'

'But you'll be leaving her out here all night?'

'You'd rather I brought her inside?'

'No but . . .'

'Cows are hardy creatures well used to life outdoors.'

'But the rain?'

'Won't bother her in the slightest.'

'Are you sure?'

'Positive.'

'How are you sure?'

'Because she's indestructible.'

Teena still stood beside Sally in the rain, her strawberry smell starting to make Sally hungry. Sally watched her. She looked so soft and smooth and creamy that Sally wanted to bite a chunk out of her. She'd taste like cake and have no bones just icing, no muscle just sponge cake, no blood just strawberry jam. In all her body there'd be not one human biological substance, just items fresh from the dessert tray. The walking gateau said, 'On my walk, I encountered a small shop on the edge of town.'

'A cake shop?' Sally's stomach rumbled.

Teena slapped her.

Sally stepped back, shocked, clutching her stinging cheek. 'What the hell was that for?'

'You were thinking of eating me.'

'No I wasn't. I don't eat people. You city types, you're all the same, always looking down on us, always saying we're cannibals.'

Teena said, 'Frankly you've lost me. I merely recognized the look on your face. Being beautiful, I've seen it so often.'

'Oh.' Sally watched the ground, wishing she'd kept her mouth shut.

'I'm sorry about hitting you but it was the best way to snap you out of it.' She grabbed Sally's arm and yanked her back to a position beside her, presumably Teena's idea of reconciliation. 'Now; the general store; while there I bought the ingredients needed for the anti-gravity cream.'

36

Sally still held her throbbing cheek. 'From a general store?'

'Anti-gravity cream can easily be made with household materials. After I'd finished, I had some materials left over, so I concocted a quantity of Indestructible Cream and applied it liberally. Clytemnestra's fully atom bomb proof – the first of many such cows.'

'Teena?'

'Uh huh?'

'Why would you want to make cows atom bomb proof?'

'So they don't hurt themselves when they fall from the sky.'

'Cows don't fall from the sky.'

'They will when the anti-gravity cream wears off.'

'But you've only coated one in anti-gravity cream.'

'Well . . .' Her voice tailed away. She gazed skyward.

Sally watched her. 'Teena?'

'Uh huh?

'How many cows have you coated?'

She shrugged. 'A few hundred.'

'A few hundred!?!'

'Maybe a few thousand. Frankly, after the first eight hundred, cows all start to resemble each other. I may have coated some twice.'

'And that's what you've been doing all day?'

'What else would one do on one's holiday?'

'Most people go down the beach.'

Teena looked at her like she was talking to a simpleton. 'Sally, there are no cows on the beach.' Striding forward, she gave the cow a firm slap on the flanks. The impact sent water flying from it.

It mooed, startled.

Teena opened the front door of the office and prepared to go inside. 'Coming?'

Sally watched the sodden cow, its ears at half mast. 'I don't care how indestructible she is, I'll still worry about her.'

'That's because you're a non-scientist. You view cows as people. They're not. A cow's a cow, and she won't appreciate being treated otherwise. Now come on indoors and you can show me your fridge.'

Sally stepped forward, feet splashing in puddles. Water leaked into her trainers, soaking her toes. She ignored it. When she reached the cow, she stopped. With some difficulty she pulled the cow's mouth open and placed the umbrella handle in it. Robbed of the umbrella's cover, she was instantly soaked, her clothes clinging to her like cold octopus tentacles, rain pummelling her like the skies were out to dump the world's oceans on her. With yet more difficulty she clamped the cow's jaws shut around the handle.

Teena said, 'Sally, what're you doing?'

'The umbrella'll keep her head dry.'

'Are you trying to make me look silly?'

'What? As opposed to smearing cows with anti-gravity cream and tying them to doorknobs?'

'That's different.'

'Why?'

'It's science.'

'Now then, Daisy—'

'Daisy?' Teena protested. 'Her name's Clytemnestra.'

Sally still held the jaws shut. 'Just keep hold of this umbrella all night, and you'll be fine.'

'She's my cow, you know.' Teena still held the door open.

'We don't listen to the nasty woman, do we, Daisy? She slaps people and accuses them of wanting to eat her.' And she released Daisy's jaw.

The umbrella hit the mud at Sally's feet.

'Sally, it won't work. Cows don't understand umbrellas.'

Sally picked it up, wiped its handle clean on her soaked sweater, forced Daisy's jaws apart then placed the umbrella handle between them. She pressed the jaws shut. She released the jaws. Daisy dropped the umbrella.

Teena tutted.

Sally picked it up, wiped its handle clean and put it in Daisy's mouth.

She released Daisy's jaw.

And this time . . .

. . . The cow held onto it.

'Sally?'

'Yeah?' With great difficulty she bit a generous length of masking tape from a roll. It tasted foul.

'I'd like to thank you for putting me up for the night.' Teena lay on the top deck of Sally's bunk bed, having refused the bottom one.

'Don't mention it.' Sally stood beside her, on the bunk's ladder. She took Teena's right wrist, the one nearest her, and wrapped tape around it. She yanked the wrist against the nearest bed post, held it there, and bound wrist to post.

Teena said, 'Only, some women seem to find my presence intimidating.'

'You know, that's how they feel about *me*.' She bit off another strip then leaned across and wrapped the tape round Teena's other wrist.

'Sally?'

'Yeah?'

'What're you doing?'

'Strapping you down.' Having to stretch to reach, she pressed the wrist against its nearest bedpost and bound them together.

'Sally, it's not that I'm actively opposed to bondage. As a social scientist I appreciate its therapeutic value. Lesbianism has its place also. However, as we've established that you're not attractive and I'm engaged–'

'Engaged. Engaged. You're always saying you're engaged. For someone who claims she's a man magnet, you seem remarkably impressed with yourself for having pulled. My God, even I've been engaged once. It's not that big an achievement.' She'd been engaged to Barry Sping, the paper boy, when they were both eleven. Cthulha'd put them up to it. She'd thought it cute.

Teena said, 'Look in my coat pocket.'

'For what?'

'A wallet.'

Annoyed at the disruption to her work, she finished binding wrist to post then stood up as best the ceiling allowed. Teena's camouflage jacket hung drying on the bed post. Sally felt in the pocket and retrieved a wallet.

'Open it,' Teena said.

She opened it.

'What do you see?'

'Credit cards, old tickets, taxi firm numbers, a photo–'

'Take the photo and look at it.'

She did so.

And . . . 'Jesus Christ!' She almost fell off her ladder with shock. 'What the hell's that!?!'

'My fiancé.'

'But . . . but he's huge!' The photographer (who Sally assumed to be Teena) had only managed to fit half of him

40

into the photo. You could have fitted Barry Sping into a photo and have had room left over for the Brighouse and Rasterick brass band.

Teena said, 'Huge? He's positively Olympian.' It wasn't clear whether she meant an athlete, a Greek god or the mountain. Sally suspected she meant all three.

'But he's got no clothes on!' said Sally.

Teena said, 'When one owns a work of art, one doesn't leave it covered up.'

'But that . . . that thing he's got—'

'Perhaps now you know why I'm pleased with myself?'

Sally tried to prise her gaze from it. He could have wrapped it round his neck if it had looked in any way shape or form flexible. 'But . . . but . . . there are more important qualities in a husband than a . . .' she imagined being on its receiving end, '. . . knob.'

'I can't think of one.'

'What about personality?' She tried to prise her gaze from it.

'All men have a personality. It's their personalities that're the problem.'

'But your husband should be your best friend.' She tried to prise her gaze from it.

'No. Your best friend should be your best friend. A husband's job is to satisfy his woman whenever and however she demands it.'

'And he does?'

'What do you think?'

'Jesus.' Almost feeling sorry for him, and almost afraid to touch it, she slipped the photo back into the wallet. She closed the wallet and put it back in the jacket pocket. Fingers still trembling from the sight of him she took the roll of tape from the mattress where she'd left it. 'Anyway, I'm not binding you to the bed for kinky purposes.'

'Then why are you doing it?'

'For your safety.'

'My safety?'

'Look at me.'

Teena looked at her.

'What do I look like?'

Teena looked non-plussed.

'I'm an entertainer's assistant. That's what I've always been.'

Teena studied her bindings. She clenched a fist and flexed an arm to test the tape's strength but no way was she getting free. 'So this is some sort of magic trick?'

'My last job in entertainment was six months ago. Know what I was?'

'No.'

'Assistant to Magic Keith, He Can Outrun Bullets.'

Teena frowned. 'Magic Keith?'

'I had to wear the assistant's costume; you know, with the ostrich feathers and sequins. I looked a total prat.'

'Your boss could outrun bullets?'

'No. But I didn't discover that till I pulled the trigger.'

'You shot him?'

'In the back, point blank. The bullet went clean through and lodged in a stage hand.'

'You killed them *both*?' People always used that mortified tone when they said that.

Sally said, 'The police were very understanding. They accepted it was an accident.'

'And it didn't occur to you that this Keith couldn't outrun bullets?'

'Of course it did. All the time were were rehearsing – without bullets – I kept saying, "Magic," he liked to be called Magic. "Are you sure you can outrun bullets?" He'd give a knowing wink, tap the side of his nose and say, "There's a knack."'

'What possible knack can there be to "outrunning" bullets?'

'Acceleration. Jesse Owens could outrun horses over a hundred feet because humans accelerate faster than horses. Keith reckoned it was the same with bullets. That doesn't make sense does it? Bullets are launched by an explosion, and horses aren't. But I figured he was the boss, he must know what he's doing.'

'And?'

'Three days later we buried him.' Roll of tape in hand she descended the ladder then unhooked it from the top bunk's safety rail. She carried it round to the foot of the bed and hooked it onto the rail there. 'It was the same with Madam Tallulah.' After rattling it to check it was safe, she climbed the ladder until level with Teena's bare feet. She resisted the urge to tickle them while she was helpless.

'Madam Tallulah?' Teena asked.

'The World's Greatest Escapologist. Except she wasn't. She was just some idiot. She told me to weld her into an iron casket then tip it in the river. Again the police were understanding but this is a small town, word gets round. Now no decent employer will touch me.'

'Have you considered leaving town?'

'You don't watch ITV?'

'Never.'

'Then you didn't see *When Gun Stunts Turn Bad*.'

'No.'

'Or *When Escapology Turns Bad*.'

'No.'

'Or *The World's Worst Welding Incidents*.'

'No.'

'Or *When Hang Gliders Collide*.'

'No.'

'Or *When Big Things Fall On Small Entertainers.*'

'No.'

'Or *When–*'

'All right, Sally. I get the idea.'

She wrapped tape around Teena's ankle and pressed it against the safety rail. She bound one to the other. 'Every job I do, someone ends up dead. And those shows make sure everyone knows it. But I'll prove them all wrong. I can go two weeks without killing anyone. I know I can. That's why I'm strapping you to the bed; you might roll over in your sleep and fall to your death.'

'From a bunk bed?'

'You might land on your head.'

'With safety rails in the way?'

'You might roll over them.'

'Isn't that unlikely?'

'You can't be too safe.' She bit off more tape and bound Teena's other ankle. 'Rest assured that while you're staying here I'll be doing all I can to keep you alive.'

'Sally?'

'Yeah?'

'Have you ever seen the movie Misery?'

'Oh my God, that terrible woman. Can you imagine what it must be like to be trapped in a place with someone like her?

'And what's this?' Last thing that night, Archie Drizzle the Dullness Inspector paid Safe Joe Safe's Caravan Park a surprise visit. He stood in the offices' bedroom, a middle-aged man with a brown suit, a Bobby Charlton comb-over

44

and a Gladstone bag and watched a man who was bound, gagged and chained to a bunk bed.

Stood beside Drizzle, the manager said, 'He was passing the camp, whistling. Before he could react, we grabbed him, coshed him and chained him to the bed so he can't fall over and hurt himself. We at Safe Joe Safe's are holding numerous people hostage who might otherwise hurt themselves. I think you'll agree we've taken every possible precaution to make this the safest camp not just in Wyndham but in the whole world.'

'I'll be the judge of that.' Drizzle thrust his bag into the chest of the manager, who took hold of it while Drizzle stepped forward and inspected the captive's bonds. They seemed firm enough, and the gag was tight enough to muffle whatever it was the prisoner was frantically trying to say.

But then . . .

. . . Drizzle realized what the man was wearing.

'You fool. Don't you realize what this is?'

The manager looked blank.

Drizzle said, 'This is a scientist.'

He still looked blank.

'Denied, by you, the chance to express itself through mad experimentation, his subconscious may create monsters from the id which will run loose and destroy us all.'

'Isn't that a little unlikely?'

Before the manager could react, Drizzle slapped a sticker on his forehead.

That sticker said FAILED.

nine

Morning woke Sally with the warmth of a rising sun and the twittering of birds. Her eyes opened with a string of tired blinks, adjusting to the light, and she stretched out in a yawn that extended her to her limits.

Then she relaxed, letting herself sink into a mattress that felt like love. She felt great. She felt more than great. She felt harmless. And beside her on the pillow Mr Bushy stretched out in a great long yawn that exactly mirrored her own. He held the pose then relaxed into a ball, snuggling his warm fur against her cheek. And she smiled. Could paradise be any better?

But then a thought struck her. She rolled onto her side, Mr Bushy scampering out of her way. She looked over the side of the bed. And she sighed with relief at not finding Teena on the floor dead.

Another thought struck her. She rolled over and looked over the other side of the bed, relieved at not finding Teena dead.

46

She rolled onto her back, and again sank into the mattress that felt like love. Smiling she watched the wooden slats of the bunk above and gently, so as not to wake her, asked, 'Teena? Are you awake?'

No reply. Some people had the luxury of sleeping all day. Sally had no such luxury. She had a job to do; lives to save. She sat up, cast her legs over the side of the bunk, and planted both feet on the carpet. After leaning forward for one last yawn, she stood then turned a half circle. On her toes, hands on the safety rail, she checked the top bunk, ready to see Teena asleep.

Instead, she saw a nightmare.

The bunk was empty.

'All right, Mr Landen, you've had your fun, now let me in. I've no intention of spending another night in that madwoman's home.' Early morning, Teena stood on her mobile home's front steps, her knuckles machine-gun rapping its door.

The only reply she got was the rumble of objects being moved around.

She knocked again. 'I know you're awake, I can hear you pushing furniture up against the door.'

'No, Dr Llama.'

'No?' She gazed at the door. 'What do you mean no?'

'I mean no. You should understand what that means. You are, after all, the expert linguist. You know how to say no in more languages than anyone else alive.'

'I'm fully aware of the word's general meaning. What does it mean in the context of you not letting me into my own mobile home?'

'It means you can't come in till you let me marry my bunny.'

'Marry it?' She frowned at the door. 'That bunny's a boy bunny. Since when have you liked boys?'

'I don't care. I love my bunny and won't let you take him off me.'

Lepus called out, 'Help me, female! Help me! He makes me eat celery.'

She watched the door, non-plussed.

Just to make her morning complete, Landen called, 'Help me, Dr Llama! Help me! My bunny's just sat on me.'

'Lepus, stop sitting on Mr Landen,' she sighed.

'Not unless he lets me out.'

'He can't let you out unless you get off him.'

'I don't care. I'm not getting off him till he lets me out.'

But how'd she done it? How'd she got away? Madam Tallulah hadn't been able to escape masking tape, and Sally hadn't bound her with half the vigour she'd used on Teena. And yet, when Sally'd found the tape, its sticky side had collected so much fluff it must have been unpeeled from her flesh for hours. She must have got free as soon as Sally'd climbed into the bottom bunk.

And why'd she escaped? Didn't she realize Sally was trying to help her? And if there'd been a certain pleasure in seeing Teena in discomfort, a sense of revenge for her rabbit antics, that was just a bonus and shouldn't in any way be viewed as a major part of her reason for doing it.

She tried to put Teena to the back of her mind and concentrate on her work, sticking another square of foam rubber in place.

'What's the hell's this?' asked Cthulha, to her left, watching Daisy.

Sally took the final square from the box to her right, unrolled it then pressed it in place. She ran her palms along its edges to make it stick, pressed its centre then stepped back to admire her handiwork.

It stood before her, magnificent, Wyndham's first ever caravan to be completely covered in foam rubber. You could throw yourself at it all day and never get hurt. Not that the two hippy geeks staring out of its window looked like they wanted to throw themselves at it. They looked like they wanted to throw her at something. But to do that they'd have to leave the caravan and, when she'd called round the other day, they'd refused to do so, pushing the rent out through a slot in the door. The sign on the doorknob might have said WYNDHAM FINISHING SCHOOL FOR DAINTY YOUNG LADIES but, to Sally, they were just two geeks.

She said, 'Cthulha meet Daisy. She's helping me make the camp safe.'

Hands in tuxedo pockets, cigarette in mouth, Cthulha eyed Daisy from a distance of nine inches. 'It's flying.'

'Floating,' Sally beamed.

'Jesus.'

Daisy floated tethered to the caravan door, chewing a foam rubber square Sally'd given her to keep her entertained. The cow gazed at a pink sports car parked ten feet away. Open-topped it stood so low you'd have to lie down to sit in it.

Hands in pockets, Cthulha leaned forward. Her face now one inch from Daisy's she too watched the car. 'Know what that is?'

'Moo?'

'That's my Spooder Yo-Yo.'

'A Spooder Yo-Yo?' Sally laughed. 'What the hell's a

49

Spooder Yo-Yo? It sounds like someone who got shoved out of an airlock in Star Wars.'

Cthulha attempted a withering stare. 'For your information, no one got shoved out of an airlock in Star Wars. And the Spooder Yo-Yo was the grooviest car of 1968.'

'Sure it was.'

'It was Greek,' Cthulha protested. 'The title lost a little in translation. But secret agent Carnaby Soho drove one in all her films.'

Sally frowned. 'Carnaby Soho?'

'You remember Carnaby Soho.'

'I've never heard of her.'

Everyone's heard of Carnaby Soho; pink-clad super-spy, righter of wrongs and, in later years, serial thwarter of the evil Mullineks.'

'Mullineks?'

'Queen of the mad moon lesbians.'

'Cthulha, where exactly do you get your videos?'

'You must have heard of Mullineks. Everyone has.'

'Like they've all heard of Carnaby Soho?'

'But Mullineks was even hornier than Hudson Leick.'

'Hudson what?'

Then Cthulha started singing.

'♪Carnaby Soho

making all the guys go whoa whoa.

Cruising in your Yo-Yo.

Letting through your hair the wind blow.

Carnaby Soho, do you know what you've done?

Having make the room go spun and spun and spun and spun and spun and spun and spun and spun . . . ♪'

'Cthulha, I've no idea what you're on about.'

'It was Italian.' She shrugged. 'It lost something in translation.'

'Yeah – the audience.'

Her face again inches from Daisy's, Cthulha told the cow, 'That car came with my big flash job. Want to know why you've not got one?'

'Moo?'

'Because only special people get a Spooder Yo-Yo. That's what humans get to do. We get to sprawl naked across our car at sunrise and kiss it till it hurts. Cows just get to stand around chewing grass. It must look pretty flash to you.'

Sally assumed she meant the chrome-tube tangle that jutted from it at seemingly random angles.

Cthulha told Daisy, 'My boyfriend's souped it up with some weird technology of his. Now it does six hundred miles an hour and a thousand miles to the pint. How fast can *you* go?'

'Cthulha,' Sally said. 'Not many people bother asserting their superiority over cattle.'

'Says a woman who works for squirrels.'

'I don't work for squirrels.' Suddenly she was looking everywhere but at Cthulha.

Cthulha looked upwards.

Sally looked upwards.

Mr Bushy was on the edge of the caravan roof. He looked down at them, wearing a little red crash helmet, with knicker elastic tied to his tail.

He bungee jumped off the caravan, boinged just above the ground, recoiled several feet into the air, plummeted again then hung there by the tail.

Sally turned red.

Cthulha said, 'Even I can figure out what you're doing.'

'And what's that?'

'Training it to do death defying stunts because you're so desperate to be an entertainer's assistant you'd even accept being assistant to a squirrel.'

'And why shouldn't I?' she protested. 'No one else'll

work with me, and I happen to be the best damn assistant this town's got.'

'Apart from that bit where you kill the turn.'

'This is a showbiz town. I have to be in showbiz.'

Cthulha lowered her little round shades to the tip of her nose. She looked over their rims at her. 'Sally, the fact that Charlie Williams once played a venue within ten miles of the place doesn't make it a showbiz town.' She prodded her sunglasses back into place. Hands in pockets, she watched the squirrel dangle. 'Are you leaving this here?'

Sally said, 'He likes hanging there.'

'Says who?'

'I can tell he does.'

'Does it pay rent? I can't see Uncle Al letting it stay for free.'

'Mr Bushy pays three pence a week with dropped coins he finds under caravans.'

'And Dobbin?'

'Daisy.'

'Does it pay rent?'

Before Sally could answer, Teena appeared from round the far side of her mobile home. Gaze fixed on the offices, jaw clenched, she strode towards them. If she'd been a bull (and not just engaged to one) she'd have been snorting.

Sally took it that things hadn't gone well at the mobile home.

Hands in pockets, Cthulha watched Teena all the way; 'Jesus. Imagine that spread naked across your car.'

'I take it you mean Dr Rama.'

'That's a doctor?'

'And she's not a "that". She's a woman.'

'Oh yeah. You're still into that hardline feminist "women aren't objects" crap aren't you? No wonder you never have any fun.'

Sally rolled her eyes.

Teena reached the offices, pulled open the door and entered. Its lax spring pulled the door to behind her.

Cthulha watched the door, imagining getting up to God knew what. 'So, what's the story?'

'That big mobile home.'

Cthulha glanced across at it.

Sally said, 'Her assistant's locked her out of it. So she spent the night with me.'

Suddenly impressed, Cthulha twisted her head round to stare at her, 'You gave her one?'

'No.'

'Why not?'

'I'm heterosexual.'

'Jesus.' Cthulha shook her head in disbelief and again watched the offices.

Sally said, 'I thought you were into men now. Only two days ago you were boasting about this great new boyfriend you'd found in a ditch.'

'I have, and he's okay. But you know there are times when you need a woman. No matter how hard they try men don't understand our needs. No man'll ever know what it's like to have your head swell up eight times a month.'

'Cthulha?'

'Yeah?'

'What're you on about?'

'Women's things.'

'Cthulha?'

'Yeah?'

'What're you on about?'

'Your head. You know?'

'Cthulha.'

'Yeah?'

'Women's heads don't swell up eight times a month.'

'Course they do. It's a woman thing.'

'No it isn't.'

'Doesn't yours?'

'No.'

'Then why does mine?'

'I've no idea.'

'What about the Beloved Catherine?'

'What about her?'

'Her head must swell up fifty times a day at least.'

'The Beloved Catherine's hardly a typical example of womanhood, is she.'

'No but–'

'And in her case it's down to air pressure, like a barometer.'

'Do you think that's what it is with me? Air pressure?'

'Cthulha, I long ago stopped trying to explain anything about you. And who says your head swells up? I've never seen it swell up.'

'Ninety-six times a year, you know what happens?'

'What?'

'My hat gets too tight.'

Sally glanced at the undertaker's hat. Its black ribbon flapped in the breeze.

Cthulha said, 'I can't get the thing off some nights. I have to sleep in it. First thing next morning, it's so loose it falls down over my eyes.'

'Then don't wear it.'

'That's not the point.'

'What is the point?'

'My head must be swelling.'

'Who says it's not your hat that's shrinking?'

'I measured it. It's always the same, twenty inches round.'

'Then you must have a problem that's unknown to medical science.'

Cthulha still watched Sally's offices. 'Do you think Dr Rama'd give me a medical?'

Sally reached into her jeans' pocket, found an object among the handful of coins and retrieved it. It had been screwed up into a ball. Taking care not to rip it, she smoothed it out against her upper leg, then held it for Cthulha. 'You see this?'

Cthulha cast a glance back at it and shrugged. 'It's a sweet wrapper.' She returned her attention to the offices.

Sally said, 'Daisy collected it first thing this morning and gave me it – along with two others.'

'So?'

'So what's it made of?' Sally angled it to glint in the sunlight.

Cthulha turned, and frowned at it. 'It's foil.'

'Exactly. She's collecting foil for Uncle Al's campaign.'

'Is it lead foil?'

'They don't wrap sweets in lead.'

'Why not?'

'It's poisonous.'

'But how could it know about Uncle Al's campaign?'

'Animals sense things. They're not too bright but they sense things.' Unlike Cthulha who was not too bright and sensed nothing.

'And she thinks a sweet wrapper'll impress him into letting her stay?' Cthulha shoved her face into Daisy's. 'Bye bye, Dobbin. You and your sweet wrappers are on a one-way trip to the abattoir.'

ten

Long after Cthulha's departure, Sally fixed the last foam rubber square to the last caravan. She ran her palms around its edges and pressed its centre. She held the pose then checked her watch; nine-thirty and daylight fading.

She dismounted her step ladder and stepped back to admire her handiwork. Perfect. She looked left. She saw caravans. She looked right. She saw caravans. She turned half circle. She saw caravans.

And she'd done it. Every caravan in that park, all fifty-eight of them, was now covered from top to bottom in green foam rubber.

She looked down. The ground was too hard. Tomorrow she'd have workmen dig it up and replace it with foam rubber; likewise the trees that dotted the camp, and the perimeter fencing. Soon this would be the softest, bendiest, bounciest caravan park on Earth.

And the hanging baskets some guests had hung up to

make their drab lives more bearable, she'd confiscate them in case someone got tangled in their chains and strangled to death.

And the caravan whose tyres were a dangerous shade of black; first thing tomorrow she'd paint them grey.

And that nervous-looking cat needed tying to something.

Barely able to wait for tomorrow, she untethered the cow from the ladder. 'Come on, Daisy.'

'Moo?'

'Let's see if your mistress has had as great a day as we have.'

'And what's this?' Archie Drizzle stood outside the offices of Flaccid and Placid's Caravan Park.

The manager stood beside him, a young man far too pleased with himself for Drizzle's liking. Drizzle decided he must be Flaccid, though there was no sign of Placid. Flaccid said, 'As you can see, we've covered the entire site with foam rubber. I'm sure you'll agree this is the safest park, not only in Wyndham but the whole world.'

'I'll be the judge of that.' He thrust his Gladstone bag into the chest of Flaccid, who took hold of it while Drizzle stepped forward to inspect the nearest caravan. It was indeed completely covered in foam rubber; green foam rubber. A nice safe colour.

As Drizzle tugged the foam to check it was properly glued, Flaccid said, 'Take as long as you like. We've nothing to fear from close inspection.'

And it seemed he was right.

But then . . .

. . . a thought struck Drizzle.

He stepped back and took in the entire view; a whole caravan park covered in foam – not just caravans but offices, trees, the ground.

'You fool,' Drizzle demanded. 'Don't you realize what you've done?'

Flaccid shrugged blankly.

Drizzle said, 'You've turned this entire camp into one big sponge. If an asteroid were to hit this site, immediately after heavy rainfall, the impact could squeeze out a tidal wave so huge it would deluge the entire North Yorkshire coast, drowning us all.'

Flaccid frowned. 'Isn't that highly unlikely?'

Drizzle slapped a sticker on Flaccid's forehead.

It said FAILED.

'No, Gary. No one could be having a worse time than I am. I've been locked out of my mobile home, my assistant's out of control, I've a giant rabbit sitting on him, my host's a psycho. How could you be having a worse time than me?' Teena paced Sally's kitchen, arguing with her cell phone.

The phone said bzz.

'Baboons?' Teena said. 'How can you have been kidnapped by baboons? There are no baboons in Blackpool.'

The phone said bzz.

'Tanzania? How the hell did you get from the Pleasure Beach to Tanzania?'

Bzz.

'What giant squid?' she said.

Bzz.

58

'Captain Nemo?' she said.

Bzz.

'Jules Verne?' she said.

Bzz.

She stood still and frowned. 'Gary, are you making this up?'

Bzz.

'All your holidays are like this?' she said.

Bzz.

'Then why do you keep taking them?'

Bzz.

'Gary, there is such a thing as taking optimism too far.'

Bzz.

'Right! That's it! If this is what holidays are like, you can keep them! I won't be taking another!' She prodded the phone's Off button like it was the eye of her worst enemy then held the phone like she was about to throw it at the wall. She thought better of it and placed it on the table. She stood fuming until she noticed Sally leaning against the doorpost, watching her. 'You heard that?' Teena asked.

'Every word.' As far as Sally'd been able to work out, Gary was Teena's lodger. He was also her bridesmaid. She'd wanted him as her best man but the vicar wouldn't stand for it. He'd said it might cause confusion if both bride and groom had a best man. She'd said that was easily solved. She'd have a best man and her fiancé wouldn't. But the vicar had insisted – even after a prolonged bout of finger proddings and Do-You-*Know*-Who-I-Ams. He'd said it would be the same at any cathedral. It was a standard part of the wedding ceremony.

So now Gary Yates was her bridesmaid. She'd said it would do him good since he was totally besotted with her.

Seeing her marry another man would give him a sense of closure and finally convince him there was never going to be anything between her and him. He might blub now but he'd thank her for it later.

'I take it you'll be staying in a hotel for the rest of your holiday, what with your host being a psycho,' Sally said.

'And not be able to keep an eye on those two? No chance. I'm staying right here.'

Daisy doggie-paddled upside down between the two girls.

Teena glared at it as though ready to punch it. 'And what's that doing in here?'

'Because she's been such a good girl, helping me foam rubber the camp, I'm letting her live indoors from now on.'

'And do I get a say in this?'

'None. You don't live here, remember?'

Teena fumed some more. She opened her mouth to say something then thought better of it. She opened her mouth again then thought better of it. She glanced around as though seeking inspiration. Then at last she said, 'His reputation's built entirely on me, you know.'

Sally frowned. 'Your bridesmaid has a reputation?'

'Not Gary – Landen.'

She frowned deeper. 'Mr Landen has a reputation?'

'Because he was my first college lecturer, the scientific press said he'd discovered me – like I was some lost tribe. I wasn't lost. I knew precisely where I was – Oxford. And I'd discovered myself long before he came along. He thinks he's so clever. Well . . . well . . .' Her clenched knuckles turned white by her sides.

'Well what?'

She just stood there, anger stopping her conceiving the

60

revenge she thought he deserved. Then she spotted something, something on the worktop by the sink. She headed for it, ravenous strides devouring the ground between her and it.

At the worktop she unplugged the TV aerial, opened the window, shoved the TV out then shut and fastened the window. She clattered aside unwanted items, the electric tin opener, the whisk, the coffee blender. Each hit the floor with a clank until at last she lifted the one object she wanted. A yank at its cable tugged its plug free of the wall socket.

'Could you treat my property with a little more respect please?'

'Never mind that.' She eagerly studied the object's black plastic. 'Let's see how clever he is when this gets through with him.'

'Teena?'

'What?' Her gaze was fixed to the thing like Cthulha's had been fixed to her.'

'That thing you're holding?'

'Yeah?'

'Your deadly revenge?'

'What about it?'

'You do know what it is?'

'Of course.'

'And it's . . .'

'A sandwich toaster.'

Just so long as she knew.

'Teena?'

'Uh huh?'

'What're you doing to my sandwich toaster?'

61

'The usual.'

'Which is?'

'Making a mind control machine.'

Sally sat facing Teena across the kitchen table as Teena reassembled the sandwich toaster. She'd already reassembled it five times, none of which had produced whatever result was desired. Each time, she'd point the thing at Sally, press its ON switch then look at her like she was a major let down. Then she'd start scrabbling away at the thing again. Frankly, Sally didn't think she knew what she was doing.

In order to scavenge parts for her mind control machine, she'd dismantled every piece of electrical equipment Sally had and left it in pieces around them on the floor; her fridge, her microwave, her coffee blender, her radio, kettle, electric blanket, video recorder, her plastic flower that danced when you shouted at it – and the rest. If she wasn't determined to be the best caravan park manager on Earth, Sally would have swung for her.

At a table covered with cogs, wires and assorted circuitry, Teena held a screwdriver to the sandwich toaster. Daisy watching intently over her right shoulder, she said, 'It's a simple yet complex device incorporating one connection for each connection of the human brain. Much as I'm loathe to take such action, finding it a plain nuisance, drastic steps are required if I'm to re-enter my mobile home.'

'But mind control?'

'Uh huh.'

'Is it really that urgent you get back inside?'

She stopped screwdriving and watched Sally across the table. 'Have you seen my face?'

'It looks okay to me.' Sally shrugged.

'It looks okay? Do you know how beautiful I am?'

'I'm sure you're gorgeous.'

62

'Yesterday morning I was one hundred and forty-seven per cent too beautiful. A burden but bearable. Now, according to Browning's Attractivity Index, I'm two hundred and ninety-three percent too beautiful. Three hundred percent is the figure at which female beauty would kill.'

'How can you be getting more beautiful? We're all stuck with what we've got.'

'Adversity makes a woman more attractive. Once I'm back in the mobile home and my adversity level retreats, so my beauty levels should normalize.'

'You're not a nuclear reactor, you know.'

'Some forces are stronger than any nuclear explosion, Sally.' She resumed screwdriving. 'This sandwich toaster will turn Landen into a walking robot. Then I'll make him open the door.'

'And then?'

'I'll hit him.'

'?'

Teena tightened a screw deep within the machine. 'Concussion therapy's a valid part of any psychiatrist's toolkit.'

Sally watched the weedy device which looked like it couldn't even toast sandwiches anymore. 'And this thing could do all that?'

'No brain can resist its waves – apart from mine.'

'What's so special about yours?'

'I'm too strong-willed. Its rays would simply bounce off my cerebellum and hit bystanders.'

'Isn't there an obvious flaw in this plan?'

'None. I've thought of everything. I even have the right sized fuse.' She held up the plug as proof. 'A luxury in mind control circles.'

'But how could it work on a man with no brain?'

'It couldn't.'

'But Mr Landen has no brain.'

63

'Nonsense.' She tightened a screw deep within the device.

'No, listen to me.' She reached across and held Teena's arm to stop her working. 'He's got no brain. You know that wing nut on top of his head?'

'What about it?'

'When you first arrived, and you told him to pay the week's rent while you went veil buying, he unscrewed the wing nut and removed the top of his head. I almost passed out. Then he reached inside and pulled out a wad of notes. Teena, I've seen inside his head. There's nothing in there but a tub of margarine.'

Teena shook her arm free but kept working at the machine. 'Mr Landen has one of the finest brains in England. I've seen it myself.'

'When?'

'Whenever he's removed it.' She tightened another screw.

'Removed it?' Sally's gaze scampered all over her.

Then Teena stopped work. Then she did nothing. Then she put the screwdriver down. Then she stared at the far wall. Then she said, 'Ah.'

'Ah what?'

'To enliven his lectures, Mr Landen often removes his brain. For demonstration purposes he passes it round his students. As a joke, one of them must have substituted a tub of margarine for his brain and he placed it back in his head; an easy mistake for a brainless man to make.'

'What sort of idiot would play a trick like that?'

'We shouldn't be too hard on the students. I'm sure they were just being high-spirited.'

'But they'd have to be complete morons.'

Teena said, 'I remember hearing once about a young student who played the same trick using a goldfish she'd won at a funfair. Of course, in her case, she was very young and very sorry for any harm she'd caused and wouldn't dream of doing such a thing now.' She turned red and shifted uncomfortably in her seat. 'That goldfish was swimming round in there for two months before anyone got suspicious.

'That may explain his odd behaviour since coming away with me. I'd been putting it down to lust but total brainlessness would provoke identical behaviour in a man.'

'Teena?'

'Uh huh?'

'How can a man live without a brain?'

'Many people live without a brain.'

'No one I know does.'

'Are you sure?'

Uncle Al leapt to mind. She pushed him aside.

Teena said, 'When autopsied, one in thirty people are found to have had little or no brain function in life. It's a mystery of modern science. Statistically speaking, you know someone with no brain.'

Cthulha leapt to mind. Sally pushed her aside.

Teena said, 'The media exaggerates the brain's importance. For a woman such as myself, a brain's indispensable. But for an average person, like you, its main use is as ballast whilst swimming.'

'So your invention won't work.'

'No.'

'And you've ruined my sandwich toaster.'

'Yes.'

'And you've ruined my washing machine.'

'Yes.'

'And you've ruined my TV.'

'Yes.'

'And I can't have coffee.'

'No.'

'And I can't watch TV.'

'No.'

'And I can't do the washing.'

'No.'

'So what can I do?'

Teena shrugged. 'Is there anyone you know whose brain needs controlling?'

'Only yours.'

eleven

Last thing that night, Teena lay on the top bunk, reading Stephen Hawking's *A Brief History of Time* and scrubbing out the wrong bits. One of these days she was going to have to have a word with Mr Hawking.

'Teena?' Sally appeared in the doorway. Clearly hiding something behind her back she beamed, 'I've been thinking.'

'Yeah?'

'As you don't like being sellotaped to your bunk at nights, I've thought of a better way to keep you safe.'

Teena squinted at her distrustingly. 'And that'd be . . . ?'

From behind her back, looking far too proud of herself, Sally Cooper produced a full set of, 'Chains!'

'You do realize this is a waste of time?' Teena said. 'I

possess three doctorates in escapology. I can get out of this whenever I want.'

Did the girl never stop boasting? She lay with her wrists, head, midriff and right ankle chained to the bunk's safety rails. You'd have thought that'd be enough to shut anyone up. The one part of her still free was her left ankle which Sally was in the process of securing.

Standing on the ladder, Sally told her, 'For the last time, I'm not trying to keep you prisoner. I'm trying to save your life. Is it too much to ask that, for just eight hours, you try not to escape? My job's on the line here you know.'

'Well forgive me my selfishness.'

'There's no call for sarcasm.'

twelve

The plain girl's hallway. Two AM.

In darkness, Daisy the cow clamped her jaws round the bedroom door handle, ignored its bitter metal taste and pulled it downward. Silently, silently she nudged the door ajar.

It creaked.

Daisy stopped.

Pulse raised, ears pricked, she listened hard, fearing discovery. But the only sound was the comely girl moaning, 'Frankie Howerd,' in her sleep before turning over in her bunk and settling down again.

Confidence growing, Daisy lowered her ears and pushed the door fully open.

And, murder in mind, she gazed in at two sleeping girls.

They dreamed their little dreams, oblivious to her treacherous intent, one in chains, one free. She could float in there, take their pillows and smother them as they slept. They would never even know they'd been killed.

Anticipation mounting, she made her move to do just that.

But no. Where would be the style in that? Where would be the recognition? She had other plans for them, plans more worthy of a cow of her literary repute. Again clamping her jaws around the handle, she pulled the door to until it clicked. Sleep tight, little girls. Sleep well. For tomorrow you may die.

Now in the kitchen, Daisy closed its door behind her then 'swam' to the room's far corner.

By the washing machine stood her target, the pedal bin. She glanced around making sure she remained undiscovered then pressed the pedal. The lid flicked open. She looked inside.

And she smiled.

Discarded in that bin, a jumbled mass of wires and plastic, lay the one thing she needed to initiate her master plan.

Teena Rama's mind control machine.

In the entrance hall, mind machine and a hair grip in mouth, Daisy swam to the front door. There she placed the machine on the Welcome mat and the hair grip in the door lock.

Legs paddling she floated upward to undo the top bolt.

Legs paddling she floated downward to undo the bottom bolt.

Now the tricky part – but how tricky could any task be for a cow of her intellect? She clamped her jaws around the hair grip and jiggled it in the lock till it produced a pleasing clunk.

She released the hair grip. She clamped her jaws around the door handle. She lowered it. And she pushed.

The door opened.

Perfect.

After again checking she'd not been seen she opened the door fully. A cold breeze blew in. She ignored it. She collected Teena Rama's mind machine from the floor. And she took it into the night.

In moonlit darkness Daisy arrived outside the front door she sought. And she placed a mind control machine on the front step of the one person who'd know how to use it.

thirteen

Morning woke Sally with the warmth of the rising sun and the twittering of birds. Her eyes opened with a string of tired blinks, adjusting to the light, and she stretched out in a yawn that extended her to her limits.

Except she couldn't.

She'd been chained to the bunk.

fourteen

'Shut up, I'm coming.' She was coming with a hacksaw, a chain dangling from her right wrist, her jaw clenched and her teeth grinding. Sally strode into the kitchen, summoned by a phone that had started to ring as she sawed through the last link of the last chain. She'd still have been chained to the bunk if not for Mr Bushy getting the saw from the bottom drawer – and he'd never have done that if she hadn't spent weeks teaching him the rudiments of stage mind-reading. A mind-reading squirrel, who wouldn't pay good money to see that?

At the phone, she dropped the saw into the sink. When she got the rest of the chain off her wrist she'd wrap it round Rama's throat, yank it tight and strangle her.

The phone was still ringing. She answered it. 'Hello?'

'Is that Sally?'

'Yeah.'

'Sally who?'

'Sally Cooper,' she sighed.

'Good. Because if you're Sally Dunstable tapping my niece's telephone, let me tell you, young lady, I have lawyers – and I don't care how big your brother is.'

'Who the hell's Sally Dunstable?'

'This is your Uncle Al.'

'Uncle Al who?'

'The one who raised you and suckled you between his teats when you were a mere whelp.'

'You didn't suckle me between your teats. You don't even have teats.'

'But I ordered Miss Go-La-Go-Go to suckle you between hers. And, as I own Miss Go-La-Go-Go . . .'

'Uncle Al?'

'What?'

'You don't own Cthulha.'

'Of course I do. I have a receipt.'

'Owning people's illegal.'

'Since when?'

'Since donkeys' years ago.'

'Is this true?'

'Yes.'

'Then why did no one tell me?'

'Like they should need to.'

'But I paid ten pounds for her.'

She frowned. 'You paid *who* ten pounds for her?'

'The man beside her at the bus stop.'

'What bus stop?'

'The one where I first met her.'

'And who was he?'

'I don't know.'

She'd unchained herself to have conversations like this? 'Has it ever occurred to you that he was just some bloke waiting for a bus?'

'Then why did he take the money?'

74

'Because he could spot a mug a mile off. And Uncle Al?'

'What?'

'All those people you employ at your house; the butler, the maids, the cooks.'

'I know who I employ.'

'You don't own any of them.'

'What?'

'You heard.'

'What about Mr Dunnett?'

'No.'

'Miss Jones?'

'No.'

'Mr Sondheim?'

'No.'

'Mrs Howams the gardener? I must own her, she's old.'

'Not even her.'

'But I give her money.'

'So?'

'Doesn't that count for anything with these people?'

'No.'

'You'd think they'd be glad of the chance to be owned by me.'

'Let me give you an example to clarify the point.'

'I'm all ears.'

'You buy your groceries from Davey Farrel's?'

'Of course.'

'And you give him money?'

'He insists.'

'And you don't think you own him. So why do you think you own your staff?'

'I don't own Davey Farrel?'

'For God's sake.'

'But this is madness.'

'No. It's sanity. I know you're not familiar with the concept.'

'But–'

'Look,' she told him. 'Your customers give you money.'

'Yes.'

'And does that mean they own you?'

'Don't be ridiculous.'

'Why am I being ridiculous?'

'I'm a higher form of life. It'd be a mockery for them to own me.'

'Good God.'

'Just because you've lost the argument,' he said.

'Anyway, Cthulha didn't suckle me.'

'But–'

'She refused. She took one look at one of those pumps that promote lactation, and panicked.'

'But–'

'Remember that scare? The Beast of Jansen's Lea? Half wolf, half something else, all terror? Cthulha took me out into the big woods by Jansen's Lea, claiming wolves always suckle abandoned kids. When she couldn't find it – like it ever existed – she left me to find it for myself then set off in search of her dealer, wanting to know what it was he'd been selling her. I was eight.'

'I suppose Miss Go-La-Go-Go *was* going through one of her more irresponsible phases at the time.'

'When hasn't she been?'

'But my original point stands.'

'Which is?'

'I ordered other people to make considerable sacrifices for you. And never forget it.'

'Oh, then you must be that Uncle Al – the one who never lets me forget a "kindness".'

76

'"That Uncle Al"?!? Just how many Uncle Al's do you think you have, young lady?'

'With any luck, just the one. But I thought I'd see how you like being mistaken for someone else.'

'My constant enquiries as to who you are, are purely for your own protection.'

'Sure.'

'Do you want Sally Dunstable to discover your private doings?'

–sigh–

'Well do you? Do you?'

'No, Uncle Al, though I'm sure she's desperate to.'

'And that's why I always double check your identity.'

'No; you do it to remind me how unimportant I am before you launch into a conversation that'll end with you trying to scrounge off me.'

'Nonsense.'

'It's blatant. You're the most blatant person I've ever met.'

'Excuse me?' he protested.

'Did you get my letter?'

'Indeed I did. That cow . . .'

'What about her?'

'Send him over.'

'Her.'

'I'm sorry?'

'Cows are "Hers". "Hims" are bulls.'

'Regardless, send him over.'

'You want to thank her?'

'Thank a cow for sending me sweet wrappers? Of course I don't wish to thank a cow for sending me sweet wrappers. Do you take me for a fool?'

'Then . . . ?'

'I wish to offer him an executive post.'

fifteen

'Miss Go-La-Go-Go.'

'Sod off.' Mid morning. Uncle Al's mansion. Cthulha sat at his Reading Room table sighing. How was she meant to wrap his stupid head in foil if he kept interrupting her? 'My name's Gochllagochgoch,' she complained adding yet more foil to the head. 'I've told you a billion times, it's Welsh.'

'And are you Welsh?'

'No,' she groaned.

'Then where are you from?' Like he didn't know.

'Bradford.' She sighed emptily.

'Then, Miss Go-La-Go-Go, I'd like to show you something.'

'I've seen it.'

'Miss Go-La-Go-Go!!!'

'Look, do you want me to go over there and join you or do you want me to sit here and wrap your stupid head in foil? I can't do both.'

'Put that head down! Now!'

Half ready to deck him she placed the decapitated head on the table, with the aplomb of someone sticking a cabbage on a spike. She was glad to get rid of it. Wrapped in lead it weighed a ton.

'And be more careful with my Beloved Catherine.'

'That head is not your Beloved Catherine.'

'How dare you.'

'It's a Japanese sniper's head you bought in a car boot sale.'

'Nonsense.'

'Beloved Catherines don't have gouges where the shrapnel was removed.'

'Nonsense.'

'Beloved Catherines don't have rising suns tattooed on their foreheads.'

'Nonsense.'

'It never fools anyone, you know. They all know you just call it your Beloved Catherine to make them think you deserve pity.'

'And what's wrong with that? Everyone wants to be pitied don't they?'

'Jesussake.' Ensuring her chair legs dug deep into the oak floor, she stood up, rattled her chair to annoy him further, then set about crossing the forty feet that separated her from him. Her footsteps echoed around the oak panelled room.

He was an even bigger pain than he'd been before he'd had his 'personality' downloaded into the machine that hid the room's entire south wall; a great, black, pointless bank of lights, monitors, valves, screens and circuitry – most of which served no purpose. And there were the squiggly little noises it emitted, copied from the bridge of the Starship Enterprise.

She stood before him, cigarette in mouth, hands in pockets, all stroppy defiance. 'So, what do you want?'

'Miss Go-La-Go-Go, do you remember our first meeting?'

She remembered standing at a bus shelter twelve years earlier, spraying her name all over it in big red letters that no one could miss, then kicking it to see how big a dent she could make before anyone complained.

She remembered ignoring a voice that said, 'Young lady? Over here,' until she'd realized it was her the voice was calling a lady.

She remembered looking up to see the world's longest car, parked kerbside, a man looking out the back, waving money at her and saying, 'You look like a woman who could motivate me.'

Well she'd discovered early that she could motivate men to do all kinds of things, though most involved the removal of clothing.

He'd brought her back to this place, just outside town, covering more land than she'd ever known existed, him walking alongside her through long dry corridors, offering her a drink, trying to make her feel welcome, trying to make it so she'd like him. As though liking him was ever going to come into it.

Now watching the computer he'd become she shrugged and said, 'Who could forget?'

'And you remember the man stood beside you at the bus stop?'

'What man?'

'Damn! She was right.'

'Who was?'

A small hatch opened before her. A sink plunger extended from within. It held three small objects. He said, 'My niece pushed these through my letter box yesterday evening.'

80

She squinted at them, battling to bring them into focus. 'So?'

'Do you know what they are?'

'Sweet wrappers.'

'And how many are there?'

'Three.'

'And do you know who collected them?'

'A cow.'

'No.'

'No?'

'It was a flying cow.'

'Yeah, like I couldn't fly if I had the time.'

'Miss Go-La-Go-Go, how many sweet wrappers have you collected for me?'

'None. I've been collecting lead foil.'

'And of what use to me is lead?'

'To wrap around your stupid head.'

'Why would I wish to wrap foil around my head?'

'Because you said–'

'Wrapping my head in sweet wrappers collected by a flying cow will gain me publicity. You have gained me no publicity; not one reporter, not one TV camera–'

'Publicity.' She sneered. 'You said you were doing it for some bloke called Blighty.'

'I find it astonishing that my motivational coach has less instinct for PR than a farmyard animal.'

'So now you want me to get you sweet wrappers? Well isn't that hunky dory? After I spent the whole of last night running round bribing nuclear technicians for you. None of which you've paid me for, I might add.'

'Miss Go-La-Go-Go, I'm not an unreasonable man–'

'Only because you're not a man.'

'–I don't expect a woman of your abilities to walk the back streets seeking sweet wrappers – any more than I expect you to return to walking those streets for money.'

'Good! Because I–'

'I expect you to leave this building and never return.'

'What?' Her cigarette fall from her mouth.

His valves flashed furiously. His squiggles made sounds even she'd never heard before. He said, 'From now on, that cow shall be my motivational coach.'

sixteen

Daisy the cow placed her nose against Aloysius Bracewell's front doorbell and pressed it. Through the oak panelled door she could hear the bell ring in the hallway.

While awaiting an answer, she turned a half circle and looked down the wide avenue that linked the mansion to its wrought iron gates a quarter of a mile away. With her cow vision – an eye on either side of her head – she watched the manicured lawns to either side of her, with their flower beds, ponds, lakes, fountains and strolling herons. Perhaps this should be her headquarters when her plans came to fruition. Yes, yes, her the finest of cows living in a grand country mansion. It was only right.

The front door creaked open behind her. After a suitably timed pause, she turned to face it, and a balding man in his late forties stood before her. He wore a suit and the casual air of the manager of a small but friendly building society. He was the type to give you an extra percent interest on your savings just to show you not all financial institutions are soulless money grabbers. She decided he must be Charles Dunnett, officially Bracewell's butler but, according to the plain girl, really his main business adviser. Bracewell thought it good management to not let his staff feel in any way important.

Dunnett said, 'Yes, Miss? Can I be of help?'

Tipping her head forward, she offered him the introductory note the plain girl had given her.

His footsteps echoing around them, Dunnett led Daisy up a grand staircase whose polished banisters reflected her face back at her. A chain of too-large paintings hung from the oak panelling to her left. They depicted what were clearly meant to be Bracewell's distinguished forbears. But they all shared a face: a dull greengrocer's one you wouldn't trust with sixpence.

She sniffed one. It stank of linseed. The paint was fresh. These were paintings done by some hack to make it look like Bracewell had breeding when the only breeding he'd ever had was pigeons. His ego was too big to allow his ancestors a face other than his own.

At the top of the stairs, Dunnett headed right. She followed him. He led her along the landing and past a series of oak panelled doors. Each bore a brass plate that revealed the room's function. She passed a Library, a Drawing Room, a Master Bedroom, a Sick Bay, a Bridge – and a Transporter Room?

Dunnett: 'I must say we rarely get cows visiting us.'

Cows had judgement.

He said, 'But then we rarely get animals of any persuasion,

unless one counts Miss Gochllagochgoch, which I rather fear Mr Bracewell would. Personally, I had rather a soft spot for Miss Gochllagochgoch, finding her total lack of respect for anything, herself included, a refreshing change from the stuffy conventions of a big house. Still, I'm sure that once we get to know you we'll discover you have many endearing qualities of your own.'

The paint smell was stinging her nose. She shoved it against his double breasted jacket, shut her eyes and, with a huge, closed-eyes blast, sneezed into it.

She wiped her nose dry on the fabric then withdrew.

She watched him, provocatively, to see how he responded. If he wanted a fight she was ready for him. As though he stood a chance against her cow strength and mastery of wu-su.

Dunnett watched the heavy mucous drip from him and onto the floor. If it bothered him he didn't let it show. She wondered how he'd respond to a French kiss.

He still watched the mucous. 'Then again, perhaps having you here will be just like having Miss Gochllagochgoch still with us. Now, if you'll excuse me, I'll check Mr Bracewell's availability.' He stepped toward the nearest door which swished open. Electronic twiddlings, beepings and gurglings came from the room within. Not looking altogether trustful of the door, he stepped through into the Reading Room. The door swished closed behind him.

With malicious impatience she floated staring holes in that door. Muffled voices seeped out from within but she didn't prick up her ears to hear better. She didn't care about Aloysius Bracewell, his gutless flunkie or anything they might have to say to each other.

The only thing of any interest in that room was the key to the one thing she coveted.

Would their muffled debate never end? She hadn't come here to listen at doors. She'd come to divine and conquer, to rule and replace. But at last their voices did stop, shortly followed by approaching footsteps. She prepared herself mentally, as a great actor prepares for a role.

The door swished open and Dunnett stood before her. He stepped through the door before it could trap him. It swooshed to behind him. He'd wiped the mucous from his person. Good! Why should she the finest of cows have to deal with dirty people? And perhaps when the house was hers, she'd keep him on and ride him around the house on Sundays. A butler of her own. Yes. Yes. A splendid idea.

Her future lackey said, 'Uncle Al will see you now.'

'Uncle Al? Introducing Miss Daisy the cow.' Now in the Reading Room, Dunnett stood by the door.

She floated impatiently beside him, watching the computer that filled the far wall.

'Excellent, excellent.' Bracewell's lights flashed in excited zig zags. His sound effects twiddled busily. 'Mr Dunnett.'

'Yes?'

'Do I have my Friendly Voice on?'

'I believe your Friendly Voice is on Maximum. I'm sure anyone would believe anything you tell them. No matter how stupid it might be.'

'Why thank you, Dunnett. That'll be all,' and Dunnett

departed. Now it was just the two of them. Through narrowed eyes, Daisy watched him.

'Come in, my dear. Come in. Don't be afraid of me, just because I'm awesome and this is the grandest mansion you've ever been in. Think of me as your Uncle Al and treat this room like it's your own field.'

She doggie paddled to the room's centre then stopped there. Tail swishing she waited for him to speak.

Uncle Al said, 'You may be wondering why I invited a pretty young thing like you here. Don't worry, it's not for sexual favours.'

'Moo?'

'Oh I know people say I'm mad just because I had myself downloaded into a computer and talk to cows and buy those plates advertised in colour supplements . . .'

To her left, twenty-five rows of plates hung from the wall. She wanted to smash the lot.

'. . . But those plates are collectors' items and will one day be worth millions. And they only cost thirty pounds new. The fools who make them, then sell them so cheaply, are the mad ones, for not seeing the true worth of their own products. You see those? Those are My Star Trek plates, faithfully reproducing Gene Roddenberry's greatest triumph. See the gruff yet kindly face of Dr "Bones" McCoy. See Mr Spock raise a quizzical eyebrow. See the boyishly determined face of Captain Kirk give the fatal order, "Shoot to kill," their expressions superbly captured by the most acclaimed artist since Michelangelo. And look,' he enthused. 'He's even signed some.'

'Moo?'

'Look at that map.'

A map of the world filled the wall to her right. All the places that had once been the British Empire were pink. She swam across and inspected it. The other continents had been left unmarked but enough black dots covered Europe to make it look as though the plague was back.

'You see those black dots?'

'Moo.'

'Each represents a caravan park. You may know I own the biggest chain in Europe. I mean of course a chain of caravan parks, not a literal chain. What use would I a computer have for a big chain? But dominance of Europe is not enough. Like Alexander I must expand or die. Not that Alexander expanded. By all accounts he remained the same size throughout his career. But he did expand his empire. As must I. I mean of course that I must expand my own empire, not Alexander the Great's. His empire is long gone and such an undertaking would anyway be dangerous.

'But I aim to launch a chain of trailer parks in the US. For America is full of potential customers. Trailer park trash I believe they call them – though, being British and therefore more sensitive to the feelings of others, I prefer to call them future nephews and nieces.'

'Moo?'

'But to expand I need a publicity and motivational coach. Having received your sweet wrappers, I believe you're the man for the job. Naturally you'll be given all the pies you can eat and a straw hat that will make you look endearing to tourists. So, what do you have to say about that?'

She had nothing to say about that.

'Yes. Well. You don't have to decide straight away.'

She ignored him, tail swishing, still watching the map. Let him sweat. She had better things to do with her time. Soon every territory on that map would be hers to use as she saw fit.

She turned, and floated to the long table at the room's centre. A Papermate pen lay on the blotter pad. She collected it in her mouth and held it steady with her tongue.

Ignoring its bitter metal taste, she began to write.

Daisy gazed out through the Reading Room window – or viewscreen as it was labelled – and watched the lawns that stretched for miles around. Those herons would have to go. They were too leisurely. She'd replace them with mules, great lines of tap-dancing mules.

'Just read these ideas, Dunnett.' Behind her, Bracewell showed his re-summoned 'butler' the marketing notes she'd written.

'I'd read them better if you'd keep the sink plunger still, sir.'

'I'm sorry. I tend to wave it around when excited. Is this better?'

'Much.'

'Do you know who came up with these ideas, Dunnett?'

'I think I can guess.'

'And what do you make of them?'

'They're highly impressive.'

Uncle Al said, 'You probably don't believe a cow produced them. You probably think ideas this good must have been written by me and I'm just pretending it wrote them to make it look like I didn't make a mistake hiring a cow.'

'Uncle Al, it never occurred to me for one moment that *you* might have produced ideas such as these.'

'Why thank you, Dunnett. I always appreciate your faith in my judgement.'

'In all the years I've known you, you've never once given my level of faith in you one reason to vary.'

'With ideas like these we could control the American market within six months.'

'I'd say five.'

'Five?' Bracewell's excitement grew. His twiddling sounds were louder than ever.

Dunnet said, 'And it's certainly an improvement on Miss Gochllagochgoch's last suggestion.'

'Exactly. How was I supposed to shove my caravans up there? What kind of marketing strategy was that?'

'You know, Uncle Al, sometimes when people give you advice, they don't really mean it.'

'They don't?'

'Shall I explain sarcasm to you again?'

'Will this "sarcasm" help me launch more caravan parks?'

'I wouldn't have thought so.'

'Will it get me in the Guinness Book of Records?'

'It's unlikely.'

'Then don't bother with it. And, Dunnett?'

'Yes?'

'Contact the Development Department immediately.'

'The Development Department?'

'Tell them; the US – we invade at dawn.'

'I'm sure they'll be delighted.'

When Dunnett had left, Daisy turned to face Bracewell.

'As for you, my fine, uddered beauty, your first pie will arrive within days.'

Was she meant to be impressed?

'In the meantime, if I can do you any favours? Perhaps gambling or drugs debts that need clearing? I know what you young people get up to these days. Or perhaps you'd like to buy some Swing records? There's a little record shop in town. I own the proprietor. I'm sure a discount can be arranged.'

As though such trifles would interest her. She turned

towards the window again and gazed down at the only thing she'd come here for.

It stood glossy and empty in the mansion forecourt . . .

. . . Cthulha Gochllagochgoch's 1968 Spooder Yo-Yo.

seventeen

–Sigh–

'Something up, babe?'

Damn right there was. Last thing that night, Cthulha sat up in bed, listlessly pushing her nipples around her chest. Round and pink, they reminded her of the headlights of the car she'd lost with her job.

Bridget Fonda looked down at her from the opposite wall, half facing her, half turned away from her. Wet, bedraggled and pouting, she held a gun like it was a purse. The word ASSASSIN hung over her head in big red letters, followed by a cast list. She looked like Cthulha felt.

Bored with trying to make them meet in the middle, she released her nipples, let her hands flop onto her lap and sighed. 'Cheer me up, Roddy.'

Roddy McDoddy was sat beside her, drawing in a large sketch pad. Held like a hammer's handle, his marker pen scritchety scratchetied across the page. 'Why don't you take a look what I've been drawing, babe?'

She tried to. It made no sense to her. She took the pad from him and held it at arms' length. It still made no sense. She held it closer then further away then closer, trying to find the ideal viewing distance. There wasn't one. She gave in and pressed it against her nose.

'Why don't you wear your glasses?' he asked.

'I don't need them.' She pressed it tighter against her nose.

'I'd noticed.'

She said, 'It's you.'

'Me?'

'You draw fuzzy.'

'How can I draw fuzzy.'

'You do everything fuzzy.'

'You weren't saying that twenty minutes ago.'

She didn't believe this; for the last ten minutes she'd been regaling him with her woes. And all that time, what had he been drawing? He'd been drawing cows – cows like eight-year-olds draw cows, stick figures with cross eyes, and tongues hanging out the sides of their mouths. A circle with lines coming from it was either the sun or a flying hedgehog. 'Are you sure you're the new Rembrandt?' she asked.

'I'm planning a summer exhibition.'

She let the pad fall onto her lap then groaned.

'Something up, babe?'

'You know, some boyfriends might have the sensitivity not to sit up all night drawing cows on the day their girlfriend lost her job to one.'

He took the pad back. 'They ain't cows, babe.' He placed it on his lap and resumed drawing.

'Then what are they?'

'Buffaloes; a mighty herd sweeping majestically across the plains.'

'A herd? You've only drawn two.'

'Buffaloes are difficult. It's the fingers. There's too many of 'em.'

'Roddy?'

'Yeah?'

'Buffaloes don't have fingers.'

'They don't?'

'No. And they don't have cheeky grins either.'

He stopped scribbling, held his drawing at arms' length and gazed at it. 'My masterpiece is ruined.'

'Who could tell?'

He started drawing again. 'Regardless, I'll give this to the Indian Nations of America as a sign of unity with the indigenous peoples of the world.'

'I'm sure they'll be delighted.' More likely they'd stick an axe through his head. 'Anyway, buffaloes are just a type of cow. The cow that got my job, its nose drips. How can you lose a motivational coach's job to something whose nose drips?'

'It's a bum rap.' He drew on.

'All my life I've only wanted two things. You know what they were?'

He shrugged, still drawing.

'A pink Spooder Yo-Yo and to be nice like Bridget Fonda. And now the car's gone, I'll have reached twenty-six–'

'Thirty-one.'

'–without achieving either ambition. No one should reach twenty six–'

'Thirty-one.'

'–without achieving a single ambition.'

He drew on. 'You want to be the chick who talks to her socks?'

'What?' She frowned at him.

'That chick you want to be, she thinks her socks are

people. She talks to 'em. Then she pretends they're talking back, but it's just her speaking through the side of her mouth. She's crazy, man, crazy.'

Cthulha watched him, her frown deepening. 'Bridget Fonda talks to her socks?'

'All the time.'

She watched him some more. Either Fonda was keeping something from the world or . . .

Then it dawned on her. 'Do you mean Shari Lewis and Lambchop?'

He shrugged, still drawing.

'How could anyone confuse Bridget Fonda with Shari Lewis?' she complained. 'They're completely different. Bridget Fonda was in Single White Female. You know; "Hello. Can I be your flatmate?", "Okay. But only if you don't kill my boyfriend with my shoes. Ha ha."'

'She killed her boyfriend?' he drew on.

'No. Her flatmate killed her boyfriend.'

'What for?'

'Drawing cows.'

He didn't take the hint.

'But that's what they said at drama school. They said, "Cthulha, stick with it. One day you could be the new Bridget Fonda." And like a mug I gave it up for love.'

'I heard you gave it up for vice.'

'Who's telling this story?'

'Then why don't you *be*?'

She took the pad from him and let it rest on her lap. She'd heard artists were sensitive about having their work screwed up and she'd probably need him in a good mood for what she was about to ask. 'Roddy?'

'Yeah?'

'You know that arrangement we have?' She turned another page, still plucking up courage.

'What arrangement?'

'This one. The one where we . . . we . . .'

'The one where I make love to you, and you scream hysterically, banging your head against the wall till you orgasm?'

'That's the one.'

'What about it?'

'Well.' She went red.

'Yeah?'

'I was thinking.'

'Yeah?'

She swallowed. 'Maybe you should pay me for it.'

'Huh?'

'Now I don't have a job, I'll need the money.'

'Why should I pay to give you an orgasm?'

'Because that's what men do.'

'I don't.'

'You wouldn't go into a shop and take goods without paying.'

'I'm not taking. I'm giving.'

'Are you saying I'm not worth it?'

'Yeah.'

'Are you saying I'm too old?'

'Yeah.'

'You know, this isn't making me feel very attractive. I used to make a living out of sex. Now even my own boyfriend won't pay me for it. I might as well face it, I'm just a washed up old–'

'Like Toulouse-Lautrec, I see dignity in those women polite society scorns. Where others might call you "slapper"–'

'Excuse me!' she protested. 'I have a genuine medical condition brought on by childhood trauma.'

'You're not going to start on about that Lizzie Henthorpe chick again?'

'Yes I am going to start on about "that Lizzie Henthorpe chick". An experience like that'd unbalance anyone. Want me to show you my certificate that officially states I'm not a slapper?'

'You wrote that yourself.'

'Professor Tiberius Steinbeck of Wheatley University wrote it. Want to call him and check? You know where my phone is. He'll tell you. My sex addiction's a pathognomic condition deserving of sympathy.'

'Then why not get therapy?'

'That'd be right. My boyfriend wants me to give up the one pleasure I have left in life.'

'What I'm saying is, where those less enlightened might call you "slapper", I see the divine spirit within and refuse to debase it.'

'And refusing to debase my spirit's supposed to pay my bills is it? Do you think a house like this comes cheap? Three storeys high, perched on a cliff edge, directly over-looking the sea? It's pure Hitchcock. Can you even begin to imagine what my mortgage is?'

He shrugged.

'Some boyfriend you turned out to be.' Tempted to tear it in half she pressed the pad against her nose. On this page a stick figure reclined on a bed, in a pose taken from *The Venus of Urbino* by Titian. She recognized it from one of Uncle Al's *Classic Paintings* plates, the ones he used to lick gravy off. Bendy spikes that were either hair or deadly radiation jutted from the figure's head. Its day-glo green eyes faced opposite ways. She squinted at it, tilting it from side to side, trying to make sense of it.

'Roddy?'

'Yeah?'

'What's this meant to be?'

He took a peek. 'That? That's Dr Tinashta Rama.'

She watched him, amazed. 'Teena Rama? You know Teena Rama?'

'I met her yesterday. Inspired by her classical beauty, and great jugs, I decided to draw her nude. I think I caught her lines.'

She watched him, amazed. 'Teena Rama posed nude for you?' Maybe she'd do the same for Cthulha.

'No. I forgot to ask her—'

—groan—

'—so I used my imagination.'

She pulled a face at the pad. 'This is how you imagine her?' She ogled the picture some more, trying but failing to get aroused by it. 'Why's she got frying pans stuck to her chest?'

'What frying pans?'

'There.' She pointed at one.

'They ain't frying pans.'

'Then what are they?'

'Mammaries.'

'But they've got handles,' she said.

'Don't be ludicrous. A woman as lovely as Dr Rama don't have no handles.'

'Then what are they?'

'Luggage labels.'

She looked at him. 'Luggage labels?'

He snatched the pad back, flicked backwards through it and resumed work on his buffaloes.

She said, 'Why don't I be what?'

'Huh?'

Before I asked about the nude sketch, you said why don't I be.'

'I was asking—'

'Yeah?'

'—This Fondu chick.'

98

'What about her?'
'If you want to be her . . .'
'Yeah?'
'. . . Then . . .'
'Yeah?'
'Why don't you be?'

eighteen

Last thing at night Teena lay on the top bunk, reading Richard Dawkins and turning each page with a growing sense of disbelief. Able to bear no more she flung it at the wall. It bounced off, then hit the floor, like a wounded duck. She considered leaping from the bed then jumping up and down on it till it was completely flattened but it lay there dead so she didn't bother.

'Teena?' Sally stood in the doorway, holding something behind her back. She wore the smirk of one in on a secret. 'I've a surprise for you.'

'Does it involve chains?'

'No.'

'Does it involve masking tape?'

'No.' Her smirk widened. Teena could have written whole papers on that girl's psychiatric condition.

Teena peered at her. 'Then what *does* it involve?'

Sally paused. Then, from behind her back, she produced, 'A sledgehammer!'

No way would she escape this. It might have seemed drastic, it might have seemed OTT, but it had to be done. She had to be saved from herself.

Not that she seemed to care. She just lay in bed, reading another of her endless supply of books, left wrist between safety rail and mattress as Sally hit the rail with the sledge hammer. Soon that rail would be bent out of shape enough to hold that wrist captive.

But the hammer weighed a ton. Stood on her ladder, she cast aside the handle, letting its head rest on the mattress then wiped sweat from her forehead with her lead-heavy arm. Her arms hurt. Her back hurt. Her head hurt. Her armpits were pools of sweat. And did Teena look grateful? Did she buggery. She just turned another page like Sally wasn't even there. She was posh. She was probably used to having people run around after her in her big house in Wheatley where everything was made of silk. *Well, Princess Polka Dot, if I missed with my next blow and broke your wrist, how cool would you act then?*

'Are you all right, Sally?' She turned another page, not noticeably concerned with Sally's well being.

'I'm fine,' she gasped.

'Very good.' She turned another page.

Sally gripped the hammer's handle, braced herself, and with all her might, hoisted it above her head. She narrowly avoided having its weight pull her backward off the ladder, and again brought hammer down on rail. When this was done she'd trap the other wrist, and her ankles, and maybe her neck. She'd enjoy trapping her neck. Then she'd crawl off somewhere to die, happy in the knowledge that she'd won at last.

'Sally?'

'What?' Gasp pant wheeze.

'Has anyone ever told you, you have an over-competitive streak?'

nineteen

Morning woke Sally with the warmth of the sun, the twittering of birds and the chattering of chimpanzees. Her eyes blinked, adjusting to their exposure to daylight. She smiled, flexed herself all over then stretched out in a great long yawn that extended her body to its limits.

Except she couldn't.

Her head was stuck between the railings at Wyndham Zoo's elephant house.

twenty

'As you'll see, we at Toothless Tony's Gummy Caravans have taken every possible precaution to ensure that ours is the safest camp, not only in Wyndham but the world.'

'I'll be the judge of that.' Archie Drizzle stood outside the site's offices, Toothless Tony beside him, a curly-haired young man too full of himself for Drizzle's liking. Gazing down at the thing that lay on the ground before him, Drizzle asked, 'And what's this?'

'Fido, the bubble-wrapped dog.'

The collie lay on the ground, on its back, legs in the air. Just its face uncocooned, it lay motionless except for its lazy panting.

Still watching it, Drizzle said, 'Is he all right?'

'Fido's kept permanently drunk so he'll lack the co-ordination to do any damage.'

Drizzle thrust his bag into the chest of Toothless Tony, who took hold of it while Drizzle stepped forward, squatted on his haunches and inspected the dog. It seemed to be securely enough wrapped and its crossed eyes and happy demeanour suggested it was indeed paralytic.

But then . . .

. . . it dawned on him.

Still squatting, he looked back toward Toothless Tony. 'My God, man, do you know how dangerous this dog could be?'

Toothless Tony looked blank.

Rising to his feet, Drizzle said, 'The bubbles in that bubble-wrap might contain ozone-destroying gases. The moment children start popping those bubbles – as children are guaranteed to do – that gas could ignite the Van Allen Belt, forcing us all to live in submarines at the bottom of the sea.'

'Isn't that a little unlikely?'

Drizzle slapped a sticker on Toothless Tony's forehead. It said FAILED.

Old Mr Johnson's Rottweiler fancied himself as quite the proper little lady and, on sunny days, would parade around the camp, in his Easter bonnet, seeking the admiration of others. If anyone tried to remove it, he'd leap on them and rip their throats out.

Sally decided not to try and remove it.

She sat him on her lap, at her kitchen table and set about bubble wrapping him. By now she had him seventy percent covered though it would have been easier if Mr Bushy hadn't kept popping his bubbles.

Daisy floated around the room, vertical like a sperm whale before it dives into the depths for squid. Davey Farrel had told her all about squid – every chance he got. He and Cthulha's mother should have got together.

The front door creaked open. No-nonsense boots clomped into the entrance hall and wiped on the doormat. Mr Bushy scurried for cover and Sally's heart sank.

Now Rama stood in the kitchen doorway, a cat who'd caught its mouse. She hugged a red bucket to a silk, polka dot dress that seemed to have been sprayed on. It just about covered everything it needed to and had straps a fly could snap.

Sally sneered, 'You think you're so clever.'

Boots clinking, Rama strode across to the window. 'I am clever. If I say so myself, few could have performed the elephant house feat without waking you. I take it you've finally learned your lesson?'

'What lesson?'

Rama rolled her eyes like Sally was the one in the wrong.

'I could've been killed,' Sally complained. 'I could've–'

Rama opened the window, pushed the TV out then closed and fastened the window. She turned to face Sally, backside resting against a cupboard 'You were in no danger. Indian elephants are renowned for their placidity. African elephants, on the other hand, would have torn you to shreds.'

'And if there'd been a fire?'

'They could have put it out with their trunks.' And she burst out laughing like she'd said something hilarious.

Sally wasn't laughing. She could still feel the rashes on her neck where the bars had chafed it until the fire brigade had shown up. 'And what are those meant to be?'

Teena looked down at her feet. 'These? These are my Emma Peel boots.' She did a twirl to show off their thigh-high, folded-back-down-to-the-knees, suedeness. Their three-inch

106

heels made her over six-foot tall. A six-foot Teena Rama was a scary thing.

Twirl completed she grinned at Sally. 'So, what do you think?'

'If you're so concerned about men lusting after you too much why don't you try wearing underwear?'

'A woman has a right to wear whatever she chooses, without harassment. Clearly feminism has yet to reach Wyndham.'

'And you think you're Emma Peel?'

'I like to think she and I are cut from the same cloth, yes, and that, given the chance, I could rescue Steed from the same situations she did. And look.'

'At what?'

'They come with big buckles at the top.' She slapped one to make it clink. 'It was Gary's idea. I called him this morning to see how his baboon ordeal was going and remind him he has to be back in time for my wedding. After a few minutes blubbing and pleading with me not to get married, he asked me what I've been up to. When I told him about flying cows and mind control machines, he said I was doing it wrong. Apparently, when on holiday, women do frivolous, girlie things. After researching the subject in the local library, I decided he was right. Gary right about something, who'd ever have thought it? So I asked myself, what have I always wanted but have never got round to buying? I couldn't think of anything. Then it struck me – Emma Peel's boots. Not that I approve of stereotyped thinking that seeks to modularize behaviour into male and female templates.'

'Gee,' Sally said flatly. 'You sound more frivolous already.'

'Why thank you. I do my best.' Still beaming, she strode to the table and placed the bucket on it. A Davey Farrel price tag dangled from its handle, at the end of some string.

She said, 'Those cliffs by the sea; the ones topped by the Hitchcock house.'

'Splatter Cove?'

'Has anyone ever scaled them?'

'Why do you think they're called Splatter Cove?'

'This afternoon I'll be conquering them.'

'You're doing this on purpose!'

'I can hardly climb them inadvertently.'

'You're deliberately doing dangerous things to annoy me. You're wearing dangerous footwear! You're climbing dangerous cliffs!'

'Tempting as the thought is of planning the rest of my life around annoying you, I try to act in a slightly more mature manner. I'll be climbing the cliffs purely for my own pleasure.'

'And you'll be conquering them with a bucket?'

'The bucket's not for rock climbing.'

'I thought it might be for scooping your remains into after you fall to your death and ruin my life.'

'I won't be falling to my death.'

'You have safety equipment?'

'No.'

Sally stared at her, blank.

Teena said, 'Only amateurs use equipment. The experienced climber needs just her fingers and toes.'

'Then what's the bucket for?'

'I need your brain.'

Sally bit off more sellotape, and bubble-wrapped the dog's left hind leg. 'You mean you need to pick my brains about some idea you've had?'

'No.' She pulled out a chair and sat facing Sally across the table. She manoeuvred her chair till it was just so, pulled a stray rag away from her face, got her pert backside comfortable then said, 'I need your brain – in this.' Her perfect fingernails tapped the bucket once. 'As my mind control machine won't work on Mr Landen, the logical alternative is to remove his margarine and replace it with a more useful brain. Then I may be able to talk some sense into him.'

'But it wouldn't be him. It'd be me.'

'Of course it'd be him. It'd be him with your brain.'

'Which'd be me.'

Teena looked at her like she was simple. 'You don't understand brain swapping, do you, Sally?'

'I don't believe this.'

'Is something the matter?'

'You've completely lost it.'

'On the contrary, I've never seen things more clearly.'

'Then answer me this. How can you swap his brain for mine when you can't get him out of the mobile home?'

Teena leaned back in her chair, smug. 'I've an idea.'

'It's crap.'

'You've not heard it.'

'I don't need to.'

'As is my wont, I've been seeking an elegant solution to this problem. But, from watching you perform your duties, I've realized that some conundra demand child-like simplicity.'

'Are you calling me thick?'

'Not at all. I merely admire your directness in problem solving. You wish things to be safe, so you foam rubber them. When you run out of things to foam rubber, you bubble wrap things.' She glanced at the dog. 'I could super-evolve that dog for you, by the way.'

Sally sighed.

Teena said, 'Gary watches Star Trek. I don't know why. I've a horrible feeling he thinks it's real. Regardless, it features aliens called the Borg. When faced with a problem, do you know what the Borg do?'

'They shout and hit things?'

'That's Klingons.'

'Oh.'

'When they encounter resistance the Borg assimilate it. You have a similar mentality when it comes to safety.'

'And you think brain swapping's simple?'

'Perfectly.' She toyed with the bucket's label. 'Of course, I'll return your brain when I'm through with it.'

'Teena, you can't remove my brain.'

'On the contrary. It's a simple operation lasting twenty-seven seconds – twenty-five if you don't demand anaesthetic. With a surgeon of my skills there really wouldn't be much pain.'

'There'll be no pain–'

'I wouldn't say I was that good a surgeon.'

'–because you can't have it.'

'Sally . . .' Teena reached across, interlocked her fingers with Sally's and looked her in the eyes. 'I really need this favour. And, as camp manager, you do have certain duties to your tenants.'

Sally yanked her hands free, resolving to keep them by her side from now on. 'My duties to my tenants don't include giving them my brain.'

'I'm afraid they do. The lease I signed with your uncle stipulates that during my stay I can remove any of your organs I see fit. He was adamant. I wasn't keen, seeing no use for the clause and doubting its legality. But clearly your uncle's a man of some foresight.'

'Foresight? He doesn't even have hindsight.'

'Of course, as your psychiatrist, I wouldn't force you to'

'You're not my psychiatrist. Dr Steinbeck's my psychiatrist.'

Teena frowned. 'Dr Steinbeck of Wheatley University?'

She shifted uncomfortably in her seat, like Supergirl hearing the word Kryptonite.

'That's him.'

'That clown.'

'He says he's your old psychology tutor.'

'I learned nothing from him.'

'That's funny, he says the same. And for your information Dr Steinbeck helped me come to terms with all those entertainers' deaths. He's fantastic.'

'Fantastic? The man's a quack. And as for his ideas on hypnotherapy, it's a wonder he didn't have you running round convinced you're a chicken.'

'He's got you sussed.'

'No he hasn't.'

'How's your sister?'

'I don't have a sister.'

'He says you do.'

'When did he say that?'

'On the phone, forty minutes ago. I call him whenever I'm depressed. He doesn't even charge me. He's great.'

'Well isn't he a saint?'

'He says you're a prime example of a spoilt child who feels displaced in her parents' affectations by a younger sibling. Your entire motivational force is to outdo your sister because she was always the clever one.'

'Clever one!?! Excuse me but I have forty-seven degrees, twenty-two doctorates, ninety-seven honorary titles and a hundred and forty-seven arts and science awards. She has one "A" level.'

'Not that you're counting.'

'And if she's so clever, how come she's living in a squat, and busking for a living?'

'Because she doesn't have anything to prove. Unlike you, she can spend her life having fun.'

111

'I know how to have fun.'

'When have you ever had fun?'

'Right now. I've just bought these boots. That's a fun thing to do.'

'No. You bought a pair of boots guaranteed to get you noticed. You're wearing a dress guaranteed to get you noticed. Everything you do's designed to get you noticed.'

'Nonsense.'

'You can't even settle for being the pretty one because you're a mass of insecurities about your looks. That's why you run around measuring them all the time. And it's why, despite all your achievements, you're not properly famous; you daren't go on TV in case they light you badly. My God, I bet even I have more self esteem than you do!' Fed up of her, Sally hugged the rottweiler to her, pushed her own chair backwards as noisily as Teena always did, and carried the dog towards the door.

'Where are you going?'

'Out!'

'Out where?'

'To have more than a word with my uncle about his "clauses", then to return this dog. Then I'm going to see Cthulha. Friends; I have friends. I don't suppose you have any.'

'I have countless friends.'

Sally yanked her coat from the hook on the door and slipped her arm into one sleeve as best she could while carrying a fully grown dog. Old Mr Johnson's Rottweiler had to be carried everywhere. If you took it for a walk, you had to carry it all the way or it turned nasty. If you threw it a stick, you had to carry it to where the stick had landed or it'd turn nasty. For a dog in touch with its feminine side it had a distinctly masculine take on aggression. Trying to get her other arm in the other sleeve, staggering under the dog's weight, she told Teena, 'For some reason Cthulha wants to shag you.'

'So does Dr Steinbeck. Did he tell you that before launching into ludicrous character assassinations? Did he tell you I rejected him and he's been carrying a grudge ever since? Did he tell you that?'

At last she got the coat on. She opened the door, ready to leave.

Still seated, Teena complained, 'And what should I do with my bucket?'

'Try crying in it.'

The front door slammed behind her and Sally's footsteps receded across the compound till they were gone. And Teena sat glowering at the bucket on the table. Its price tag flapped in the breeze from the door slam. A swipe of her arm sent the bucket flying. It hit the fridge, then the floor, then lay there on its side.

She leaned back in her seat, arms folded, jaw jutted, legs sprawled as they saw fit. She felt at her nose. It had never mended properly; no matter that everyone else said it had and was now her best feature. She could still feel where that bitch had 'accidentally' broken it when she was ten.

Clytemnestra mooed.

Teena ignored it.

It mooed again, attention seeking.

She watched it. Floating before her it began to spin like the bone in *2001*. So? Was she meant to be impressed by a cow that made redundant cinema references while she was trying to sulk? Anyway, *Solaris* was a far better movie.

But a brain, where could she find a brain at short notice?

Preferably one whose owner wouldn't legally need to give permission.

Akira, she'd do – her 'beloved' sister who'd have thought of a solution in one second flat then spent the rest of her life rubbing it in, getting her friends to laugh at her; 'Poor slow Teena. Always the family dunce, always the last to catch on.' Then, when she'd almost (but not quite) finished laughing; 'Teena, you shouldn't take it so seriously. You know I'm only teasing.'

Oh really? Well I've noticed you're not coming to the wedding. Or if you are, you're keeping quiet about it. If you do, you'd better not try to steal back my Man Who Does – not after all the effort it took to get him off you in the first place. You can stand there humiliated as I walk down the aisle with 'your' boyfriend. Akira, you fat, ugly cow, I'd just love to get my hands on your brain and . . .

. . . Brain?

. . . Cow?

. . . Brain?

. . . Cow?

Teena leaned forward in her seat, suddenly riveted by Clytemnestra's antics.

She'd just had the greatest idea ever.

twenty-one

Roddy McDoddy stood dry-mouthed at the centre of Wyndham's bustling Argos store. He glanced around, expecting an officer of the law to place a hand on his shoulder and say something clichéd before taking him in. In front of Roddy, a catalogue lay shut on its stand.

He gazed to his left. A big chick was stood beside him, big enough to squash him if she decided to jump on him. But she studied her catalogue, paying him no mind.

He gazed to his right. A normal sized chick was beside him, studying her catalogue. She looked nice. She had blonde hair. He inched closer to her till he was touching her. She ignored him but if she jumped on him it wouldn't hurt so much.

He glanced around again, senses on full alert but saw just kids, men, women and crazy cats. All of them had eyes only for their catalogues.

Feeling happier he turned to face his catalogue. He turned it onto its front – it weighed a ton – and opened it from the back. After again checking no one was watching he stood on tip toes and placed a sucker tipped finger at the head of the catalogue index.

Silently mouthing each category heading, he ran his finger down the index.

He was looking for one word.

The word was Gun.

twenty-two

'Mr Landen? Answer me or face the consequences.' Teena stood on her mobile home's front steps and, with the I-mean-business air of the FBI rapped the door as hard as its foam rubber covering allowed. And if she didn't really have a plan for getting him out of the home, she had a suitable brain and that was a start.

'Go away!' He called from inside.

'Is the rabbit still sat on you?'

'No. He's gone looking for carrots.'

'Where?'

'On the other side of the chair.'

'Which other side of the chair?'

'The other side from the one he's on now. But when he gets to it, it's not the other side anymore. It's become "this" side, and the side he started from is suddenly the other side. He says that if he can only get to the other side of the chair before it becomes this side of the chair, he can find all the carrots of Valhalla. So go away.'

Right. As he was determined to be difficult, that gave her every right to take whatever action she deemed necessary. 'Mr Landen?'

'What?'

'I've an offer for you.'

'An otter?'

'Not an otter. An offer. You do know what an offer is?'

'You always have otters. You have more otters than the devil.'

'Frankly, you've lost me.'

'I wish I had.'

'This is an offer you'll like.'

'Is it a big otter?'

'An offer, for God's sake! I have an offer for you!'

'Will you let me keep my bunny?'

'No I will not. That bunny's reserved for the camp manager.'

'Then stick your otter up your–'

'Listen to this.' She prodded Clytemnestra who was floating alongside her, tethered to the door handle. The action provoked a long moo. Teena asked, 'Do you know what that was, Mr Landen?'

'I know.' He sounded suspicious.

'And what was it?'

'My bunny.'

She frowned at the door. 'Mr Landen, have you been rubbing your head against the radiator again?'

'What if I have?'

She should have known it. His margarine had melted. But if he was too stupid to realize his bunny couldn't be out here while it was in there perhaps she could use that. 'Do you love your bunny, Mr Landen?'

'More than anything. We're going to be married.'

'And do you know what I'm stood beside?'

'What?'

'A Caxton printing press, circa 1490.'

He gasped, shocked.

'That's really not very shocking,' she said.

'Oh.'

'Please try and be shocked at appropriate moments, or I'm wasting my time here.'

'Yes, Dr Llama.'

She said, 'It's the type of printing press where you turn a huge vertical screw to bring the plates together. I'm holding your bunny bound and gagged between those plates.' She awaited a response. She didn't get one. She said, 'You may gasp now.'

He did so.

'Mr Landen?'

'Yes?'

'If you don't come out . . .'

'Yes?'

'I'll squash your bunny.'

'No! No!' he cried.

'No! No!' cried the rabbit, also too stupid to realize he couldn't be out here if was in there. 'Scary little man, don't let her squash me!'

She turned, ready to descend the front steps. All around her, pallid faces peered out from behind the net curtains of surrounding caravans. So? Let them watch. Let this be a lesson for them in how a scientist solves a problem.

She skipped down the steps, turned, and took up position by the door.

She readied herself. 'Mr Landen? I'm holding the screw, and I'm t-u-r-n-i-n-g it . . .

'No, scary little man! Stop her!'

Now she heard furniture being flung away from the door,

presumably by the panic-stricken rabbit. Landen lacked the strength to throw furniture around.

The door flung open, startling Clytemnestra who was still tethered to it. And Landen blundered out, clearly having been pushed by the rabbit.

Before he could react, she grabbed his ankles, swung him round and, with all her strength, smashed him against her mobile home.

Landen slumped over one shoulder, Teena carried him up the steps and into her mobile home. She stopped in the doorway. 'Lepus? Are you in here?' No. He wasn't. He'd just crashed out through the wall, leaving a new hole beside the one she'd repaired the other day. It didn't matter. She'd retrieve him later. She had more pressing concerns.

She carried Landen to her kitchen table, deposited him there then headed for the cupboard that contained her brain surgery equipment.

twenty-three

The moment she got back from Cthulha's, Sally sat at the kitchen table and opened HarperCollins' *Encyclopaedia of Entertainer's Assistants*. It was definitive, much better than Macmillan's; nine hundred pages, fully illustrated, the one she always read when depressed. It profiled every major assistant of the last hundred years, all the way back to the great days of music hall.

There was Betty Hawes, assistant to Gonzales the Human Flea, who upon his death turned out to be neither Gonzales, human nor flea.

And here was Tillie Moskowitz, for ten years assistant to Rattlesnake Bob, He Prods Live Rattlers. She'd started out with the Great Osmosis but walked out on him during his first performance, seemingly preferring the company of rattlesnakes. The Great Osmosis? Whatever happened to that loser?

And of course there was Lillian Clapthorpe; three whole pages devoted to her. Twenty entertainers she'd worked with and turned down forty more. She grinned toothlessly out at Sally; assistant to Rajah Singh, He Fights Live Tigers – except, in the photo, the live tigers looked suspiciously like sheep. Sally figured not many people in Victorian times had ever seen a live tiger – or a sheep.

The frightening thing was, the sheep seemed to be winning. The Rajah's expression said, 'Oh God! Get them off me! Help me! Anyone!'

And what was Lillian Clapthorpe doing?

She was smiling.

The one rule of assisting, always smile like nothing's going wrong.

Sally knew now what she'd done wrong after shooting Magic Keith. Disorientated by the gasping, shouts and shrieks from the audience, she'd stood there, one hand holding the gun, the other over her mouth. Horrified she'd watched the two bodies sprawled on the floor, desperately hoping they'd get up and wave to the audience before running off stage in triumph.

But they didn't.

The bastards just lay there.

The stage lights were too strong, too hot, the audience too loud. Not knowing what to do. Not knowing who to turn to, to run to. Alone on stage, small, vulnerable, with a murder weapon, looking around for anyone who could help her; the director, the technicians. But there was no one; just light, heat, noise, and the blackness of the stalls.

But then . . .

But then . . .

In her mind, the noise had faded, like she was suddenly underwater, and everything was slow motion.

And she knew what to do.

She turned to the audience, ignored their cat calls, and the missiles that bounced off her. To her they were no longer real. She held her arms out to either side and let the gun hang loose from her right hand.

And she said the one word she knew would get her out of trouble.

She said, 'Ta-daa.'

Ta-daa? What the hell was she thinking off? You don't shoot people then go, 'Ta-daa.' You smile like nothing's gone wrong. That's what Lillian Clapthorpe would have done.

No wonder they'd stormed the stage trying to get at her. She had to be rescued by the director who grabbed the gun in one hand, her in the other, and shot some of the audience to clear a path to the fire exit.

The image faded away.

Now she sighed and touched the book's glossy paper as though that might empty her into it and record her in its pages alongside her idols. But she knew she'd never be included among them.

Neither would she lose her sense of guilt about what she'd said to Teena. What was all that stuff about having friends? She didn't have friends. Not unless she counted the staff at Uncle Al's house. No one wants to remain friends with someone whose presence guarantees death. And even with Uncle Al's staff she could always sense them backing away from her as though expecting something big to drop on them just for speaking to her.

In all the world she had one real friend – Cthulha. And some friend *she* was. Apart from her, Teena was the only person who didn't act scared in Sally's presence. And like a genius she'd had to fall out with her.

The front door creaked open. Bootsteps clomped into the entrance hall then wiped on the doormat.

Mr Bushy scurried for cover.

And Teena stood in the kitchen doorway, a cat that had

got its mouse. She clutched the unconscious Landen to a silk, polka dot dress that seemed to have been sprayed on. It had straps a fly could snap.

Sally said, 'You've got him out of the mobile home then?'

Teena smiled. 'Uh huh.'

'And you hit him?'

Teena smiled. 'Uh huh.'

'And you'll be sleeping in the mobile home from now on?'

Teena smiled. 'Uh huh.'

'Thank God for that.'

Teena entered the room. Didn't those boots chafe her thighs when she strode like that? Sally imagined her running for a bus. Suddenly she'd accelerate and the friction would ignite her, leaving just two charred boots on the pavement, like the legs of Ozymandias. The fire brigade would arrive and scratch their heads trying to work out where a burnt pair of Emma Peel boots had come from. Then they'd find the ashes within and guess the terrible truth.

Landen draped over a bare shoulder, Teena opened the window, shoved out the TV then closed and fastened the window. One of these days, Sally was going to ask her why she always did that.

Teena headed for the table. She deposited Landen on it. His hand flopped onto the encyclopaedia's open pages. She pulled out a chair and sat facing Sally. She manoeuvred the chair till it was just so. She manoeuvred her backside till it was just so. She pulled a stray rag away from her face and tucked it behind one ear. 'I will indeed be spending the rest of my holiday in my mobile home.'

Sally plucked up her nerve and prepared to apologize for what she'd said earlier. 'Teena, I–'

'Mr Landen on the other hand has elected to spend the rest of his holiday with you.'

Sally watched him. He didn't look in any condition to elect anything. 'He has?'

'Uh huh.'

Sally removed his hand from her book and placed it by his side. 'And how does he reckon on that?'

'Because he's dead. I've killed him.'

twenty-four

'Okay, Davey boy, open that till and throw your money at me. You've just hit pay dirt.' Cthulha stood beaming, in the open doorway of Davey Farrel's general store, a tiny place on the outskirts of town with too few shelves and too much stock. She had a plan that couldn't fail and a wardrobe that couldn't miss. She was so proud of herself she was scared she'd explode.

Davey wasn't going to explode. He was stood with his back to her, a cardboard box under one arm, taking tins from it and placing them on a shelf. Look at him, the twenty-four-year-old lump of male scrumptiousness in his Davey Crockett hat and Buffalo Bill jacket with tassles. Did he know the effect he had on a woman?

Moving her lips as she read, she checked the writing on her palm.

'Is this a stick up?' he asked.

'Davey, I told you before, that stick up thing was just a joke.'

'I don't remember laughing.'

'You never laugh at anything.' Satisfied with what her palm said, she stopped reading.

'The police didn't laugh either.' He put another tin on the shelf.

'Cops being famous for their sense of fun.' Disappointed by her lack of impact, she let the door fall shut behind her. Its bell tinkled then died.

Davey's ices box hummed beside her; five-foot long, three-foot wide, three-foot high with a glass lid. Its stickers said, WALLS, LYONS MAID and HÄAGEN-DAZS. Lifting its lid, she leaned forward and gazed in at choc ices, lollies and ice pops. The cold made her exposed flesh goose-pimple. She didn't care; it sent her horny.

She leaned further over the box, supported its lid with the top of her head then cupped a breast in each hand. She manoeuvred them into the position that would best catch the coldness then held them there waiting for it to send her nipples hard. In her experience, male pliability was in direct proportion to female nipple protrusion; proof that there is a God and she's female.

'Cathula?'

'Yeah?'

'What're you doing?'

She was aware of him watching her across the shop but didn't look at him. She had a job to complete first. She said, 'I'm making myself desirable for you.' She moved her breasts around some more to get the full cold effect. She figured that when she could no longer feel them they were ready.

He said, 'Yeah that's really desirable; you leaning over a fridge, your head against its lid, squeezing your waps.'

'Excuse me but did it never occur to you that, when you go on a date, there are little tricks a young lady

127

does beforehand to emphasize her feminine wiles?' She manoeuvred them some more.

'And that's one of them is it?'

'You'd be surprised what we get up to.'

'I'd be shocked – if that's typical.' And he resumed shelf stacking.

She continued working at it. 'It'll be worth the effort when you're putty in my hands. And if you were any kind of man you'd know it.'

His only response was the sound of tins being stacked.

But what should she have? A choc ice? A lolly? Something more exotic? She settled on the raspberry lolly to the left. She took it from the box, removed the wrapper, screwed it up and threw it in the ices box. Let someone else dispose of it; she was on a mission. She closed the lid, looked down at her nipples – they were like golf balls – took a bite at the lolly and headed for Davey.

Now stood behind him she took another bite of her lolly. She watched his hard-as-bowling-ball buttocks through his jeans as she sucked ice. 'You still run that lookalikes agency?'

'I suppose.' He put a tin on the shelf.

She grabbed his left buttock.

'Cathula? What're you doing?'

'Sexually arousing you so I can manipulate you into doing whatever I want.'

'If you're trying to manipulate me, is it a good idea to tell me in advance?'

She slipped her hand down inside the front of his jeans, took hold of what she found there and started working at it. 'It doesn't matter with men. Even if they know you're after something, they'll still let you do it. Once the old fella's up, he's in charge of you; and right now, I'm in charge of him. Did I ever tell you God's a woman?'

128

'If you want something, why don't you just try asking –
like anyone normal would?'

She frowned. 'Davey?

'What?'

'How long have you had trouble producing an erection?'

'I don't have trouble producing an erection. You have
trouble producing an erection.'

'We'll see about that.' She removed her hand from
inside his jeans then started patting in the appropriate
region.

He put another tin on the shelf. 'Now what are you
doing?'

'I'm patting it at just the right rhythm to produce maximum response. Another trick women know and men
don't. You see how men would gain so much wisdom
if they'd only listen to women?'

'This is the Twenty-First Century, men do listen to
women.'

'They never listen to me.'

'I can't imagine why.'

Still patting she asked, 'How many lookalikes you got
on your books?'

'None.'

'None?' She stopped patting. 'It's supposed to be a boom
industry.' She resumed patting.

He put a tin on the shelf. 'There's no one round here
looks like anyone you'd want to meet.'

She gave up on the patting. Clearly there was something
medically wrong with him or he was just plain gay. She
took a step back. 'Look at me, Davey.'

'I . . .'

'Look at me.'

And, reluctant, he turned to face her.

Now she had his attention, she pulled lank, freshly bleached hair away from her face and wrapped it behind one ear. She checked her nipples were still erect. They were starting to lose it, so she tweaked them between thumb and forefinger, another feminine trick men never dreamed existed, and took three steps back.

To best show off her proud new look she raised her arms like she was a plane about to take off. The look was a pink tie-dye bikini top, savagely cut-off jeans and a goldish ankle bracelet. And if the hair was bleachier than she'd intended and lanker, so what? She looked great. She looked better than great. She looked Hollywood. Grinning like a loon, she did a dainty three-sixty-degree turn, bare feet scuffing floorboards.

Again facing him she let her arms flop to her sides. 'So,' she asked, head high. 'What do you think?' She bit off the last piece of lolly and tossed the stick aside. It hit the floor with a 'tic'.

He said, 'Will you be paying for that lolly?'

She sighed. 'Forget the lolly. Who am I?'

'Cathula Go-La-Go-Go.'

'Gochllagochgoch!' she complained. 'And it's not Cathula. It's Cthulha. You always make it sound like "Dracula". It's a beautiful Welsh name that probably means something and has nothing to do with horror.'

'Whatever.'

'But I remind you of someone?'

'Yeah.'

'Who?'

'Cathula Go-La-Go-Go.'

'No,' she insisted.

'No?'

'I remind you of Bridget Fonda.'

He looked at her, clueless.

She said, 'This is her *Jackie Brown* look, her greatest ever role.'

'Bridget Fonda?'

She waited for him to spot the blatant resemblance.

He said, 'The woman who talks to her socks?'

'For Godssake! Does no one round here watch movies?'

He turned and resumed tin stacking. 'I'm too busy, working all hours God sends me, to watch movies.'

'Hold that tin up.'

'What?'

'Hold that tin of beans up.'

'It's spaghetti.'

'Just hold it.'

He turned to face her and held it up.

'Ask me what it says.'

'Cathula, with your eyes, you'll never read it from this distance.' He was twelve feet away.

'Ask me.'

So he sighed, 'What does it say?'

'Stavely's beans. 30p.' And she grinned, awaiting his amazement at the sudden improvement in her eyesight.

He looked at it. 'It says Heinz Spaghetti. 420g.' And he put it on the shelf.

'It says Stavely's beans,' she insisted.

'It says spaghetti.'

'It says Stavely's beans.'

He again turned to face her. 'And what the hell are Stavely's beans? There's no such things as Stavely's beans.'

'Stavely's beans? Everyone's heard of Stavely's beans. They're practically a gay icon.'

'I've never heard of them and I run a shop.'

'You need to get out more.'

'You need to get out less.'

'But can you believe this?'

131

'I'm trying not to.' He lifted the hatch and went behind the counter.

'All my life I've been unfocussed and now I know why.'

He did beepy things with his till.

When he didn't ask her why, she said, 'I was the wrong woman. But the moment I tied this bikini top on and became the Fond, her weird healing powers kicked in and, for the first time in my life, I could see.'

He looked at her funny. 'Weird healing powers?'

'Hollywood stars have weird healing powers. Everyone knows that.'

'Do you *know* how scary you are?'

'Of course I do. Now I'm the Fondster I even know you're not my brother.'

'It's written on your palm.'

'It's always been written on my palm. But now I can read it.'

He didn't look impressed. The jerk. How would he like it if she jumped over that counter and punched him one?'

But then; 'Davey?'

'Yeah?' He was still beeping his till.

'If you never watch movies . . .'

'Yeah?'

'. . . how do you know your lookalikes look like who they're meant to look like?'

'Because they say they do.'

'Well I look like Bridget Fonda. Am I hired?'

'I suppose so. Though I can't see there'll be much demand for a woman who talks to her socks.'

twenty-five

'It's happened again! It's happened again!'

'What has?'

Incredulous with horror, Sally stood over Teena and despaired, 'Just when I thought it was safe, I've killed another one!'

Teena was sat at the kitchen table, sipping a glass of water as though nothing untoward had happened. How often would Sally have to punch her head to make her pay for this mess? Teena said, 'Sally, you didn't kill him.'

'Then who did?'

'I did.'

'Because I made you.'

'I'm sorry?'

'Dr Steinbeck didn't cure my Touch of Death.'

'Oh?'

'He just put it on hold so it could leap out at me when least expected.'

'Can Touches of Death leap?'

133

'You think this is funny?'

'I'm just intrigued by your Touch of Death. I've never read of one in any medical book. Would it by any chance be a concept Dr Steinbeck introduced you to?'

'He says there's no such thing. But there is. And my Touch of Death can do whatever it bloody likes.'

Teena took a sip of water. 'Sally, I killed him. You weren't involved.'

'It's my camp. I'll get the blame. I'll lose my job. All those TV shows'll say I did it. Couldn't you have waited till after the Dullness Inspector called?'

'I find your concern for Mr Landen touching.'

'I'm not the one who killed him, remember?'

'Clearly he wasn't going to lie down while I removed his brain, therefore I had to render him unconscious. Lacking the time to buy anaesthetic, I used more robust means. With a skull as thick as his and the mobile home covered in foam rubber–'

'You see? It was my fault!'

'–With a skull as thick as his and the mobile home covered in foam rubber, it was hard to know how hard to hit him. So, to be on the safe side–'

'Safe side!?!'

'–I used maximum possible force.'

'You great steaming, doll-faced, Barbie-shaped twat!'

'Perhaps it *was* the wrong option but patience has never been a virtue of mine.'

'And if he's dead, how did he "elect" to move in with me?'

Teena shrugged. 'As his psychiatrist and friend–'

'Psychiatrist? You didn't even notice he had no brain!'

'An easy mistake to make.'

'And as for being his friend, it's a wonder you even noticed he was dead.'

'And what's *that* supposed to mean?' Now Teena was getting angry. Good! Why should Sally be the only one?

She prodded Teena. 'It means I've never met anyone as self-centred as you.'

The prodding made a dress strap fall off Teena's shoulder. 'Self-centred?' she snapped, pulling the strap back into place. 'Everything I do is for the welfare of others.'

Sally glanced at the corpse on her table. 'Yeah. I can see that.'

'Bafflingly Mr Landen was rather fond of you. As his psychiatrist and friend, I knew that in the event of his demise he'd want to be with you.'

'So he can stink out my place instead of yours?'

'He won't be stinking out anyone's place.'

Sally went round the table and pulled out a chair, banging its feet on the floor and sat facing Teena. 'We'll have to hide him.'

Teena said, 'We won't need to hide him.'

But where could they hide him? In a cupboard? In a desk? On the roof? In the hot water tank? None of them seemed likely to fool anyone. Nor were they overly hygienic.

Then it came to her, an idea so perfect you could sell it to a jewellers and have them think such a gem must have come from outer space; 'Bruce Wayne!'

'I'm sorry?'

'Bruce Wayne.'

'I can assure you, Sally, pleasing though the thought may be, Batman won't be coming to our assistance.'

'Not Bruce Wayne – Bruce Wayne.'

'I see.' She didn't look like she saw.

Like Sally cared what she saw. 'He runs Wyndham's other big caravan site.'

'Sally, Bruce Wayne's a multi-millionaire playboy who

dresses his youthful wards in tights. I doubt he has time to be running caravan parks.'

'Not that Bruce Wayne – a different Bruce Wayne. He's a short, fat, ginger bloke with a beard.'

'This isn't your friend who thinks she's Bridget Fonda?'

'That's someone else.'

'And people mistake you for the king of the Ewoks?'

'I'm nothing like him.'

'I see.' She didn't look like she saw.

Sally pressed on. 'The other day he loaded his guests onto Mr Scraggs' mystery tour then waved them goodbye. The moment it left he had their caravans shoved off the cliffs at Splatter Cove. He reckons nothing's safer than a caravan park without caravans. If we throw Landen off Splatter Cove, people'll think he did it.'

'Sally, we can't frame an innocent man.'

'Course we can. It'll be easy.'

Teena held her gaze. 'No, Sally, we can't.'

And she deflated like a slashed tyre. 'You're right. We can't.'

'Thank God for that.'

'No one'd believe he'd done it.'

For some reason Teena sighed.

But the more Sally thought about it, the more she knew there must be an answer. But what? Why did her brain always switch off when matters of life and death were involved?'

But then . . .

But then . . .

She had it!

It was simple!

It was brilliant!

It wouldn't even cost any money.

She watched the photo in her open encyclopaedia. It was

the one beside the picture of Rajah Singh sheep-fighting. In it the Rajah was losing to another thing he was trying to pass off as a live tiger; 'A rug!'

'I'm sorry?'

'We could flatten him out and pass him off as a rug, like one of these tiger-skin ones.' She held the book up open to show Teena.

'Admirably imaginative though that solution is, we'll be neither throwing Mr Landen off a cliff nor passing him off as a novelty rug.'

'Why not?'

'Both courses of action might do him further harm.'

'Further harm? Teena, he's dead.'

'And anticipating that subduing him might require the use of lethal force, I took the liberty of buying this.' Her camouflage jacket had been hung over the back of her chair since that morning. From its pocket, she produced an object. She placed it on the table. It was a Penguin paperback, cream coloured.

Sally watched it, unsure what to make of it.

Teena's nod invited her to take a look. She closed the encyclopaedia and put it to one side. She reached across, pulled Teena's paperback toward her then turned it the right way round. Teena pulled the encyclopaedia toward herself, opened it, propped it against the table edge and browsed through it. The paperback's cover featured dramatically lit Steam Age types watching a dead bird in a glass jar.

And Sally's jaw dropped.

Heart in mouth she watched Teena. 'You don't mean?'

Cool as you like, Teena turned another page of the encyclopaedia and took another sip of water.

But Sally stared at the paperback, almost afraid to read the five words in its title.

Those words were, *Frankenstein: Or the Modern Prometheus*.

twenty-six

'Get it out and put it on the table.'
   'I don't like–'
   'Put it on the table.'
   'Are you sure about this?'
   'Put it on the table.'
   'But . . .'
   'Put it on the table.'
   'But . . .'
   'Put it on the table.'
   'But . . .'
   'Have you never seen *The Assassin*?' she complained.
   'Never.'
   'Never? Everyone's seen *The Assassin*.'
He just shrugged. The man was unbelievable. There Cthulha was, sat at her kitchen table, wearing a fixed grin, tight shoes and a little black dress that showed everything every time she leaned forward. She had a clitoris like a beach ball, a cervix like a cooling tower and nipples that

still hadn't come down from her second bout with Davey Farrel's ices box. She had a horrible feeling they were stuck like that. But so what? It wasn't like she used them for anything. Besides, that wasn't the point. The point was she was up for it; and what was the little grey jerk doing? He was playing hard to get.

She tried again. 'Put it on the table.'

'But why?' He sat facing her, in a white dinner jacket that was supposed to make him look CIA but only made him look C&A.

She said, 'That's what happened in the film. Bridget's boss takes her to a fancy restaurant. It's the first she's ever been to, because she's always been a druggie and not had nice enough hair.'

He frowned. 'She's never been to a fancy restaurant?'

'Never.'

'Even though she's a Hollywood star?'

'No. No. Listen to me. In the movie she's not a star, she's a condemned killer. In the restaurant she's grinning and happy and Bridgeting it up big-time coz she's just so happy.'

'And then?'

'Halfway through the meal, you know what her boss lays on the table?'

'Her?'

She chose to ignore the remark. 'What her boss lays on the table . . .'

'Yeah?'

'. . . is a box.'

He gasped. Too right he did. She had him in the palms of her hands. He said, 'What kind of box?'

'It doesn't matter. Say it's a hat box. It's wrapped in a big ribbon – like you get around cake boxes? Her boss says, "This is for you." Now she's grinning so wide her

139

face'll split; "For me? A present?" Maybe it's flowers or chocolates, a dress, something a young lady like myself would want. When she opens it, you know what it is?'

Eyes wide, he shook his head slowly.

She said, 'Guess.'

He said, 'A Flymo?'

'A Flymo!?!' She stared at him.

He shrugged. 'Everyone'd like a Flymo.'

'I've just said it's in a hatbox, for Godssake. How big do you think they make hats?'

'Maybe they make 'em big in America.'

'Not the size of lawnmowers!'

'Oh.'

Cretin. She forcibly reclaimed her composure. 'The thing in the box is . . .'

'Yeah?'

'. . . a *gun*.'

He gasped, hooked by her story-telling prowess. 'But why?'

'He's only taken her to the restaurant so she can kill someone.'

'Him?'

'No.'

'The waiter?'

'No.'

'The cook?'

'No.'

'The guy who parks the cars?'

'No.'

'Man this is crazy. So who does she have to kill?'

'Some bloke.'

'Some bloke who?'

'It doesn't matter who.'

'Why's she got to kill him?'

'That's what her boss does. He works for the CIA. He's a killer.'

'Then why doesn't *he* shoot the guy?'

'She's got to shoot him.'

'Then why's he there?'

'To give her the gun.'

'So there are two CIA assassins in one restaurant?' Roddy asked.

'You see how exciting this is?'

'But they've only one gun between them?' he asked.

'Yeah . . .'

'Does her boss get to have the gun next time round?'

'No. I . . .' *Jesus.*

'Is that how secret agents work? They take it in turns to have the gun?'

'Okay it sounds stupid when you put it like that. But it's the big scene, the Not Bloody Likely moment.'

'The . . . ?'

'*The Assassin* is *My Fair Lady* with bullets. In *My Fair Lady*, Eliza Doolittle lets herself down at a posh do by saying, "Not bloody likely," showing she can never escape her roots.'

'She talks to the animals,' said Roddy.

'That's Dr Dolittle,' she said.

'He don't talk good,' he said.

'That's Eliza Doolittle,' she said. 'In *The Assassin* Bridget lets herself down by shooting the place up, proving she can never escape her violent past. I could go through all the parallels, one by one, if you like.'

'I could live without it, babe.'

'Anyway, the restaurant moment's the one where she commits herself to being a killer.'

'I thought she already was one.'

'She was. But now she's a nice killer'

141

'How can you be a nice killer?'

'By smiling – like this.' Sitting bolt upright, Cthulha gave a smile apposite for any company.

Roddy looked suitably impressed. 'Wow. And is *he* a nice murderer?'

'Who?'

'Her boss?'

'Not half. She wants to shag him. So did I.'

'Then why does he want her to be a murderer?'

'Forget it.' Sighing she propped her chin on one palm. 'Did she get to eat dessert before he pulled the gun?'

'Forget it.' She watched the ceiling.

'Did they leave a tip?'

A spider crouched up there in a web, dismembering a fly. Maybe she should have that as her boyfriend instead.

'Did he–'

'Justputthefuckingboxonthetable!'

What was it with him? Sometimes it was like he didn't understand things on purpose. Chin still propped on palm, she watched him. Was he stupid? Was he perverse? Was he just toying with her?

But then, she realized; he was stalling!

'No I'm not.' He shifted guiltily in his seat.

'Yes you are. You're stalling. That's why you pretended not to understand the film, to waste time.'

'I just don't see why you want me to give you a gun. Guns are bad news, babe.'

'The gun's not the point.'

'Then what is?'

'Authenticity. She was given a gun, so, to be true to the scene, you have to give me a gun.'

He again shifted guiltily, his face like he was seeking an emergency exit. 'It has to be a gun?'

'JUST GIVE ME THE SODDING BOX!'

He rose, pushed his chair backward then disappeared under the table, to get the box he'd had hidden since before she'd entered the room. Bridget hadn't seen hers in advance, why should Cthulha? But, Jesus, a gun of her own. The people she could scare with it. That'd show Sally. 'No, you can't borrow my gun,' Sally always said. 'You're not responsible enough to borrow weapons.' *Well, excuse me, but how many entertainers have I ever killed?*

Something was wrong.

He'd been down there forever and still no sign of his return. She looked down, her view of the floor blocked by her legs. 'Rod? You still down there, Rod?'

His head reappeared across the table from her. 'Here you go, babe. Don't wear it all at once.' With much grunting, unhfing and straining he hauled the box out from under the table. One last heave and it hit the table. It stood at the table's centre, like the obelisk from *2001*. She'd hated *2001*; *Quatermass and the Pit* did it way better.

Roddy sat back down, purple faced, gasping for breath.

Her gaze scaled the box's heights. Jesus, the size of the thing. You could hide a body in it and have room left over for a bus.

Then she noticed the five black letters down its side:

F

L

Y

M

O

She stared at him. 'Is this a lawnmower?'

'No.' He shifted guiltily in his seat.

She stood up, pressing on with the charade. In case he hadn't totally messed up, she feigned the appropriate innocence. 'A present? For me? What is it? A dress?'

'Only if it's made of lead.'

'If this is a lawnmower . . .' she grunted, almost putting her back out pulling the box toward her. To reach the box's top, she climbed onto her chair then onto the table. Teetering on black stilettos, she used a fingernail to puncture the twin strips of sellotape that sealed the box. She dug her fingers into the gap and yanked back its twin cardboard flaps. She looked inside. Whatever was in there was wrapped in the world's entire supply of tissue paper. She told Roddy, 'Role playing's not exactly your strong point is it?'

He shrugged.

She rummaged. Whatever was in there was no Flymo. It was too small and sat atop a pile of paper which filled the box almost to the brim. Lawnmowers? The cheeky little sod had just been teasing her. The object was wrapped in yet more paper, and more sellotape than you could imagine. She felt at it through the paper.

And her heart missed a beat.

The thing had a handle, cold and hard – one that could only belong to a gun.

'Why're we doing this?' Roddy asked.

'Because it's sexy.'

'It is?'

'It's what boyfriends and girlfriends do. They role play.'

'They do?'

'It maintains a healthy sexual relationship.'

'Do we have a healthy sexual relationship?' he asked.

'Too right we do.'

'What about that thing you always make me do? Is that healthy?'

'I've told you a million times, that thing I make you do is not dangerous and it's not illegal.'

'Then why doesn't it feel right?'

144

'It doesn't matter how it feels for you. It does it for me. That's all that matters.'

'Then why won't you let me tell the police?'

'You try, and you're dead. But my point is, all around the country, right now, blokes and babes are role playing in the privacy of their own homes.'

'Why?'

'It gets them in the mood.'

'What mood?' he asked.

She was going to swing for him in a minute.

He shifted uncomfortably in his seat.

'Now what's up?' she asked.

'It's my underwear.'

'What about it?'

'I made it myself from knotted hankies.'

Giving up on him she took the object from the box. It was heavier than you'd expect but she'd read somewhere that a loaded pistol weighs eight pounds.

That must have meant it was loaded!

In a flurry of rustling she started to tear away its wrapping. At last she got her first glimpse of the glossy black handle.

And she frowned.

Baffled, she hurriedly unwrapped the rest of the object then stared at it. 'What the hell's this?'

'An iron,' he said.

'An iron?' She glared at him, tempted to jump across the table and hit him with it. 'What use is an iron?'

'Argos don't do guns. The nearest they do is irons. So I got you that. I figured you might not want one so I bought you twenty, to make up for it.'

She glowered at him. 'There are nineteen more of the things in this box?'

'Each individually wrapped.'

'Jesus Christ.'

'You can hold them like guns and point them at people.'

'I'm meant to be a ruthless killing machine, for Godssake.' She dropped it back into the box. 'What am I supposed to do with these? Smooth my victims to death?'

'They have five settings.'

'Are any of them "Kill"?'

'No.'

'Jesus.'

Her mobile phone beeped. Having lost the will to live, she climbed down from the table then the chair then let her backside hit the chair. She took the phone from the table and punched the appropriate button, all the while staring at Roddy. 'Don't think I'm finished with you, pal.'

He just shrugged.

Phone against her ear, she asked, 'Hello?'

'Cthulha?' A voice crackled at the other end.

'Yeah?'

'It's Davey Farrel.'

'Davey? What do you want?'

'Be at Giorgio's in half an hour.'

'But . . . but that's the fanciest restaurant in town.'

'I know. There'll be a package and a job waiting for you.'

twenty-seven

With a thud Sally deposited Landen's corpse on Davey Farrel's counter. It landed between two open magazines. The one to the left featured metal diving suits of varying design. In red felt-tip Davey had ringed a big yellow suit. The second magazine lay open at the small ads, with an ad in the middle highlighted. Read upside down it said, NEW LUNGS AT REASONABLE RATES. If Sally'd been Scooby Doo's Velma she'd have called it a clue, except clues weren't her strong point. But she could imagine Davey running round his shop, in a mummy suit, trying to scare off customers. For now, he stood behind his counter, beeping his till.

Fighting the urge to walk straight out of the shop, she gathered her courage. 'Davey?' Her voice was an octave too high. 'I need the biggest favour anyone's ever done anyone.'

'Yeah?'

Her legs were trembling so much it was a wonder she'd

even got Landen there. 'My unconscious friend here wants to live in your ices box.'

'Why?'

Her mouth dried. A lump ran down her throat and lodged in her stomach. 'He wants to break the world record for surviving in a freezer.'

'And what's the world record?'

'Four days.' Her voice rose another octave.

'Sally, living in an ices box for four days'd kill a man.'

'That's why it'd be a world record.'

He looked sceptical.

'Davey,' she pleaded. 'We're talking about this man's life's ambition.'

'If he weren't already dead.'

'Dead?' Her pulse set off like a bullet. Half expecting the entire Wyndham police force to crash in, guns blazing, she insisted, 'He's . . . he's not dead.'

'Sally, he's stiff as a board.' Davey prodded the corpse.

'He is?'

'You could snap his arms off.'

'You're not going to – are you?'

'No.'

She gazed at Landen. 'Dead? Blimey. How do you reckon that happened?'

'You've killed him.'

'No. I–'

'Now you want to store him in my ices box till you can revive him.'

She squinted at Davey, suspicious, voice lowering to its normal pitch. 'Why would you think that? I mean the stuff about reviving him?'

'Why else would you want to put a body in a freezer? If you just wanted to dispose of it, you'd throw it off Splatter Cove, like everyone else does.'

'Then, I can use it?'

'Seeing as you're planning to revive him, why not?'

'Davey.' She leaned across the counter, flung her arms round his neck and gave him a huge hug. 'You're an angel.'

'So I'm told.'

'Why couldn't it have been your dad who adopted me when my parents fell off that trapeze, instead of Uncle Al?'

'Because he can't stand you.'

'Who can't?'

'My dad.'

She loosened her grip on his neck and looked up at his face. 'Davey, your dad loves me.'

'No he doesn't.'

'He says I'd make a great girlfriend for you. I know he only says it to make me blush, which he always does, but . . .'

'He says you're cursed and evil and he'd like to throw rocks at you till you're dead.'

'He said that?'

'All the time.'

'But he's always been great to me when I've been round your house.'

'He says he wouldn't want to hurt your feelings.'

'Oh.' She released the hug. Maybe having Davey as a big brother wouldn't be so great after all.

'But it'll cost you,' he said.

'What will?'

'Renting the ices box.'

'How much?'

'Two quid a day.'

'Done.'

'Cash up front.'

149

From her coat pocket, she retrieved two coins and placed them on the counter.

He slid them into his palm, dropped them in the till then shut it. 'You want a receipt for this?'

'No thanks.' Like she needed written evidence lying around.

He slung Landen over one shoulder, lifted the counter's hatch, and carried him to the ices box.

She followed him, watching his back all the way. Maybe when he opened it she should shove him in, lock him in then call the police. He had Landen's body. She could fabricate a motive. They'd have him bang to rights. By the time they arrived he'd be too hypothermic to contradict anything she said. And without a receipt there'd be nothing to implicate either her or her caravan park. Not good enough for his family? Cursed? Evil? She'd show them.

He lifted the ices box lid. A frigid steam rose from within, and without ceremony, he dropped Landen into it. 'That should do it.' He was about to close the lid but stopped: 'Hold on.'

'What?' She knew it. He'd changed his mind.

'I want to check something.'

'Check what?' She braced herself, ready to push him in before he could react.

He reached into the box, rummaged around, and retrieved a lolly from beneath Landen. 'Yeah, that's okay.'

'What is?' She stepped back, deciding there was no need to push him in after all.

'Kids should still be able to get at the stock with him in there.' He removed the wrapper then started eating the orange rocket-shaped lolly.

She frowned at him. 'Davey?'

'Yeah?'

'Is that hygienic?'

'Is what hygienic?'

'Keeping your lollies in with a dead body?'

He looked non-plussed. 'No one's ever complained before.'

twenty-eight

Early afternoon a man dressed as a clown stood outside Giorgio's restaurant in the town centre and tried to look interesting. He failed. That didn't matter. All that mattered was Cthulha was there, stood behind him, in her topless Minnie Ha-Ha outfit. Twin black plaits hung down over her chest, preserving her modesty. It was what the Fond had worn in Scandal, her greatest ever role, in which she demonstrated a perfect English accent. Two crows' feathers jutted from her headband, giving the world a V sign. And if the gusting wind was giving her goosepimples, she didn't care. And if Davey Farrel's mysterious package had turned out to contain nothing more deadly than a plastic tomahawk, so what? She couldn't stop grinning. My God, she was scared her face was going to stick like that.

A bunch of losers had gathered around them – and stupid looking men in vests, jeans and cowboy hats. They had words like 'Etah', 'Llik', and 'Uoy kcuf' biroed on their knuckles. Either they were Welsh or they'd written the messages using a mirror. They chewed tobacco which they kept spitting at the pavement. Sometimes they'd leave their mouths open too long and the tobacco would drip out. Then they'd wipe away the drool, with forearms as thick as their heads. What sort of turn-out was this for the reopening of Wyndham's fanciest restaurant?

The clown held his microphone to his mouth; 'Testing, lesting,' then blew into it from too close. He started to speak. Thank God for that. She'd had a horrible feeling he was about to sing – and she'd heard him sing. He said, 'Ladies and gentlemen, thank you for coming. My name's Charles Dunnett and some of you might recognize me, though dressed like this that does seem unlikely. I'd like to point out that I'm attired as a clown purely on the orders of Mr Aloysius Bracewell, the establishment's new owner. And if any bounty hunters are present I should in no way be mistaken for the man dressed as a clown who robbed Wyndham central bank yesterday.'

'Bugger,' said a tattooed knuckled onlooker, pump action shotgun over one shoulder. Cthulha'd been wondering why he'd brought that along for a meal.

'That's my beeping day wasted.' A huge woman with some kind of assault rifle spat tobacco at the pavement then left, shoving aside a kid with a beagle.

And most of the crowd drifted away, muttering, grumbling and cursing. Shotguns slung over hairy shoulders, they climbed into their 'battle' vans, slammed the doors then drove off.

Now the bounty hunters were gone, Dunnett addressed what was left of the crowd. 'Thank you for attending our grand reopening. Mr Bracewell wishes it known the new ownership will in no way take Wyndham's classiest restaurant downmarket. He also reminds you that with your first meal you'll receive a warmish carton of potato substitute fries and a lovely plastic dinosaur. Not life sized of course. Not that dinosaurs still walk among us.'

'I've seen one,' said a voice in the crowd.

'Me too,' said another.

'So have I,' said another.

'I saw two on that common by the caravan park,' said another.

'Me too,' said another.

'But they were little dinosaurs.'

'You'd think they'd have big dinosaurs in a huge town like this.'

Huge? The place had a population of thirty thousand. Jesus, the standard of people she had to perform to. They see some ducks or something and think they're seeing monsters. She sighed, full blast, hoping Dunnett would hear. Was he ever going to introduce her? She was freezing out here.

He tried to draw the crowd's attention away from their 'dinosaurs'. 'Now I know you're all thrilled to be here and can't wait to get inside and at your Uncle Al burgers, but first – as advertised on local radio – to cut the ribbon and reopen our restaurant, we have a genuine Hollywood superstar.'

About sodding time! Regardless of annoyance she forced her grin to widen, like the pro she was. The crowd oohed. The crowd aahed. And suddenly her grin was real.

She grabbed her plaits and flicked them upwards to give the crowd a flash; something to look at while they waited for Dunnett to get to the point.

They gasped and tutted, the suckers. She did it again.

A man in a suit shouted, 'Burn her! She's a witch!' and was heading for her, taking his cigarette lighter out ready to do the deed till others grabbed him, pushed him against a wall and told him it was a fact that women were

154

meant to have things like those. And they were generally regarded as a good thing though not necessarily for public consumption. He quickly put a cigarette in his mouth and pretended he'd just taken the lighter out to light it and that as always his comments had been misconstrued.

Dunnett continued, 'Courtesy of Davey Farrel's look alike agency and general store – you can't find a better range of string – I love her, you love her, she talks to her socks.' His voice raised to whip up excitement; 'Ladies and gentlemen, a big hand please – for Miss Sh-i-i-i-rley Frondle.'

One of the remaining onlookers clapped gently, clearly no idea who she was meant to be. The rest stood in blank silence watching her as though waiting for her to do something famous. A cold wind blew through. They looked like the cast of the Evil Dead with the vitality removed, but Wyndham was that kind of town.

'Bridget Fonda!' she snapped at Dunnett. She shoved him aside, grabbed the ribbon that sealed the restaurant doors and, like she was stabbing at the face of man who deserved all he got, hacked at it with the plastic tomahawk. 'Does no one round here watch movies?' she complained through gritted teeth.

'I don't,' beagle boy boasted.

'Me neither,' said the girl beside him.

'I saw one once,' added another. 'It had talking apes. Was she one of those?'

'She was! She was that chimp! How'd they teach that chimp to talk? Here chimpy chimpy chimp chimp.'

She didn't dignify his comments with a response. She was still trying to get the tomahawk through the ribbon. Sod it. She just tore through it.

'I seen that film,' said a man at the front.

'Me too,' called someone else.

'It's the only one me've ever seen,' said another

Me've?

'I too.'

I too?

'But how did the Statue of Liberty get on that alien world?'

'They never said.'

'Did the apes take it there in their space ships?'

'They didn't have space ships.'

'They had go-karts,' said a man.

The others looked at him.

He shrugged. 'Or maybe that was a different film.'

Beagle boy ventured, 'Perhaps it was the planet Earth all along.'

'Don't be stupid,' said someone. 'The planet Earth's not ruled by apes.' Then; 'Is it?'

They all looked at each other like they weren't sure.

'Who's she meant to be?' A woman asked about Cthulha as Cthulha kicked the restaurant door down.

'Shirley Frondle,' said another.

'She's just like her.'

twenty-nine

'But how can this work?' Sally was sat at her kitchen table, watching Teena use a screwdriver on the pop-up toaster she called a Shelleytron.

'It's simple.' Teena sat facing her, the well-thumbed copy of Frankenstein open before her. 'Mary Shelley's book gives no details of Frankenstein's machine. However, by reading between the lines then using fractal literary dynamics to fill the gaps, we can recreate the device and restore Mr Landen.'

'But Frankenstein was fiction.'

Teena looked her in the eyes, like an old sea dog recounting a ghostly tale. 'Sally, every word of that book is true.'

'Cobblers.'

Teena put down the screwdriver. 'Frankenstein's creature was built in Byron's Swiss villa one snowy weekend in 1816. Upon waking, it taught itself to read, write, speak and count – and developed an infallible sense of geography.

No matter where in the world it was it never got lost. In that sense I and it have much in common. Like anyone educated beyond their intellect the creature went on the rampage – not unlike Byron. The creature was of course less destructive.'

'But . . .'

'When the – male – scientific establishment learned of that weekend's events it reacted as the scientific establishment always does to new ideas – it suppressed all details.'

'Then . . . ?'

'Frustrated, Mary Shelley (then Godwin) published her diaries in fictional form, using the pseudonym "Frankenstein".'

Sally watched her, amazed. 'Mary Shelley built Frankenstein?'

'No. She built Frankenstein's monster. The scientist was Frankenstein. The creature was unnamed. Mary Shelley was last seen, harpoon in hand, chasing an unnamed monster around Hull. From that we can draw our own conclusions about its progenitor's identity.'

'It all sounds like rubbish to me.'

Teena shrugged, clearly not bothered what Sally thought. Again working on her machine, she took the plastic tomato sauce bottle from the table. She uncapped its nozzle, stuck it in her mouth and took a long hard suck on it.

'Teena, that's horrible,'

'What is?'

'Drinking tomato ketchup like it's a soft drink.'

'Tomato sauce contains all the nutrients one needs for a healthy body. And it's delicious.' She put the bottle down and continued work on the machine.

Sally watched the mass of polka dot rags on Teena's head. 'It didn't stop your hair falling out.'

'Congratulations, Sally.'

'On what?'

'I'm trying to raise the dead and you're discussing hair care.'

'I'm just curious.'

'For your information, it didn't fall out. I shaved it off then replaced it by bonding eight hundred torn rags to my scalp.'

'And why would you do that?'

'I thought my Man Who Does might like it. While no woman should be submissive to her mate, sometimes it makes one feel that bit more feminine if one's made an effort. Plus, whenever I attend a scientific conference, two geeks sit behind me and tug my hair till I'm forced to turn round and hit them. If they try it with my rags, they'll leave fingerprints by which they may be identified and prosecuted.'

'How romantic.'

'Romance is best when mixed with practicality.'

'And your Man Who Does likes them?'

'I assume so.'

'He hasn't said?'

'He never talks.' She guzzled more ketchup.

'Never?'

'Apparently, since he was twelve, he's only said three words, none of which had anything to do with anything. For his first four weeks in my employ—'

'Employ?'

'He works for me.'

'You pay him?'

'He's my house cleaner. Of course I pay him. You think I expect him to maintain my house for nothing?'

'He's your cleaner? Then that's why you call him your Man Who Does?'

'Why else would I call him that?'

'I thought—'

'For the first four weeks in my employ I thought he was mute. Then I realized; he's just deep. Sally, you can't know what a relief it is to have found a man who shares my level of depth.'

'Hold on a minute. If he never speaks, how could he have proposed?'

'Last week my parents came up visiting from Hampstead. At a strategic point in the evening, I grabbed his hand and dragged him into the kitchen, ostensibly to get the non-alcoholic wine. In reality it was so we could make full use of each other's bodies. After we'd done, and were lying on the table, gasping like landed fish, he reached behind my ear and produced a small object. That's his party trick, producing things from behind ears. I still haven't worked out how he does it.'

'And?'

'He showed me the object. It was a ring. He took my hand, which was tiny in his, and placed the ring on my third finger.'

'And then?'

'He went back into the lounge, with the wine. I just lay there, surprised, studying the ring. No words were needed.'

'Ha!'

'"Ha"?' Still screwdriving, Teena frowned. 'What do you mean, "Ha"? That's my big scene. It's not something you "Ha" at.'

'You made it sound like he walked into the living room – where your parents were – naked.'

'Of course he did. He wanted them to see what their daughter was getting, that she wasn't settling for second best. He knew I'd want him to – without me even having to tell him. Once I'd got dressed I re-entered the lounge and sat beside him on the sofa. Not as his fiancée but

160

as a doctor, I pointed out areas of interest on his body. Holding it between thumb and forefinger, using a pencil as a pointer, I explained how the hard ridges of his erect penis give me maximum pleasure on both the upstroke and downstroke and how his high quality sperm guarantees that any children he produces – should I ever decide he'll have any – will be of the highest quality.'

This had to be the most appalling thing she'd ever heard. 'Why didn't you give them a demonstration and shag him in front of them?'

'You think I should have?'

A tattered photo lay face up on the table. Teena'd left it there when she'd first come in. Sally picked it up and studied its monochrome. 'What's this for?' It showed a bunch of men with musical instruments.

'You may recognize those gentlemen?'

'No.'

'You should.'

'Why?'

'Those are Bobby "Boris" Pickett and his Crypt Kickers.'

'Who?'

'They had a 1973 Number One with the song "Monster Mash" – written in 1962.' She smiled at her own humour. 'I thought that was appropriate to our purposes.'

'And of what relevance are they?'

'How much have you heard from Boris Pickett and his Crypt Kickers lately?'

'I've not heard anything from them ever. Are they dead?'

'Who knows?' Teena took the photo from her and studied it. 'But if my Shelleytron can revive the chart career of Boris and his Crypt Kickers . . .'

'. . . It can revive anything?'

Teena attached bulldog clips to the photo's top corner

then wired the clips to the machine. A 1920s telephone crank handle jutted from its side. She cranked it vigorously like she was about to phone God.

Finished cranking she checked the machine for flaws. 'Everything looks in order. Perhaps you'd like to do the honours?' She placed the Shelleytron in front of Sally.

Sally watched it, wary as to why Teena'd delegate the task of activating it.

'It won't bite you,' Teena said.

'You're sure about this?'

'I wouldn't ask you to do it otherwise. I merely thought that, after killing so many, you might appreciate the chance to resuscitate something.'

Sally extended her hand, stopping it just above the toaster's lever then watched Teena.

'It's perfectly safe,' Teena said. 'It produces less voltage than a TV's remote control.' She squirted the last of the ketchup into her gaping maw.

'You're sure?'

Teena unscrewed the bottle's cap, placed it to one side then held the bottle up to the light. One eye shut, she gazed into the bottle to see what was left inside. She stuck her finger into the neck, ran it around scooping out the last dregs of ketchup then licked her finger clean.

Sally took a deep breath. She closed her eyes and counted down from three to zero.

When she reached zero, she pressed the lever.

thirty

So what? So what if no one had known who she was meant to be? She'd been great. She'd been better than great. That was all that mattered – that and the fact she'd been paid. Cthulha patted the wad of bank notes in her breast pocket. And if no one in the whole town had ever seen any movies? That just meant she could pass herself off as anyone; Robert Mitchum, Gregory Peck, Jack Douglas. She'd have the market sewn up; the only look alike in a town where no one knew who anyone looked like. And unknown to them she'd be laughing at them because all the while they thought she was John Wayne in *True Grit* or Charlton Heston in *Moses* or a chimpanzee in fucking *Planet of the Apes*, she'd be Bridget Fonda in *Doc Hollywood*, her greatest ever role.

Heading back from the restaurant, she headed down a town centre street she'd never before walked down. To preserve her modesty, she wore her black tuxedo over her Minnie Ha Ha outfit. The first rule her mother had ever taught her; 'Cathyellah,' (she'd never been able to pronounce it), 'never show anything for less than a fiver.' Her mother, always the moralist.

She arrived at a low step. She stopped, and read the sign above the door; RODDY'S CRAZY RARE WAXINGS, MAN. IF YOU'RE SQUARE, KEEP OUT. AND HE'S AN ARTIST TOO, DOLL. YOU SHOULD SEE HIS AURA. IT GOES BANG BANG A BOOM. As record shop names went, Cthulha always felt it lacked a certain something. Music she wouldn't touch with rubber gloves leaked out into the street.

And, plucking up courage, she stepped through the garish plastic strips that separated RODDY'S CRAZY RARE WAXINGS, MAN. IF YOU'RE SQUARE, KEEP OUT. AND HE'S AN ARTIST TOO, DOLL. YOU SHOULD SEE HIS AURA. IT GOES BANG BANG A BOOM from the real world.

Jesus, the place was like another planet. Stood just inside the doorway, Cthulha looked around, trying to ignore the sick-making smell of dope and the bad lighting. RODDY'S CRAZY RARE WAXINGS, MAN. IF YOU'RE SQUARE, KEEP OUT. AND HE'S AN ARTIST TOO, DOLL. YOU SHOULD SEE HIS AURA. IT GOES BANG BANG A BOOM was smaller than her living room, and her living room wasn't huge since part of it had fallen into the sea and she'd had to have a new exterior wall built. The counter stood to her left, racks to her right. Some mambo thing pounded from the speaker on the far wall. Roddy always claimed it was the coolest record shop in Wyndham, and he should have known. However crap an artist he was, he was Joe Cool when it came to music; she'd never managed to sit through more than ten seconds of any record in his collection. That made this the most embarrassing place in town to try this. It was also the only record shop whose proprietor she was bonking. That made it the least embarrassing place to try this.

Roddy was behind the counter, joint in mouth, doing

Wilson, Kepple and Betty's sand dance – only, it was like his feet were super glued to the floor. Then he was 'surfing'. Then his arms were out before him, his feet running on the spot. Now he was Wilson, Kepple and Betty.

She looked around again. All the customers were mamboing wildly, some balanced precariously atop the racks. A girl in a psychedelic, 60s mini-dress was Pan's People dancing on the counter. Her badge said, CALL ME MJ, whatever that meant.

Still dancing, Roddy gave Cthulha a wave. She waved back feebly. Now he was chicken dancing.

Able to delay no longer, she crossed to the nearest rack and found the 'B' section. She tipped forward and flicked through a bunch of vinyl singles in dog-eared sleeves. Why was she even here? One moment she'd been heading home, the next she'd been gripped by a weird urge.

Failing to find what she wanted, she tipped the singles back into place and glanced across at Roddy. It was funny but all the while she hadn't been able to see properly, it had never struck her how weird he looked. It was like there was something he was keeping from her.

She gathered her courage, stepped forward like Lizzie Henthorpe had all those years earlier, and approached the counter. She rested her fingers on the counter then checked to either side for eavesdroppers. She saw none.

Pan's People girl was still grooving away on the counter, too far gone to notice anything Cthulha might have to say, so Cthulha leaned forward and said, 'Psst,' at Roddy.

He didn't notice.

She half-shouted half-whispered, 'Roddy?'

'Yeah, babe?' Now he was Human League dancing.

'Monster Mash by Boris Pickett and the Crypt Kickers.'

'What about it?'

'I want a copy.'

Still dancing, he laughed, 'You want a copy of Monster Mash?'

She grabbed his sweater's polo neck and yanked him half over the counter. Her hand over his mouth, she ordered, 'Keep your voice down. You think I want everyone to know?' She glanced around, checking no one had noticed. They hadn't. Deciding it was safe she released him.

He composed himself, flexed his shoulders like Del Boy then picked up the joint he'd dropped when she'd grabbed him. He said, 'Sorry, babe.

Then he threw himself at the floor and laughed like a chipmunk.

thirty-one

There was something odd about Daisy the Cow. There had been ever since Mr Landen's death. She seemed to have lost her verve, taking to floating aimlessly till she hit something. Then she'd stay there till Teena came and dragged her away. It wasn't that she seemed unhappy; she looked more than content blowing bubbles through her toy pipe. She just seemed distracted.

Maybe she was in mourning for Mr Landen. Maybe the novelty of life indoors had worn off. Or maybe this was normal cow behaviour. Sally didn't know. So, as Daisy drifted around her kitchen, Sally took another bite of the world's most over buttered toast and – seated at the table – got on with her breakfast.

Outside, footsteps approached. They stopped at the front door. The letter box opened. Something was pushed through it then hit her Welcome mat. The letter box shut and the footsteps receded.

Chewing toast, she leaned to her right and peered out at

the entrance hall. The object now lying on her mat was a rolled-up newspaper. She didn't know why it was there.

Lighter, busier footsteps approached. The front door creaked open and Teena entered wearing just a white vest and polka dot boxer shorts. She looked like she'd just spent the last two hours in front of the bedroom mirror making herself look like she'd just climbed out of bed. She collected the paper from the mat, unrolled it, opened it and had half read it before reaching the kitchen.

'What's that?' asked Sally.

'The RODDY'S CRAZY RARE WAXINGS, MAN. IF YOU'RE SQUARE, KEEP OUT. AND HE'S AN ARTIST TOO, DOLL. YOU SHOULD SEE HIS AURA. IT GOES BANG BANG A BOOM news sheet.' Teena headed for the window. She rolled up the paper and tucked it under one arm. She opened the window, pushed the TV out then closed and fastened the window.

Sally frowned. 'RODDY'S CRAZY RARE WAXINGS, MAN. IF YOU'RE SQUARE, KEEP OUT. AND HE'S AN ARTIST TOO, DOLL. YOU SHOULD SEE HIS AURA. IT GOES BANG BANG A BOOM news sheet? I don't buy the RODDY'S CRAZY RARE WAXINGS, MAN. IF YOU'RE SQUARE, KEEP OUT. AND HE'S AN ARTIST TOO, DOLL. YOU SHOULD SEE HIS AURA. IT GOES BANG BANG A BOOM news sheet.'

Teena headed for the table. 'You do now. I ordered it.' Teena pulled out a chair and sat at the table. She unrolled the paper, opened it and read it, her face hidden behind it. 'I wanted to receive this week's chart as soon as it came out.'

'The chart!' Mouth full of toast, Sally snatched the paper from her, spread it out flat across the table and excitedly studied it. 'You mean Boris Pickett's on it?'

'Why don't you take a look?' Teena sighed sardonically.

Sally didn't care what Teena had to say. She was too busy devouring the chart's upper reaches, seeking Boris Pickett but – she looked at Teena – 'It's not here. Your machine didn't work.'

'Why don't you look further down?'

Her gaze descended from 1 to 10, from 11 to 20, from 21 to 30. Still no Boris.

She dropped further, encountering records she'd never even heard of. She was Jacques Cousteau in his yellow submersible, descending way beyond human experience. Strange life forms would drift into view, be caught in her spotlight, then swim away, never to be seen again.

She descended further, into a realm where light, heat and hope were strangers, the pressures at that depth making her street cred's hull creak, groan and grind till it threatened total collapse.

And, just when it seemed she was to sink into an abyss of obscurity that even John Peel couldn't navigate, she hit rock bottom.

She stayed there, scraping the seabed of hipness, where only primitive invertebrates and monsters from Doug McClure films belonged. And there it was, hiding behind rocks, covered in sea weed. 'Number 100?' She frowned. 'Boris Pickett's only 100?'

Teena helped herself to Sally's toast. 'There are limits to the wonders even science can perform. Regardless, this proves the technology works.'

Sally glanced at her, almost afraid to ask. 'You mean?'

Teena bit off a lump of toast. 'Tonight, Sally, we raise the dead.'

thirty-two

'Davey?'

'Yeah?'

'Why are you wearing a cape?'

'It makes me look more interesting to girls.'

'Believe me it doesn't.'

He ignored her, head down, scribbling notes in the doorstop-thick ledger on his counter. Dangling half way down his back was a white, triangular cape as worn by Vegas Elvis and Evel Knievel. It had to be the stupidest thing Cthulha'd ever seen.

Not that what he wore mattered. What mattered was what she was wearing. So she stood across the counter from him, fit to burst with pride. 'Davey?'

'What?'

'Look at me.'

'Why?'

'I want to show you something.'

'I've seen them. Everyone's seen them.'

'Look at me, Davey.'

Reluctant he put his pen down and looked at her.

She took a step back. Arms outstretched to either side, she did a three sixty degree turn that couldn't fail to show off the glories of her beehive wig. It weighed a ton. She was hoping her neck didn't snap.

Turn completed, she grinned bigly. 'Guess who?'

'Al Pacino.'

She frowned at him. 'Al Pacino?'

'He had hair like that in some film or other.'

'Davey, this is a beehive. Al Pacino didn't have a beehive in any film, and never will.'

'Isn't he supposed to be an actor?'

'A brilliant and versatile one who can play a wide variety of roles.'

'And he's not willing to change his hair style?'

'He's not going to have a fucking beehive is he?' she said.

'What was that film he was in?'

'He's been in loads.'

'It had gangsters.'

'That narrows it down,' she said.

'I mean the big one.'

'*The Godfather*?'

'They all wondered round in it with hair like that.'

She gazed at him, numb. 'You know, I'm really struggling to think of anything to say to you.'

'I wouldn't bother then.'

She took a deep breath. 'I'm Mandy Rice-Davies in *Scandal*, for Godsake; Bridget's greatest ever role, in which she displays a flawless English accent.' She bit a chunk from the raspberry lolly she'd got from the ices box upon entering the shop.

He said, 'Ah.'

She said, ' "Ah" what?'

'You still want to be Bridget Fonda?'

'Being the Fond's the only reason I have to live.'

'Ah.'

She peered at him, concerned by the way the conversation was going. 'Davey?'

'Yeah?'

'Don't tell me "Ah". Tell me about tonight's job.'

'There won't be a tonight's job.'

'There'll always be a tonight's job. I'm in demand.'

'Not this night. There's been a change of plan.'

'What change of plan?'

He shut his ledger and pushed it aside. 'I'm sorry, Cathula. I won't be needing you anymore.'

'But . . . but you can't drop the Bridge-meister. She's the mistress of a million roles, versatile beyond belief. She has a role suitable for any occasion.'

'I'm not dropping her.'

'Then . . . ?'

'I'm dropping you.'

'But . . .'

'I have a new Bridget Fonda.'

'You already have a Bridget Fonda – me.'

'But my new one's much more like her than you are.'

'No one's more like her than I am – except Bridget – and I refuse to believe she's accepted a job at a crummy Wyndham lookalike agency.' Then it struck her; 'She hasn't, has she?'

'No.'

'Good. Because if she had I'd have had to sort her out.'

'You can't sort out a film star for being more like herself than you are.'

'I could sort out anyone. I'm from the streets.'

'Regardless, I have a new girl.'

'Oh yeah?' she challenged.

'Yeah.'

'Then let me see this "lookalike". We'll see who's queen of this ersatz castle.'

'But how could you do this to me, Davey? How?'

'It's not me. It's my dad.'

'Your dad?'

'He wants rid of you.'

Cthulha's own footsteps echoed around her. Water dripped from the ceiling high above, narrowly missing her. 'But your dad thinks I'm great. When I go round his house, thinking I'm your sister, he says that if he were ten years younger he'd show me what a blow job is. I know he only says it to make me blush, which he never does, but he–'

'–Says you're a slut and a whore and he'd like to throw rocks at you till you're dead.'

'He said that?'

'All the time.'

'But he's always so nice to me.'

'He wouldn't want to hurt your feelings.'

'But you could have stood up to him, Davey. You're the apple of his eye. If you'd refused, he'd have given in. It's the least you could do after all I've done for you.'

'You?' He was still walking three steps ahead of her, his back to her. 'What've you ever done for me?'

'I used to give you cigarettes when you were a kid. That must count for something.'

'You remember my aqua-lung?'

'Who could forget? Me and Lizzie Henthorpe used to sit on the wall at the top of Carvey Street and say, 'Look.

Here comes little Davey Farrel with his aqua lung. What a pillock.' The girls had been fifteen. Cthulha's mother had moved to Wyndham the year before.

'Well, thank you,' he complained.

'Davey, the sight of an eight year old dragging a full size aqua lung around Wyndham is not impressive.'

'And you and Lizzie Henthorpe were impressive?'

'A meteorite hit her.'

'Who?'

'Lizzie Henthorpe.'

'No, Cathula, it didn't.'

'You remember Johnny Dane?' she said.

'The kid with the motorbike?'

'All the girls had a thing about Johnny. Me too. One day we spot him working on his bike. Lizzie says she's going to ask him out. Like she's got a chance. This is after six months of plucking up courage. She jumps down off the wall, unstraightens her dress, untidies her hair, and girds up her loins (though Johnny Dane'd done a pretty good job of girding up her loins just by standing there). She sticks her best smile on and takes a step forward.'

'And?'

'Bang, a meteorite hits her, smack in the grin: Kills her instantly. Chance in a billion. It's never happened to anyone before.'

'Cathula, that's horrible.'

'That meteorite was four hundred million years old. It came from Mars. It had a fossil in it, a big, weird thing like a whale.'

'A whale!?! How big *was* this thing?'

'Huge. Bigger than a street.'

'Cathula, that's not a meteorite, that's a planet. Lizzie Henthorpe was hit by a planet.'

'It was worth a fortune. If it hadn't killed her, she'd've

174

been a billionaire. In one go she lost her date, her teeth, her life and her Martian whale. Most of Carvey Street went with her. If I'd been stood three feet to the left, I'd've gone too.'

'Jesus. How come I never heard about this?'

'You were always too wrapped up in your aqua lung to notice what was going on around you.'

'She offered to show me her knickers for fifty pence.'

'What happened to that aqua lung? It was like one day you didn't have it anymore.'

'On my eighteenth birthday I threw it in the canal then walked away. I cried all day.'

'It was only a lump of tin, Davey. Most boys had friends. We tried to point that out to you.'

'And it never occurred to you to ask why I always had an aqua lung with me?'

'We knew why you always had an aqua lung with you.'

'Why?'

'You were a pillock.'

'No. I wanted to be an undersea explorer, to be the first man to see the giant squid alive. And I would have if not for you.'

'Me? What did I ever do?'

'All those cigarettes you gave me . . .'

'What about them?'

'They gave me the lung capacity of a Smartie tube. I can't dive below ten feet without the pressure making me pass out. I can't swim anywhere except the local swimming baths. You don't find many mysterious squid in swimming baths.'

'Then where do you find them?'

'The ocean depths, twelve thousand feet down.'

'Can you dive to twelve thousand feet with an aqua lung?'

'No – thanks to you. So now I'm stuck running my dad's corner shop.'

'It's not a corner shop. It's in a cul-de-sac.'

'You said it. Cathula, all you've ever done for me is destroy my life.

'Some men would thank a woman for that.'

'Like who?'

'Off the top of my head I can't think of anyone but . . .'

'Sometimes I wish I was dead. And no one cares.'

Those light fittings along the wall were great; sort of Victorian, sort of not. She might get some for her hallway, if Roddy approved. She said, 'So this is about revenge?'

'No.'

'Then what is it about?'

'Business.'

'Davey?'

'Yeah?'

'How come you keep your other look alikes in a dungeon?'

He was leading her down the narrow stone staircase of a circular chamber far below his shop. Before now, she'd never even known it had existed. The steps spiralled from the wall to her left, their right edge terminating in a sheer drop to a stone floor some five storeys below.

He said, 'It's not a dungeon. It's a basement.'

'Big difference.'

'And she's here because she's new in town.'

'I was new in town once. They didn't lock me in a dungeon. Even Uncle Al never locked me in a dungeon, however much he was tempted to.'

'It's not a dungeon. She's staying here till I can arrange proper accommodation. Before my dad bought the shop, this place was renovated as student flats. It's perfectly habitable. But it's only temporary. I'm seeking five star accommodation for Annette. That's why she's down here. I've not yet found a hotel she likes.'

'You never offered to put me in a hotel.'

'You're not Annette.'

'Annette? She even sounds like a dweeb.'

'I have high hopes for her.'

'What is it? She promised to open her legs for you if you gave her the job? You think I wouldn't do that? Let me tell you, matey, I've spread 'em for worse jobs than this and will do in the future. Don't go crediting me with ethics I don't have.'

'Annette's not that kind of girl.'

'We're all that kind of girl. And every bloke's that kind of bloke.'

To her right a green hatch was inset in the brickwork. She stopped to look at it and wonder what lay behind it.

Still walking, Davey said, 'Bridget Fonda wouldn't say bloke.'

Casting glances back at the hatch, she trotted down the next few steps till she was just three steps behind him again. 'You don't even know who she is, for Godssake.'

At last they reached the stair bottom. A tight arc of three green doors confronted them.

'Davey?'

'What?'

'Have you brought me here to kill me?'

'What?'

'Because I killed your aqua lung dream, you're going to kill me and leave my body down here where it'll never be found?'

He watched her, unimpressed. 'Is this what watching films does to you?'

'Female paranoia's Hollywood greatest export.'

'Then thank God I don't have time to watch them.'

177

He stepped forward and, left cheek against it, tapped the middle door. 'Annette? It's Davey. You've a visitor. Don't be shocked when you see her. She's not your twin sister, just someone who looks like you.' And after a pause Cthulha assumed was to give this Annette time to ready herself, he opened the door that would bring Cthulha Gochllagochgoch face to face with her nemesis.

'Well?' he asked. 'What do you think?'

She thought she was seeing the world's most over decorated room, with its wall-sized mirror and Art Deco chaise longue, diamond studded chandelier and full drinks cabinet, the Steinway in the corner, Egyptian artefacts, Monet prints, and candles flickering in soft focus. It was like something Norma Desmond would have had before her films got small. The one thing Cthulha didn't see was a look alike. Stood beside Davey in the doorway she asked, 'So where is she?'

'Right here.'

Cthulha gazed into the room harder. What was it? He thought Bridget was an invisible id monster? 'Right where?'

'Right here.'

'Right here, where?'

'Right here, here.' He pointed at where she was supposed to be but wasn't.

She watched him. 'Davey, there's nothing in there but a cow.'

And there wasn't. It stood at the room's centre, brown and white, gazing out at them as it chewed an Action Man.

Davey said, 'But she's just like Bridget Fonda.'

178

'No it's not! It's nothing like her! It's a cow. Bridget's a babe. How can a cow be a babe?'

'She doesn't need to be. It's like Rory Bremner. He doesn't look like the people he imitates. That doesn't stop him being them. Like him she just needs to convey the impression.'

'And how could it do that?'

'By a mastery of facial expressions.'

'Yeah. Right.'

He said, 'Annette?'

Its ears pricked up – as though Cthulha's ears couldn't prick up.

And Davey said, *'Single White Female.'*

Davey Farrel's performing cow ran through all of Bridget Fonda's *Single White Female* faces; 'You've been cheating on me? Get out!', 'Of course you can be my flatmate', 'You can hear us bonk through the ventilator grille?', 'My puppy, my puppy, my poor dead Andrex Puppy', 'Why can't you keep your clothes on?', 'Why's there blood on my stiletto?', 'Why's my boss dead?', 'Why's my pervy neighbour dead?', 'Why am I tied up?', 'Why am I in the lift?', 'Why am I in the laundry basket?', 'Stitch that, bitch!' and more, much more, every expression from every scene – and some that weren't even in the film.

Then Cthulha realized . . .

It wasn't doing the general release version. It was doing some sort of director's cut! It was line perfect. It even did the brief flicker of the lip rumoured to have been cut from scene eight.

Each successive expression made her feel the size of that Action Man, and almost as mangled. It was true, all of it; that cow could eat her for breakfast – and by the look on its face, it would, given the chance.

'She does John Wayne too,' Davey said. 'And Charlton Heston.'

'What about Jack Douglas?' She clutched at straws.

'She does the entire Carry On gang.'

'Davey.' Bitter tears welled in her eyes as she looked up at him. 'That's sick.'

'*You* can only do a third of those facial expressions.'

'I could learn to do more.' But she knew she couldn't.

'You don't need to. I have Annette.' He closed and locked the door. 'We should go now. She needs her sleep.'

'You were never concerned about my lack of sleep.'

'Things change.' He headed back up the steps.

Cthulha stayed behind, watching the door. Maybe she should barge in, and fight that bastard to the death. But she'd seen the size of it. It'd been fed growth hormones or something. And *she* was so slender and lovely. Why couldn't he have hired the real Fonda? The real Fonda she might have beaten, if she'd hit her with things. Whatever Cthulha hit that monster with, it'd still flatten her.

She turned and headed up the stairs, three steps behind Davey, bottom lip trembling, legs heavier with each step. 'Who the hell teaches a cow to do film star impressions?'

'Farmers.'

'Farmers?'

'They've been hit by BSE, and EU subsidy cuts. They've had to find new uses for their livestock. Some sell them as novelty chairs, some as paperweights. These . . . people I met, they let me have a job lot. Animal celebrity look alikes, it's the industry's future.'

Clunk, a green hatch in the wall fell open. A sheep stuck its head out and baaed at her.

She stood glaring at it. 'What the hell's that?'

Davey said, 'Martin O'Neill.'

thirty-three

'Davey?'

'Yeah?'

'Where is he?'

'Where's who?'

'Mr Landen.' There to collect the body, Sally stared into the frigid whiteness of Davey's ices box. She saw just lollies, choc-ices and a stuffed emperor penguin lying flat on its face.

Davey said, 'Ah.'

She looked across at him, baffled. He stood behind the counter, rubbing the back of his neck, uncomfortable. And for some reason he was wearing a cape. He said, 'He's gone.'

'Gone?'

'Gone.'

'Davey, he's dead. How can he have gone? It's not like he could have got up and walked out.'

'If I said he had, would you believe me?'

'No.'

'If I said a bunch of cows took him would you believe me?'

'No.'

'First thing this morning, three cows came in, ostensibly to buy lollies.'

'Davey, cattle don't buy lollies.'

'Neither did these. The lolly buying was a ruse. While one tried to distract me by dropping lollies on the counter, pretending it wanted to buy them, the other cows dragged your friend from the ices box.'

She gazed at him, numb. 'Davey, what're you on about?'

'That's what happened. I swear it.'

'And you didn't notice what these other cows were doing?'

'Of course I did. They were cows. How could I miss something that size?'

'And you let them take him anyway?'

'Sally, you weren't there. They were the toughest looking cows I've ever seen.'

thirty-four

'Teena, we have to do something.'

'I *am* doing something.' She was stood in her own kitchen, cross-legged, arms folded, backside against the table, and watching her own feet.

'I mean about the cows who took Mr Landen.' Sally had just run through the whole story of her visit to Davey Farrel's.

'I *am* doing something about the cows who took Mr Landen.'

'Teena, all you're doing is tying your shoe lace.'

'No. I'm politely waiting for you to finish your tale. Then I can show you something.' Laces tied, she stamped her foot on the floor to get the shoe just right then tilted her head back towards the thing lying behind her on the table.

Sally peered over Teena's left shoulder. She saw a plain white shroud covering an object whose outline revealed nothing of its nature. Glancing at Teena she asked, 'What is it?'

'The solution to all your problems.'

'How many bullets does it fire?'

'Bullets?'

'To stop them.'

'Stop who?'

'The cows.'

Teena tutted, disapprovingly.

'Haven't you listened to a single thing I've said?' Sally demanded.

'No.'

'Why not?'

'It's nonsense.'

'Teena, listen to me, evil cows are on the loose.'

Teena was watching her shoes again. 'And these "evil" cows, where are they now?' If she didn't stop smirking, Sally was going to belt her one.

Sally said, 'I don't know where they are now. Secrecy must be part of their plan.'

'Then how do you propose to shoot them?'

'I've no idea.'

Teena said, 'That has to be the best plan I've ever heard. I reckon that from now on I should do anything you say . . . Before going to extremes, we must lure those cows to this camp, where I can take Mr Landen from them. No force will be needed. They're just cows and will surrender without a fight.'

'If they're just cows, why did they steal a corpse?'

'Clearly they mistook him for a bail of straw.'

'Good God.' Sally turned her back on the girl.

Teena said, 'Now, we have two problems: one, how to lure a herd of cattle here; two, once we've recovered and revived Mr Landen, how to keep him occupied until his real brain arrives. Did I mention that I've contacted Oxford for his brain to be sent here?'

Like Sally cared. What did Teena keep in that closet over

there? Maybe Sally should go over and break it open. There might be something in it she could hit her with.

Teena said, 'What would a man newly returned from the dead need to keep him busy?'

Sally'd given up on this conversation.

Teena said, 'Once more taking our lead from *Frankenstein*, we can conclude that Mr Landen needs a mate.'

'A mate?' Sally slowly turned toward her.

'While you were out on your wild cow chase, I was resolving to build him a wife.'

'What *is* this? First you want to make me a boyfriend, now you're building your assistant a wife. What next? Mother-in-laws?'

'Mothers-in-law,' Teena corrected her.

'Teena, You can't build that thing.'

'Why not?'

'It'll go wrong.'

'Nonsense.'

'Everything either of us does goes wrong.'

'As a scientist I object to my world class experiments being lumped in with your career disasters.'

'Then name me one thing you've tried since you've been here that's worked.'

'Everything.'

'Everything? The talking rabbit? The mind control machine? The concussion "therapy"?'

'–Have all been valuable experiences supplying me with knowledge I lacked at the start of this venture.'

'Teena, don't build it.'

'But I already have.'

Sally stared at the shroud, an icy horror gripping her. 'You don't mean?'

Teena stepped away from the table, turned, and gripped the sheet's nearest edge.

And, in the style of a bad magician, she yanked away the shroud that had once hidden; 'The Bride of Landen'.

'Just how impressed are *you*?' Teena stood back, shroud in hands, clearly delighted with the lifeless thing that lay on her kitchen table.

Sally wished she could share her enthusiasm. Instead she watched it, numb. 'This . . . this . . . thing is meant to be the Bride of Landen?'

'Uh huh?'

Sally watched its blood red face, soulless eyes and slit-like mouth. Teena Rama was mad – no, beyond mad. She was a woman who'd seen every horror film and missed the point of them all, not taking them as a dire warning but as a source of inspiration.

'So?' Teena still awaited Sally's verdict.

'It's . . .'

'Yes?'

'It's . . .'

'Yes?'

'It's . . . it's a balloon.'

Tied to the table, by a piece of string, the 'Bride of Landen' bobbed in a breeze that blew in from under the door.

Teena said, 'It's more than a balloon. It's all a cow could want in a wife; it's red, it bobs and it has a smiley face marker-penned on it.'

'But why?'

'My research – conducted on hands and knees, in a field, shows that cows find balloons more fascinating than any other household item – even sink plungers. With this we can lure the cows back to the camp and grab Mr Landen.'

'And the smiley face?'

She arched a suggestive eyebrow. 'Just a little something for the ladies.'

'Are you completely insane?'

'Not at all. No one wants to marry a grumpy face.'

'And no one wants to marry a balloon. Even Cthulha wouldn't marry a balloon, and she'd marry anyone stupid enough to ask.'

'But my research . . .'

'Sod your research.'

'I beg your pardon?'

'Does the word "instinct" mean nothing to you?'

'As a modern young woman I perform a carefully planned regime of instinct exercises before retiring to bed each night and–'

'Teena, look at it.'

She did so.'

'Would you marry that?'

'Uh huh.'

'You would?'

'If I were a cow.'

'And if you were something vaguely resembling human – which you're not – would you marry it?'

'Of course not.'

'Why not?'

'It's a balloon.'

'Now do you see my point?'

Teena stroked her chin, deep in thought, watching her creation. 'You know, I believe I do see your point. You're saying I should strip off the armour of scientific principle and run naked – so to speak – through the fields of endeavour. I should create something I myself would want to sleep with were I a cow, as that would provide a more accurate template of desirability.'

'But creating something that ambitious is impossible. So now you can abandon this whole mad scheme.'

'Sally, I don't know how a woman of such limited intellect did it but you've made me realize what a fool I've been.'

'Thank God for that.'

'How could I not have seen it before?'

'Seen what?' Sally peered at her, not liking the newly inspired glint in her voice.

But Teena watched her creation, eyes a-gleam. 'You want me to give that balloon an eighteen-inch penis.'

thirty-five

'So where is he?'

'Where's who?'

'You know who I mean.' Sally stood across the counter from Davey, teeth grinding, patience thin. Clearly she'd never sort this mess out by relying on Teena, a woman whose solution to swallowing a fly would be to swallow a horse and cut out the middle men. So, taking her lead from Inspector Morse, she'd decided the best place to launch an investigation was the crime scene.

'I know nothing.' He tried and failed to look innocent.

'Where's Mr Landen?' she repeated.

He looked everywhere but at Sally. 'The cows took him.'

'Where'd they take him?'

'How should I know?'

Before he could move she grabbed his collar and yanked him across the counter. She gripped his stupid cape so tight around his throat his face turned purple. 'Listen,

189

Davey, and listen good. I've six hundred grand and my show business career riding on this, so I'm in no mood for messing. Ten minutes ago, I got a phone call. Know who from?'

'No,' he croaked.

'Cthulha.'

'Oh.'

'Being a pathetic cry baby, as soon as she got home, she phoned me about the animals in your cellar. I refuse to believe the sudden appearance of livestock after you're visited by evil cows is coincidence. You sold Landen to those cows in exchange for performing animals. You saw a chance to make some real money.' She glanced at the two magazines lying open on his counter. 'You were probably hoping to buy one of those fancy diving suits and a new pair of lungs so you could go deep-sea diving. Well let me tell you, Davey, you're too late.'

'W-what do you mean?'

'That girl who comes into your shop?'

'Which one?'

'The polka dot one whose chest you address all comments to.'

'She's lovely.'

'She kills men.'

'No!'

'Yes! you want to know how she does it?'

'No.'

'Those sharp, hard breasts of hers that you so admire? She impales men on them then leaves them on the floor, bleeding to death, as she laughs. And she has a lodger.'

'So?' he croaked as she tightened her grip on his throat.

'He's seen a giant squid alive.'

'No!'

'Yes! And he has holiday snaps to prove it. So you see,

you did the dirty for nothing. And there was a report on last night's radio, straight after the one about the mysterious Mata Hari figure who bonked her way through the entire male work force at Sellafield in one night then drove off with a load of stolen lead foil in a car too fast to catch. It said a job lot of performing animals have been stolen from Wagglow's Farm. Eyewitnesses said the thieves looked like cattle. So now you're going to tell me all you know.'

'But I can't betray those cows. They're my best customers.'

She tightened her grip. Eyes bulging, he turned indigo. She said, 'That string in your stock room.'

'What about it?'

'Want the authorities to hear how you came to have so much?'

A guilty sweat poured from his forehead. 'You . . . wouldn't tell them that. No one'd tell them that. It'd blow this whole town apart.'

'I'd tell them that and a whole lot more.'

And – to give him time to think it over – she released him.

He stood behind his counter, face regaining its normal colour. Watching the floor, he rubbed his throat while considering his options. Like he had any.

'I'm not waiting forever, Davey.'

He said, 'When the cows were leaving . . .'

'Yeah?'

'They mooed something among themselves.'

'Yeah?'

'I'm not sure but . . .'

'Just tell me what it was.'

'It might have been . . .'

'Yes?'

'It might have been . . .' He took a deep breath then

191

said, 'The Wyndham Finishing School For Dainty Young Ladies.'

She frowned. 'Cows said all that?'

'Or they might just have been going moo.'

thirty-six

'My dear girl,' said a Terry Thomas voice, 'guess who?'

Ten seconds earlier the doorbell had dragged Teena away from her balloon research. Now she stood in her front doorway, gazing out at her visitor. Brow furrowed she ventured, 'Mr Landen?'

'You recognized me?' Mr Landen – hanging in mid air, from a small propeller – sounded impressed. But then, he was a human brain suspended in fluid in a laboratory specimen jar – and he'd never looked better.

'Who could fail to recognize that cerebral cortex,' she beamed, suddenly struck by an urge to tidy herself up.

'I've had compliments on it.' With each syllable, smoke puffed from his trademark cigarette holder protruding from a grill near his jar's base.

'But the jar?' she said. 'The propeller?'

'Just a little something I had the girls in Cybernetics whip up. I thought it'd better enable me to see what

193

my ever-leggy ex-student's been up to with my body. Something sexy, I hope.'

'Ah.' She gazed at the floor, still holding the door open.

'Does one detect the merest hint of a snaggeroo?'

She forced herself to look him in the eyeballs and was again the five year old about to be told off for replacing his brain with a goldfish. 'I'm afraid it's more than a hint.'

'Then how about I come in and you tell me all about it?'

thirty-seven

'Open this door or I shoot my way in!' Sally stood outside the caravan whose sign declared it to the be the WYNDHAM FINISHING SCHOOL FOR DAINTY YOUNG LADIES and rapped its door as hard as its foam rubber covering allowed.

For reassurance she touched the bulge in her coat's inside breast pocket. It was Magic Keith's gun, the one Cthulha was always trying to borrow for reasons never given. Shooting evil cows was probably allowed; livestock was bred to be shot. Whatever happened the Dullness Inspector shouldn't hold it against her. But with luck she wouldn't have to use it. Just showing it should get her what she wanted.

She knocked again, ready to draw the gun, but heard the door unlock and unbolt.

Tentatively it opened.

And the two geeks in lab coats stood before her.

They said, 'Yes?' They had long hair and goatee beards and the only way she could tell them apart was that one wore a badge that said DR DAN and the other a badge that said DR STEVE.

'Which of you bastards stole my tenant?' she demanded.

'We beg your pardon?' They tried to look innocent.

She said, 'I've a tenant, four foot tall, dead. Your cows took him. I want him back.'

In a high-pitched Bristol accent, Dr Dan said, 'Miss Cooper, I can assure you we have no cows here. We're a highly respectable model agency.'

'Respectable,' Dr Steve echoed in a high-pitched Bristol accent.

'We groom the world's top models as superstars.'

'In a caravan?'

'Fashion's a highly mobile industry; one week Paris, the next London, and the next–'

'Wyndham?' she said.

The pair descended into a guilty, shoe-watching silence that said it all.

'And if this is a model agency,' she said, 'then what's *that*?' She prodded the contraption that dangled from Dr Dan's left hand. Its tubes clinked together as she touched them.

'This?' He looked down at it, doubtfully, then, gripped by a sudden inspiration, held it up. 'Why, this is a device for helping super models retain their disturbing thinness.'

'It sucks out all their body fat,' Dr Steve said.

'If we have it on full,' Dr Dan said, 'it sucks out their bones, for that extra thin look so beloved on the Milan catwalks.'

She glared at the idiots, not even trying to disguise her contempt. 'It sucks their bones out?'

'Both of them.' Dr Dan said.

'It's highly fashionable,' Dr Steve said.

'Would you like your bones sucked out?' Dr Dan asked. 'We could do a discount.'

'You can't live without bones,' she informed him.

'Super models can,' Dr Steve said.

'No they can't,' she said. 'And that device is no slimming aid.'

'Well.' Dr Dan leaned, arms folded, against the door frame, clearly confident he could bamboozle the 'girlie' with science. 'Why don't you tell us what you think it is?'

She said, 'It's the business end of an electric cow milker. Anyone could tell you that.'

'Super models need milking too,' Dr Steve said.

'Mustn't have their udders exploding on the catwalk,' Dr Dan said.

'Super models don't have udders,' she said. She looked at the machines metal tubes. 'They don't have four breasts either.'

The men gasped.

'For a top model agency you don't seem to know much about models,' she said. 'And what's that?' She pointed to the thing that had been stood between the two men since they'd first opened the door.

It was a cow.

It was a cow chewing an Action Man. Its big green eyes gazed out at her. She'd always thought cows had brown eyes.

'Naomi!' Dr Dan cuffed it behind the ear.

'Moo?!?'

"What're you doing here? Haven't we told you to avoid drafts? Do you want us to suck your bones out again!?!

'Moo?'

Fed up of this, Sally barged in past them.

'Wait!' complained Dr Steve as she headed down a

corridor too long for the caravan it was in. 'What're you doing?'

'Isn't it obvious?' She didn't look back at him.

'No.'

'I'm taking charge.'

thirty-eight

'. . . And you've no idea where my body is?'

'None.'

'Dashed odd.'

Teena led Mr Landen's brain into her kitchen then stopped by the table. She turned to face him as he hovered at the room's centre, and said, 'The camp manager's set off to find your corpse. Frankly, she's no chance. Keen though she is she's not the brightest of people.'

'How does she look?'

'Plain.'

'Not too bright and a Janey Plain Face? Seems the poor little thing has nothing going for her.'

'She does have a natural enthusiasm.'

'My dear girl, when hunting wayward corpses, enthusiasm comes a poor third to looks and brains.'

'I suspect you're right. Though, as a philosopher, I wish niceness was what it took to locate corpses.'

'If that were the case, my dear, you'd be knee deep in them.'

She watched her tennis shoes and blushed with all the modesty she could muster.

He said, 'This king-sized tottie you're building, when do I get to meet that?'

'You already have?'

'I have?'

She waited for him to cotton on.

He didn't. His eyes swivelled on their stalks, taking in the entire room, looking everywhere but where they should have been looking.

To drop a hint she gave a slight cough into the side of her fist and inched nearer the table – though not enough to be completely blatant. She nudged the table with her hip. He didn't catch on. She nudged the table again and coughed once more.

Now he gazed at the ceiling, looking for his Bride. 'You really should see someone about that cold, my dear. Don't want you getting chesty.'

She nudged the table again, hard enough to shift it a couple of inches and coughed three times into the side of her fist. He didn't cotton on, so she kicked it, hard.

At last he seemed to get it. And Sally'd been surprised Teena hadn't noticed his brain was missing?

He looked down at the table and at the sheet covering her creation. Like a big top the shroud rose in the middle as though supported by an eighteen inch projection. And he said, 'This is it?'

'Mr Landen.' Too proud for words, ready to tug, she gripped the shroud. 'Prepare to meet your wife.'

200

'What's this meant to be?'

'A caravan park.'

'It's a shoe box.'

It stood on a table in the middle of a field Archie Drizzle had been invited to by its 'manager', a small, grey man with large, black almond-shaped eyes and sucker-tipped fingers.

The manager said, 'It's Roddy's Womb-Tomb-A-Boom-Boom-Room. But look!'

'At what?'

'It's full of caravans!' He shook the box to rattle the two toy caravans within. 'And it comes complete with all the latest safety features.'

'Such as?'

Drizzle leaned closer, to better view its contents as McDoddy pointed out, 'Big metal spikes – hundreds of 'em. There are spikes sticking out of everything in Roddy's Womb-Tomb-A-Boom-Boom-Room. No one'd dare attack a caravan park that has so many spikes. And hang around, dad, there's more.'

A small figure lay face down at the box's centre; a blonde doll in a black leather bikini with Dynasty-style shoulder pads. Taking care to avoid the spikes, McDoddy picked up the doll and waved it at Drizzle. 'Just dig this, man.'

Drizzle watched it blankly. 'What is it?'

'The lovely Callisto, evil arch-enemy of Xena the Warrior Princess. Like a librarian, Callisto knows nothing of love and can gain sexual satisfaction only through the disembowelment of others. I've made her the site manager. Even Bendylegs Calhoun wouldn't dare attack a caravan park that had her in charge. And look!' He pointed out several buttons glued to the box floor. 'It has a minefield!'

Archie Drizzle stopped his tie from flapping in the breeze

then smoothed it down flat. 'Mr McDoddy, let me get this right. You've dragged me all the way out here to show me a shoe box.'

'That's rad, dad.'

'And its special safety features are;' he counted them off on his fingers; 'Big metal spikes . . .'

'Razor sharp, babe.'

'. . . a psychotic sex killer . . .'

'Si.'

'. . . and landmines?'

'Bang on.' Now McDoddy waved the doll around, talking through clenched teeth to make it sound like it was the doll that was speaking. 'How about it, cat? Do I get the gig?'

thirty-nine

'Miss Cooper! Miss Cooper! Come back – please!' Too gut-less to even try and stop her Dr Dan and Dr Steve hurried after her towards the door at the corridor's far end.

She ignored them, determined to get to the bottom of this. But this passageway, it seemed to go on forever. 'What is it with this place?' she asked. 'The corridor can't be this long. The caravan isn't big enough.'

They caught up with her, one to either side of her. Now all three of them were headed for the door. She couldn't help feeling they were off to see the wizard.

Breathless, Dr Dan said, 'Time and relative dimensions in space.'

She said, 'What?'

'Time and relative dimensions in space.'

'I'm still looking blank.'

'The Tardis,' Dr Dan said.

'But that's not real,' she said, 'That was just made up for some crap TV show with cardboard robots.'

'But we've got it to work.'

'How can you get it to work?'

'It's simple.'

'I don't see how.'

'Space is infinite,' Dr Dan said.

'Caravans are finite,' Dr Steve said.

'So?' Sally said.

'So there's an infinite amount of space per caravan.'

'Therefore,' Dr Steve said, 'you can build a caravan that contains an infinite amount of space.'

The scary thing was she couldn't think of why that didn't make sense. Incredulous she asked, 'You're saying this place can disappear then reappear on other planets?'

'Sally,' Dr Dan said, 'Prepare for a journey to planets that defy sanity. You may never see your home world again.'

'What!?!'

Dr Steve chuckled. 'Dr Dan tends to let his imagination run away with him. In fact we have to tow it everywhere with our Morris Minor.'

'But we're working on it,' Dr Dan insisted.

As they walked she looked up at Dr Dan. She looked up at Dr Steve. They were too tall. Teena was too tall. There was something about tall people you could never rely on. And there was something else about the duo, something she couldn't pin down. 'Don't I know you two from somewhere?'

'We wouldn't have thought so.' They tried to look innocent.

She tried to imagine them without the goatees. 'Yes I do. You . . .' Suddenly she had it. 'You're the clowns who downloaded my uncle into a computer.'

'Uploaded actually.'

'And now you're messing this up.'

'We're messing nothing up. We're conducting valuable scientific research.'

'Which is?'

'We can assure you, none of our cows were involved in the disappearance of your little friend,' Dr Steve said.

'They're far too well brought up to abduct people,' Dr Dan said.

'And intelligent,' said Dr Steve.

'Intelligent?' Finally reaching the door, she grabbed its big yellow handle and prepared to pull it. 'What're you on about? How intelligent can a cow be?'

The men stood behind her. Feet shuffling they coughed guiltily.

'Well?' She turned to face them.

After yet more coughing, Dr Steve garnered the nerve to look her in the eyes. 'Sally?'

'Yes?'

'Even the stupidest cow in this place is a genius.'

forty

'So.' Teena beamed proudly and stood well back from the table, shroud in hands. 'What do you think of your bride to be?'

Mr Landen's brain looked down at the balloon and its mighty appendage, his eyeballs taking in every detail.

She bit her bottom lip, praying for him to like it. But how could he not like it? 'I made it especially for you,' she said, hoping that would raise his opinion of it.

After moments that stretched for too long, his eyes swivelled towards her. It was hard to tell with him lacking a face but he didn't seem completely impressed. 'My dear girl, I think I didn't get here a moment too soon.'

forty-one

'When you say genius,' Sally asked, 'you mean genius by cow standards?'

'No, by human standards.' The doctors led the way along a corridor lined by doors that reminded her of when she was nine and Uncle Al had sat her on his knee to watch that late night horror sequel. As she remembered it a scientist was trying to prove his father – who'd turned himself into a giant fly – wasn't mad. He tried to prove it by using his father's matter transporter to turn everyone he met into fly people. To hide what he'd done, he then hid them in cupboards.

Even at that age it had struck her as a strange way to prove your father's sanity. But Uncle Al had said, 'Watch this closely, young Sally. One day all people will be fly people.'

Then she'd burst into tears.

Then Cthulha had gazed hard at the screen, saying that was how everyone already looked to her. Then she went off in search of her dealer, to find out just what he'd been selling her.

Sally had been fourteen before Cthulha'd realized she didn't have compound eyes.

Now two strides behind the doctors, she watched those doors, ready to grab her gun if anything leapt out from behind one. 'Those doors?' she asked.

'What about them?' Dr Steve said.

'They don't contain fly people?'

'Fly people?' The doctors laughed. 'Why should they contain fly people?'

She still watched the doors. 'You do know you're not allowed pets?' Like it was a rule ever enforced.

'Would fly people count as pets?'

'They might if you were mad,' she said.

'We're not mad.'

'Then how come you think cows can be geniuses?'

'Genii,' Dr Steve said.

Dr Dan said, 'Their intellect's way beyond that of any human.'

'What about Teena Rama's?' she asked.

'Dr Rama!?!' The duo froze. They turned to face her, leaning forward at her. 'What do you know about her involvement in this?'

She took a step back in case they turned nasty. 'Teena's involved in this?'

'No.'

'Then why did you say she was?'

'Because she doesn't know she's involved.'

'Have I missed something?' she asked.

'We can't say.'

She said, 'All I know is Teena says she's the greatest intellect on Earth.'

They turned away from her and resumed walking.

After trying to make sense of it all, and failing, she took a final look at the doors then set off after the doctors.

Dr Steve said, 'Sally, lovely though Dr Rama is, compared to our cows, she's a slobbering imbecile. In a battle of wits between her and one of our cows, she wouldn't stand a chance. And if they ganged up on her . . .' The scientists looked at each other significantly, though the significance was lost on Sally.

Dr Dan said, 'Dr Rama's intellect is natural, whereas our girls are the product of intensive hothouse flowering. Thus their brain power's way beyond anything she might muster.'

'They're on a different level from the rest of us,' Dr Steve said.

'Practically gods,' Dr Dan said.

'Sometimes I wonder if we should worship them,' Dr Steve said.

'I do worship them,' Dr Dan said.

'You never told me,' Dr Steve said.

'I like to keep my rituals private,' Dr Dan said.

Dr Steve said, 'Do these rituals involve painting yourself green, donning a Viking helmet, strapping a rubber glove to your waist and crawling round Nettos naked at midnight while mooing like an idiot?'

'They might do,' Dr Dan said defensively.

Dr Steve said, 'Then you've done a poor job of keeping it private.'

'How so?'

'You don't watch *Crimewatch* do you?'

'Ah.'

In no hurry to worship livestock, Sally said, 'So, where *are* these "gods" right now?'

'That's easy.'

'It is? Why?'

Dr Dan stopped walking. He pulled back his lab coat sleeve and checked his watch. 'It's six thirty-five.'

'So?'

'So they'll be watching *Power Rangers*.'

forty-two

'Are you sure we should be doing this, man?' Roddy looked around in case there were any witnesses.

The spineless moron. There were no witnesses; Cthulha could spot them a mile off. There was just her, him, and the cow tied to the front of Dr Rama's mobile home. Toy pipe in mouth it floated vacantly blowing bubbles, pretending to be oblivious to her. Well, Dobbin, or whatever your real name was, she'd show you oblivious.

She continued sawing through the cow's rope. She was in her little black dress – her *Assassin* get-up. 'Sure I should be doing this? I should've done this from the start. The less cows there are in this world, the better for everyone.'

'You mean the better for you?'

Stood gripping the rope between her thighs, she stopped sawing and glowered at him. 'Just who's side are you on?'

He shrugged, hands in pockets, cigarette in mouth, trying, and failing, to do it like Sean Connery as James Bond. For some reason he had the word FAILED stuck to his forehead.

And what the hell was he wearing? 'Is that my skirt you've got on?' she demanded.

'Taking a lead from a Rottweiler I once saw, I'm wearing your clothing.'

'Why?'

'To help me feel closer to you.'

'You're only two feet away.'

'I mean spiritually.'

'I bet you think that shocks me don't you? I bet you expect me to stand here mortified, going, "Oh no, my boyfriend's a bender. What did I, as a woman, do wrong?" Well let me tell you, matey, I'm not mortified. In my time I've seen everything.' She snatched his cigarette from him and took a long drag on it that filled her lungs, reduced it to a burnt-out stub, threw it down, crushed it with her stiletto,then resumed sawing.

This was taking forever. Her arm was killing her. Her shoulder was killing her. She was dripping in sweat. What sort of idiot tied a cow to a door using rope this thick?

She stopped for breath. Maybe she should give up, admit defeat at the hands of cowdom. But no! No! She had to do it. She had to win. She had to defeat them – defeat them all.

With a great heave she drew the saw back.

She pushed it forward with all her weight.

And the rope severed.

She stood back, watching the cow rise skyward like the balloon in that song by the German girl with hairy armpits. 'Go on!' she shouted. 'Fly away, you Satan horned twat! Let's see you motivate in outer space!'

And still it rose.

Now it was a blob.

Now a dash.

Now a dot.

Now gone.

She kept watching the skies, checking it didn't return. Cows were sneaky like that. You never knew where they might turn up.

Roddy asked, 'What do we do now, babe? Hide?'

'Hide?' She still watched the skies.

'That's what I always do when I've done something wrong.'

She looked at him. 'We've done nothing wrong. What we do now is flaunt ourselves. We let everyone know we've made this camp a safer place for everyone.'

'You mean safer for you?'

She chose to ignore his stupidity. 'You see that restaurant?' She nodded toward Bab's Steakhouse. It was lit up like a Reeperbahn window, its moose heads spinning wildly.

Hands in pockets, he looked across at it. 'What about it?'

'Tonight's the grand opening.'

'So?'

'So we walk in, we sit at the best table, we pick up the menu, we make our orders. And then . . .'

'And then?'

She paused for effect. Her eyes narrowed to ruthless slits. And she said, 'We eat the biggest cow on the menu.'

forty-three

'How can we not be there yet?' How many more of these corridors would Sally have to walk down? She felt like a rat in a laboratory maze test.

Dr Dan stopped by a door to her left. So did she. He rested his palm on its handle. 'As you're about to see, Sally, all our girls are safely ensconced in their TV Room.'

She eyed the door's blank greenness, untrustingly. Remembering she had a gun, she watched him and asked, 'This is the place?'

'They'll be catching up on the latest events in Power Ranger land. They'd never miss it.'

'Not even if they'd just stolen a dead man.' Dr Steve stood by Dr Dan.

'He'd be in there watching it with them,' Dr Dan said.

'Though God knows what use they could have for a dead man,' Dr Steve said. 'It's not like they'll have torn him limb from limb and are in there, right now, eating him.'

Dr Dan said, 'Dr Steve?'

Dr Steve said, 'Dr Dan?'

Dr Dan said, 'If you'd like to do the honours?'

With a flourish Dr Steve threw open the door. His hand gestured for her to take a look inside.

Keeping an eye on them she stepped forward, half expecting them to shove her in there, lock the door, and abandon her to the mercy of their killer cows.

But they didn't.

Leaning forward the three of them looked into that room.

And the scientists gasped in horror at what confronted them.

In that room, behind that TV, atop that filing cabinet, astride that radiator . . .

The cows were . . .

The cows were . . .

The cows were not there.

fourty-four

'Oh Jesus. Look at this place.' Cthulha stood at the centre of Bab's Steakhouse, hacksaw in hand. Mouth open, mind reeling, she gazed around, almost scared to speak, in case she spoiled the ambience.

'Some Day My Prince Will Come' trilled down from a speaker above the door.

Manacles hung from the ceiling; two for each table, so that one diner could torture their friend.

Bull whips hung from the walls.

An iron maiden stood by the door, a note pinned to its spikes: RESERVED FOR UNSATISFIED CUSTOMERS.

And the chairs; each chair came with a complementary riding crop.

And the walls, the walls were black and purple and green and orange and pink, and another colour she couldn't describe but that couldn't fail to send you dizzy.

And most of all, from the kitchens, drifted the smell of sizzling beef. After all humanity's searching, the blind alleys and wrong turnings, Cthulha Gochllagochgoch had found heaven just four miles from her own home.

But Sally had been right about the flashbacks; at that table over there, she could see a seven-foot rabbit trying to hypnotize a vase.

Roddy stood beside her, not looking so keen on the place. 'But what about that sign on the door, babe?

'What sign?'

'The one that said, KEEP OUT! BY ORDER OF THE CARAVAN PARK MANAGER. DO NOT ENTER! – YOU'LL DIE!!!'

'That's just Sally fussing. You know how she is. She always thinks someone's going to die. Rodders, you can take it from me, nothing bad's going to happen to me in this place tonight.'

forty-five

'Is that really a gun?' Dr Steve sat watching the bulge in Sally's coat.

'Yeah..'

'Can I play with it?'

'No.'

'Can I feel it?'

'No.'

'Can I see it?'

'No.'

They were sat at his caravan's canteen table, the place empty but for them and Dr Dan. Dr Dan was in the far corner, trying to kick a machine into giving him coffee. She was hoping it would fall on him.

She was also trying to make sense of it all. If Landen's body now had Daisy's brain and the cows hadn't taken him to eat him, the only way she could see it was that Daisy must be their leader or their god. Why else would they want him? But to be either of those, Daisy must have been even more evil than they were. So when she'd taken Cthulha's job it had been no accident but part of some dark plan. And the mind control machine had gone missing from the bin. Daisy was the only one who could have taken it. But why?

Then it struck her; Landen's body had Daisy's brain. Hadn't it said it all that when Teena'd told her about the brain swap operation Sally'd not batted an eyelid, just accepted it as a Teena thing?

Carrying three steaming cups on a tray, Dr Dan rejoined them. He asked, 'But how could this happen? How?' He pulled out a chair and sat down. 'The girls were always so well behaved.'

'When we were present,' Dr Steve said. 'Who knows what they got up to while our backs were turned?' We must recognize now that those cows were stringing us along while they finalized their brilliant masterplan.'

'But how could they be intelligent?' Sally asked. 'No matter how you reared them, they're still only animals.'

Dr Steve watched his coffee cup, gravely. 'That's not entirely true, Sally.'

Dr Dan looked at him. 'Should we be telling her this?'

'We might as well.'

So Dr Dan asked her, 'Has Teena ever told you she's gorgeous?'

'I think she mentioned it once.'

'We decided it wasn't fair that there was only one of her and billions of the rest of us.'

'We thought we'd create a Teena substitute for every man–'

'And woman.'

'–who couldn't have her.'

'For a year we attended every scientific conference.'

'Even the ones we couldn't understand.'

'Which was most of them.'

'We'd sit directly behind her.'

'Then we'd try to pull her hair out.'

'But she'd always turn round and hit us before we succeeded.'

'And she hits really hard,' Dr Dan complained.

'She broke my cheek,' Dr Steve complained.

'She broke my jaw,' Dr Dan complained.

'She broke my wrist,' Dr Steve complained.

'And this is the woman you want to fill the world with?' Sally asked.

'She's lovely,' they declared.

'She kills men, you know.' She was about to go into her breast impalement thing. It was her stroke of genius; put men off Teena by scaring them with the thing about her they most craved. And why not? Why should Teena get all the male attention? She wasn't even nice.

'We don't care,' they said.

So much for that idea.

Dr Dan said, 'Finally, at the Barry Trusk conference – our last possible chance – we got . . .' He looked at Dr Steve. Dr Steve looked at him. Dr Dan took a sip of coffee as though trying to prolong the tension. He placed his cup on the table then gently pushed it aside. 'We got . . .'

'Yes?' she demanded.

'We got a hair.'

'A hair?'

They nodded gravely.

She watched them, blank. 'That's it? You got a hair? I mean, I'm sure her hair was very nice but I can't see what–' Then she shut up.

It had dawned on her.

She watched Dr Dan, amazed. She watched Dr Steve, amazed. 'You mean . . . ?'

They nodded gravely.

She said, 'You were trying to clone her?'

'But Dr Rama's copyrighted ninety-nine-point-eight per cent of her DNA to prevent irresponsible scientists filling the world with her.'

'We had to fill the gaps with other genes.'

'We got the idea from *Jurassic Park*.'

'We bought a packet of frog genes from a local store.'

'Oh God,' she said. 'Not Davey Farrel's?'

'You know him?' they asked.

'What mood was he in?'

'Mood?' they asked.

'Did he seem bitter and twisted?'

Dr Dan: 'Now you mention it he did slam the packet down on the counter with surprising force.'

Dr Steve: 'We thought he was just being energetic.'

'Energetic?' she complained. 'You don't buy *anything* from Davey when he's bitter and twisted. You wait till he's calmed down and becomes the model of sweet reason.'

'Well no one told us.'

Dr Steve said, 'As you've probably guessed, the genes turned out to be cow genes.'

'But that was okay,' Dr Dan said. 'Everyone likes Teena Rama. Everyone likes farmyard animals.'

'But we never bargained on the average cow's capacity for evil,' Dr Steve said.

'And there was another problem,' Dr Dan said.

'Which was?' Sally asked.

'They weren't all cow genes.'

'Then what were they?'

'We'd rather not say.'

'But unlike with the Teena-cattle, we realized straight away that the other clones were dangerous, and locked them away. Those animals can never escape.'

'They're under incredible security.'

'Watched constantly.'

Dr Dan buried his head in his hands. 'But, the cows. How could we have been so wrong about the cows?'

'How?' Dr Steve said. 'Ask Robert Oppenheimer. Ask Wernher Von Braun. How many well meaning scientists have had to ask themselves that question over the years?'

'Dr Dan?' Sally asked.

'Yes?'

'If a young woman tracked down those cows . . . ?'

'Yes?'

'. . . how dangerous would it be for her to try and snatch a corpse back from them?'

'Sally.' He looked her in the eyes, reached a hand across and placed it on hers. 'If cows really *have* turned bad . . .'

'Yes?'

His hand tightened around hers. '. . . the human race has seventy-two hours to live.'

forty-six

'Are you going to be all day with this?' Legs hugged to her chest, Teena perched on the wooden chair by the wall where Mr Landen's brain had made her sit while he worked. Again she checked her watch. What was up with him? He'd been at it for nearly seven minutes.

He hovered over the table, pencil gripped in his metal claw. Humming Cole Porter songs to himself he drew his blueprint for the Bride of Landen. 'Patience never was your strong point, my dear.'

'I don't see why you're even doing this. I designed a perfectly good bride for you.'

'My dear girl, I've a reputation to preserve. I can't have people saying, "That's George Landen. His wife's a balloon, you know." How would you like it if people said, "There's Tinashta K Rama. Her husband's a colander"? And, in case you've forgotten, I once collated the nation's most exhaustive – and exhausting – survey on sexual mores. If anyone can design top class cow tottie, I can.'

'You surveyed livestock?'

'I surveyed everyone. Succeeded in debasing an angel yet?' He drew on, humming Irving Berlin.

She checked her watch again. Was it really too much to ask that others worked at her pace?

Then, click, his pencil hit the table, 'There,' he said proudly.

Suddenly she was interested. 'You're finished?'

'Indubitably.'

She stood, impatient to see what he'd drawn.

His claw gripped the paper and, humming Gershwin, he carried it across to her.

The moment he arrived, she snatched it from him.

'So how do you like those potatoes?' He asked.

If only it had been potatoes. Her gaze scampered across the paper, taking in every detail of the frog-headed monstrosity he wanted her to build. It had a giraffe's neck, a duck's body and hands like lobster claws. Gaze transfixed by its hideousness, she demanded, 'What the hell's this!?!'

'An absolute corker.'

If fury could burn, that paper would have been ashes. 'Is this a joke!?!'

'Not at all, it's . . .'

'Yes it is!' She flung the paper aside. 'It's a joke!' She prodded him backwards toward the wall. 'You're trying to humiliate me! Well, let me tell you, you chauvinistic, over-educated ponce, I've put up with all sorts from you over the years; the little digs, the insistence on calling me "dear", the liberal use of words like "hooters" and "tottie". And I've tolerated it all, in the amused acceptance that it was a post modern satire of olde worlde attitudes. But this time the joke's gone too far!' She grabbed his propeller stalk and headed for the door with him.

'Miss Rama,' he protested, powerless to resist. 'What the deuce do you think you're doing?' And he didn't sound like Terry Thomas; he sounded like Basil Brush.

'I'm doing what someone should've done years ago.' She flung open the front door, almost separating it from its hinges. 'I'm throwing you in the bin.'

'Miss Rama, I really must protest.'

She ignored the moron, carrying him to the wheelie bins outside Sally's offices.

'Miss Rama!' He said again.

'Shut up!' She threw open a wheelie bin and flung him into it.

His jar hit the bin bottom with the smashing of glass and an, 'Ouch!'

Was she supposed to care? She shouted into the bin, 'And you can come out when you've learned some manners.' She slammed down its lid then headed back for her mobile home. She'd show them. She'd show them all; the fools like him who'd never believed in her. With the materials she'd already gathered, she'd build him a bride far better than any frog-headed duck monster.

And when she was done, when she'd reduced them all to awestruck wrecks, she'd phone Dr Steinbeck because she was clearly losing her marbles again.

forty-seven

'I'm having twelve cows. How many're you having?'

'Lemme check the menu, babe.'

'What for? Flies?' Like he knew anything about food. Cthulha, on the other hand, was an expert. She was sat across the table from him, looking around for a waitress but couldn't see one. And there was nowhere to go for self service. What kind of restaurant was this?

Roddy said, 'Did you really eat someone in that scandal last year?'

She returned her attention to him. 'Everyone did. There was so much of that meat around, in pubs and restaurants and supermarkets, you couldn't avoid eating it. But I'd love to meet whoever put it there. You should have seen Sally's face when she realized what that cheap EU beef she'd been eating was. Course, for me it wasn't such a problem, on account of having eaten lots of people when I was a kid, with us being poor and my mum having that job at the morgue. On her more pleasant days she used to

226

cut my food into little space octopus shapes for me. I love my mum.'

'Human flesh, babe; what's it taste like?'

'Exactly!' she protested. 'That's exactly it!'

'What is?'

'Everyone always goes, "Uurgh, eating human flesh. That's disgusting," but the first thing they ever ask you is, "What's it taste like?" I reckon there's a cannibal in all of us. And cannibalism's good for you.'

'Yeah?'

'There's a village in France where they eat nothing but people and everyone lives to be a hundred and seven – well, apart from the people they eat, who live to be thirty.'

'Wow. Then why don't you eat it all the time?'

'You're not allowed to. I don't know what it is. It's the law or something. Anyway, Bridget might not eat people, so I figured it's probably not classy.'

'Hollywood stars, man, you can always rely on them for a guide to social etiquette.'

'Exactly.'

He opened his menu. 'But a connoisseur like me needs to check the meat against the wine list to ensure a perfectly balanced palate.'

'This is the man I caught drinking from the toilet bowl this morning.'

'I was thirsty, man. I'd had a wild night.'

'I hope you don't expect me to be kissing you any time in the near future.'

'I never did.'

'And what's that supposed to mean?'

Before he could tell her, a bull whip sliced his menu in half.

Startled, she looked at him. He looked at her. And as one they turned their gazes toward the S&M clad woman now stood over their table. One hand rested on her hip. The other held the whip. An eye patch covered each eye, another resting on her forehead. God alone knew how she could see to aim the whip. And her chest! It was like a breakout at a dirigible works.

After a suitably dramatic pause, the woman lisped, 'You won't be needing that menu, little man.'

'Why not?'

'The cook's here.'

The 'cook' leaned forward, her cleavage threatening to spill out of her PVC corset and bury Roddy beneath a combined re-enactment of the Hindenberg and R101 disasters. She cupped his chin with her fingertips then lifted his face toward her. Eyepatches gazing into his eyes, she said, 'Tonight's cow night. If it's on my table, it's a cow.'

But where had Cthulha seen her before? Sally's mother? No that wasn't it. Sally's mother was dead. Cthulha had seen her die, on the first night her parents had let Sally help with the act. Cthulha'd been in the audience, there to see Uncle Al's brother and sister-in-law in action on the trapeze; the Flying Coopers. Suddenly there were shouts, gasps and screams from the audience – and this little kid stood centre stage, holding a snapped rope, clueless about what was happening. She was cute, like a shaved Ewok with Shirley Temple's hair. Cthulha took her back to Uncle Al's and tried to convince him to adopt her so she wouldn't have to grow up in an orphanage like Cthulha hadn't. He'd refused till Cthulha'd pointed out the Ewok thing. Suddenly he grabbed the kid, picked her up and was giving her a great big hug, saying that of course he couldn't let an Ewok go to the orphanage – a Wookie might eat it. And who said Aloysius Bracewell had no heart?

Right now a lump travelled down Roddy's throat as he gazed into the cook's eye patches. Too impressed for Cthulha's liking he asked, 'What kind of cows you got, doll?'

'We have big ones, small ones, square ones, round ones, every kind of ones.'

'You got triangular ones?'

'Roddy.' Cthulha was still trying to recognize the woman, 'They don't make triangular cows.'

The cook said, 'You want triangular ones, little man?'

He nodded, gaze transfixed.

'Then we've enough triangular cows to build Cheops' Pyramid.'

He stared at her chest. 'I don't see no moo cows.'

She again grabbed his chin and yanked his head up to face her. 'We store them in a special place – just for you.'

What *was* this? She was trying to move in on Cthulha's man? At her age? She had to be thirty nine if she was a day.

'What special place?' he asked.

'A cow place,' the cook said.

That was it; Cthulha was putting a stop to this. 'Don't I know you from somewhere?'

The cook's attention remained on Roddy. 'You tell me, naughty girl.'

Cthulha pushed her chair backwards, about to get up and land her one.

But something stopped her, something that said . . .

Was she?

She was!

And Cthulha threw her hands over her mouth, in squeaky voiced disbelief. 'Oh my God! Ohmygod! Ohmygod!'

'Memory stirring, naughty girl?'
'*You're* no cook,' Cthulha gushed.
'No?'
'No!'
'Then what am I?'
'You're Queen Mullineks!'

forty-eight

One screech from the corridor sent the two doctors jumping to their feet, knocking their chairs over in panic.

'Oh God!' They stared at each other across the canteen table, mouths open, eyes wide, ashen-faced.

'What's that noise?' Sally remained seated. It hadn't sounded like any cows she'd ever heard. It sounded like the central heating system playing up. What was so bad about that?

SCREECH! There it was again. Maybe she'd fix it when she'd done with the cows.

Dr Dan grabbed her arm and tried to haul her to her feet. 'Sally, we have to get out of here!'

'Why?' She remained seated, resisting his tugging.

'The other clones we told you about, the ones that weren't cows.'

'What about them?' Now she stood, slowly, one eye on the open doorway, both ears on the noises coming from the corridor.

'They've escaped.'

'But you said they were locked up,' she said.

What sounded like scythes scraped bare concrete as though a thing of infinite malice was dragging huge claws along walls purely in order to scare them.

It was succeeding.

And it was drawing closer.

'They were safely locked up,' Dr Steve insisted.

'Then how've they escaped?' she demanded.

'My god!' Dr Dan said.

'What?' Dr Steve asked.

'They must have eaten Blind Stan.'

The duo watched each other, stares filled with dread significance.

'Blind Stan?' Sally asked.

'The wheelchair-bound man who comes in to give them their weekly run out on the common. It supplements his pension.'

'His pension?' She glared at them in disbelief. 'You left dangerous animals in the care of an old man called Blind Stan?'

'No one else would work with them.'

'They're so terrifying.'

'We told him they were labradors.'

'It seemed to keep him happy.'

'It seemed to keep them happy.'

The doctors again watched each other in horrified realization. They said, 'He must have tried to stroke them.'

'We told him not to,' Dr Steve told her. 'Like the real Dr Rama, they view it as sexual harassment.'

'He can't have had his hearing aid on when we told him.'

'That must be why he responded by giving a thumbs up and saying, "Half past seven."'

'None of that matters,' Dr Steve insisted. 'All that matters is . . .' He stopped mid-sentence, trembling, gaze fixed on the door; the first screeching had been joined by a second. Whatever was out there, there was now two of it.

'What matters now?' She demanded, glancing at the door, still seeing no danger.

His gaze was fixed on the doorway.

'What matters now?' she repeated.

He didn't answer. She slapped him. He didn't answer. She slapped him again. And again. It wasn't achieving anything but it made her feel better. She punched him in the stomach, stamped on his foot, grabbed him by the lab coat and shook him.

Sweat pouring, still watching the door, he stuttered, 'W-What matters now is . . .'

'Yes?'

'. . . the velociRamas are loose!'

forty-nine

'Queen who?' Roddy sat inspecting the remnants of his menu as though he could tape them back together again.

'Are you kidding?' Cthulha gushed, appalled by his ignorance. 'Mullineks was queen of the Mad Moon Lesbians in Miles Silkland's film of the same name.' How could it have taken Cthulha so long to recognize her? But then she'd never expected to meet the queen in a place like this. 'Queen Mullineks.' She curtsied as best as she could while sat down. 'I-I'm your biggest fan.'

'How lovely.' Mullineks sat on a throne formed by oiled musclemen in thongs. They'd appeared at the clap of her hands and had instantly arranged themselves into a chair shape.

'When I was seventeen, I used to masturbate to my poster of you all day long.'

'That's a certainly a compliment.'

'I never masturbated so much over anyone.'

'Thank you.'

'Not even Bridget Fonda.'

'Really?'

'And I masturbate over her all the time.'

'Really?' Mullineks watched the ceiling. She seemed to be losing interest in the conversation.

'And that scene in *Mad Moon Lesbians Go Cowgirl* where your girls capture Earth agent Carnaby Soho and put her in your lesbo-tron, it's the horniest thing I've ever seen.'

'I'm glad you liked it, naughty girl. It gave me a certain . . .' her tongue clicked camply in her right cheek, '. . . pleasure.'

'And Carnaby Soho?'

'She had few complaints – by the time I'd finished with her.'

Roddy looked puzzled. 'Lesbo-tron?'

Cthulha said, 'It was a machine for turning good straight Earth girls like me into mad bad moon lesbians like her.'

He was looking like he couldn't spot the difference.

'It never failed,' Mullineks told him.

Cthulha said, 'But, Queen Mullineks? Carnaby Soho.'

'What about her?'

'I could never figure it out. She made her first appearance in 1968 but even in her films from the '90s she didn't look any older.'

'That's easy.'

'It is?'

'You remember Skippy; that giant mouse?' Mullineks asked.

'I think it was a kangaroo.'

'Whatever it was, did you know they got through dozens of them every series? They were always getting run over or falling off cliffs; stupid beasts. It was the same with Carnaby Soho.'

Cthulha frowned. 'Carnaby Soho kept falling off cliffs?'

235

'Those girls were not hired for their intelligence.'

But Cthulha had to think about this. All those years, there'd been more than one Carnaby Soho? The movie industry, it was like it was all done with trickery. Cthulha asked her, 'But what're you doing here? Why aren't you out making big movies like you used to?'

'For some reason, after Miles' unfortunate suicide, I found it difficult to find acting work. I auditioned several times for *Casualty* but somehow never landed a part. It was as though I was typecast.'

'Never.' Roddy had his 'I'm going to pretend not to understand films' voice on. If he started taking the piss . . .

'It's true,' Mullineks insisted.

'And did you take those men to the auditions?' he asked.

'Of course.' She flicked a curtain of black hair away from her right eyepatch then watched her chair.

'Those men go everywhere with her,' Cthulha told Roddy. 'They're her Human Throne; ordinary men turned into adoring slaves for her pleasure.'

'In this case, I got them from the Job Centre.' Mullineks stroked the hair of the one with the Village People moustache. He was her arm rest. Cthulha could have done with giving him a good stroking herself. Mullineks said, 'This one used to be big in the City. Now he's my slave. I really can't understand why people knock the New Deal.'

'And you auditioned as a nurse?' Roddy asked.

Of course.' Another slave popped a grape in Mullineks' mouth as she said, 'I had a natural aptitude for such roles – being a lover of black suspenders.'

'And you took your Human Throne to auditions?' Roddy asked.

She answered with an affirmative shrug. A slave fanned her with a palm frond.

'And you sat on it while you auditioned?' Roddy asked.

'Of course.' She laughed, 'I'm not going to stand up for long in these boots am I?' Sat cross-legged, she wore PVC thigh-lengthers with the longest, sharpest heels Cthulha'd ever seen. Just imagine those grinding some poor man down.

'Nursing chicks go everywhere on body builders?' Roddy asked.

'Of course.'

'Er, well actually, Queen Mullineks,' Cthulha said, 'they don't really.'

'They don't?'

'No.'

'Well!!!' She banged her fist down on her arm rest, now seeing where her career had gone sour. 'Why didn't my agent tell me this?'

'Maybe he was crap,' Roddy said.

'But you're sure nurses don't have Human Thrones?'

'Positive,' said Cthulha

'But that's just gratuitous. How do the poor girls get to rest their feet?'

Roddy shrugged sardonically.

Mullineks said, 'Denied roles by directors I now know were unable to see beyond stereotypes, I returned to my first love, cooking.'

'Do you still have the lesbo-tron?' Cthulha was almost scared to ask, in case she said no.

'Of course. It's still in the packing crate from when I first moved here.' From somewhere she produced a cigarette packet. She flicked it open, flicked out a cigarette, tapped it on the packet, placed it in her mouth then lit it. She extinguished the match with a shake then cast it aside. She inhaled smoke stylishly then tipped her head back to watch the ceiling. She exhaled smoke stylishly. After a suitably succulent pause, she watched Cthulha and said, 'Would you like to find out if it still works?'

Cthulha stared at her, wide eyed. 'You mean it?'

'I never joke about my lesbo-tron.'

'Can you believe this?' Cthulha gushed at Roddy, reaching across to give him a little push.

'No.' He was probably just jealous because no one wanted to shove *him* in a lesbo-tron.

'The Queen of the Mad Moon Lesbians is going to turn me, Cthulha Gochllagochgoch, into a mad bad moon lesbian then do things to me no Earth girl should have to endure this side of the watershed. And to think I thought today was going to be the worst of my adult life.'

'And will your attractive friend be joining us?' Mullineks lazily fingered the end of her whip.

'Friend?' Cthulha asked.

'The rather scrumptious girl with polka dot rags for hair. Didn't I spot you admiring her juicy rump the other day?'

'Dr Rama? No chance. Sally says—'

'Sally?'

'The caravan park manageress.'

'Oh,' Mullineks said frostily. 'Her.'

'It seems Dr Rama's too busy, building brides, to bother with social events. Anyway, according to Sal, she doesn't ride the same bus we do.'

'How unsporting. But a bride you say? That's very interesting. Very interesting indeed.' Index fingers crooked against her lips, she reclined in her throne, descending into the silence she always used when hatching a scheme.

Cthulha looked at Roddy. Roddy looked at Cthulha. They shrugged at each other, clueless as to what Mullineks was thinking.

Roddy said, 'Maybe we should prod her.'

'Roddy, you can't prod royalty.'

'Why not?'

'You wouldn't prod Ming the Merciless would you?'

'Let's face it, babe, she's no Ming.'

'She's the nearest we're ever going to meet.'

Through with thinking, Mullineks sat up again. 'Perhaps you'd like to order now?'

Roddy asked, 'What flies you got?'

'Flies?'

Cthulha said, 'He's eccentric. He does this trick with his tongue.'

'His tongue?'

Cthulha grinned, 'Go on, Rod, show her.'

His mouth opened. He took aim. And, frog-like, his tongue shot out. Its sticky tip snatched Mullineks' central eyepatch and yanked it away from her forehead, exposing her third eye. Slap, the patch's elastic reached its limit, snapping it back into place. His tongue withdrew into his mouth. He shut his mouth then smiled at her.

'Could Miles Silkland have used that man, or what?' Cthulha was too proud of him for words.

'That's certainly a talent you don't see every day, young man. I'll see what flies we have in the kitchen.'

'Thanks, babe.'

Now she asked Cthulha, 'And what would *you* like to eat?'

'You got cows?'

'Tonight's Cow Night. Everything is cows.'

'But whole ones. I want a great big whole one flopped across this plate. And I want its head left on so I can see the look on its face as I'm eating it.'

'My naughty, if you want a whole one, you shall have a whole one. Must build up your energy levels for what follows.'

'What's the biggest cow you got?' Cthulha asked.

'How tall's your bride-building friend?'

'About five-nine. Why?'

'As luck would have it I'm expecting delivery of a cow that will stand exactly five feet nine inches tall.'

'Queen Mullineks?' Cthulha said.

'Yes, my naughty?'

'Go cook me that cow.'

fifty

'What the hell're you waiting for!?!' Sally demanded of the doctors as the scraping and screeching grew
nearer.

Dr Steve frantically rattled the window frame. 'I can't
get it open. It's jammed.'

'Then break it!'

'I can't. We had the glass reinforced to stop cows jumping
out. They were always trying to leap over the moon. With
this glass they just bounced off the windows. Even bullets
couldn't break it.'

'Then try another one!' She stood by the canteen table,
heart pounding, legs like water, half watching the doorway, half watching the doctors fiddle with the windows.
Visions filled her head of being torn apart by Jurassic Parks'
drooling velociraptors. She grabbed her gun handle inside
her coat pocket. The moment those things appeared she'd
pull the gun, start blasting, and hope she actually hit
something, though that seemed unlikely the way her hands

241

were shaking. And everyone knew handguns couldn't stop dinosaurs.

'This one's jammed too.' Dr Dan rattled another window.

'So's this one.' Dr Steve rattled the one beside it. 'It's almost as though . . .'

'—As though someone's welded shut every window in the building.' A new, cold voice came from the doorway. 'And guess who I got that idea from?'

Dreading what they'd see, the three of them turned to face the door.

'Blind Stan!?!' Dr Dan gasped.

'Blind Stan?' Sally couldn't believe what now stood before them. 'That's no Blind Stan!' she said.

'Then who is it?' they asked.

'It's Mr Landen!'

fifty-one

'Run away, young men, run away.' Now back in her kitchens, Mullineks clapped like the King of Siam dismissing his servants. 'Back to your kennels, the lot of you. I'll be round to administer your spankings later.'

And the components of her Human Throne ran out through the back door, leaving her alone.

The door slammed behind them. She waited in case they returned in search of an extra caning, the greedy boys. But they didn't return. She had them too well trained for that.

Keeping three eyes out for intruders, humming 'How Much is That Doggie in the Window', she crossed to the cupboard above the sink. There she plunged a hand deep into her cleavage and rummaged until she found something cold and hard. She yanked it free then held it up gleaming in the light. It was a key – a special key; for it guarded her greatest secret.

On tip toes, she placed the key in the lock.

She turned it.

Fingers a-tremble she opened the door.

And she smiled.

In that cupboard – a mass of wires, plastic and metal – sat all she needed to complete her deadly plans . . .

. . . a stolen mind control machine.

fifty-two

Whistling a non-specific tune to herself, Teena attached a bulldog clip to her android's nose then stood back to best admire its glories. It lay lifeless on her table, but soon it would live. And if some might call it too tall or its capacity for chaos too great, she didn't care. If this didn't win her a Nobel Prize nothing would.

She ensured the other bulldog clips were securely attached to the android's extremities, taking special care with the toes, then glanced across, and checked that the clips were all wired to the panel on the far wall. She strode across to that panel. A large iron lever protruded from its centre, salvaged from the power station she and Mr Landen had visited at the start of their holiday. She wrapped both hands round it. A lever that important had to be big, and one that big would take some pulling.

She took one last glance at her creation. From this distance it seemed more glorious than ever.

Butterflies doing a delightful tango in her stomach, Teena Rama pulled the lever.

fifty-three

'You're quite right, my dear. I am indeed Mr Landen – or at least I occupy his body.' Sherlock Holmes pipe in hand, he stood in the canteen doorway, wearing a smoking jacket.

Behind him stood the 'missing' cows, dressed as Power Rangers. Chewing Action Men, they gazed in at her.

He said, 'Having been revived by my "sisters", I adopted the guise of Blind Stan in order to gain access to these two beauties.' He nodded towards the five-foot-nine, polka-dot-dreadlocked dinosaurs that snapped, snarled and drooled at the end of the short leash he was holding.

'You gave him dinosaurs!?!' Sally shouted.

'He said he was blind,' Dr Steve protested, behind her.

'And deaf,' Dr Dan said, behind her.

'And stupid,' Dr Steve said.

'And mute,' Dr Dan said.

'Mute!?!' She said.

'That's what he said.'

'And when I first described him,' she complained, 'it never rang any bells with you?'

'You didn't say he was blind, deaf and mute,' Dr Steve argued.

'He's not blind, deaf and mute,' she said. 'He was just pretending.'

'Blimey,' they said.

'Doctors.' Landen sucked at his pipe. 'I should thank you. Without your witless help I could never have achieved my aims.'

'Which are?' She played for time, glancing around for another way out. She couldn't see one.

'Once, I was an historian, a great historian. My name isn't important but you'll have heard of me. I wrote books about the Great War. I was the only man alive who had a clue what caused it, why it ended or what happened in between. As you can imagine this made me a man in demand. But then I realized, writing books about the horrors of war was beneath my dignity.'

'Then what did you want to write about?' she asked.

'Tap-dancing mules.'

She frowned. Even some of the cows looked at each other oddly.

He said, 'My book, *Tap Dancing Mules of Passion Dale*, was a masterpiece but, shocked by my genius, the Open University had my brain put into a cow. And a cow I would have remained had I not learned of this place from a passing sheep. Rather sneakily I claimed a place amongst the girls here and mingled.'

'That's why we always had a cow too many,' Dr Steve said.

'I always wondered about that,' Dr Dan said.

'You never mentioned it,' Dr Steve said.

'It never seemed important,' Dr Dan said.

'But you were dead,' Sally told Landen, determined to ignore the idiots behind her.

'This caravan contained all the equipment needed to revive me. You see, this whole escapade – Dr Rama buying me, killing me, putting my brain into this body, you putting me in Davey Farrel's ices box – I planned it all as meticulously as the plot of one of my tap-dancing mule books. And of course I have this.' He reached into his smoking jacket pocket and pulled out something too small for her to see. He held it up between thumb and index finger.

'And what's that?' she asked. The dinosaurs were trying to stare her out. She stared back.

He said, 'It's a lock of hair from Michael Flatley. With the Flatley Gene and this place's cloning technology, I have everything I need to form a twenty four thousand mile long line of River Dancing mules.'

'But . . . ?'

'But in order to provide houses for my mules, I must remove the existing occupants.'

'You mean?'

'Yes! I have to kill the entire human race. But I'm sure you'll agree it's a small price to pay. And the process will be complete within just eight hours.' He put Flatley's hair back in his pocket and patted the pocket closed, for safe keeping.

She said, 'Eight hours? But these two said it'd take seventy-two.'

'That would be with just cows for allies. But thanks to you three, I have indestructible velociRamas.'

'Indestructible?' Dread growing, she again watched the things that drooled at her like they couldn't wait to get eating.

He said, 'I've treated them with Dr Rama's Indestructible Cream.'

'You don't know how to make that,' she said. 'You're just a writer.'

'I was there when she formulated it. I know precisely how it's made.'

'They'll rebel,' Dr Dan said. 'They'll rip you to shreds.'

'As long as I supply them with tomato sauce, they'll do whatever I say. Young ladies these days do so love a little sauce. And I've sprayed myself with Dr Rama's Indestructible Spray. Nothing can harm me. Nothing.'

Sally only had Teena's word for it that her Indestructible Cream even worked. Nothing to lose, she yanked out the gun and, before Landen could duck, opened fire on him. The blasts rang in her ears. The recoil pushed her back with each shot. But still she fired, fired till her head ached and her hand was numb, fired till the gun was burning, fired till the pistol's clip hit the floor, empty.

And after all that, Landen stood laughing, palm extended as though testing for light precipitation. 'Why,' he said, 'is it raining?'

And that was it?

That was how she died? Not on a stage? Not on TV? Not even busking in some lousy market place, performing to apathetic shoppers? It had to be in a caravan, her only audience two geeks, two reptiles and some cattle? She flung the gun at him. He caught it. He opened his mouth and swallowed it. He always had had too big a mouth. The smug bastard. If he wasn't indestructible she'd have marched over there and given him the kicking he deserved for robbing her of her glory.

Except he was indestructible.

And so were his 'pets'.

One of them winked at her.

She looked around for a way out, or for something to hit them with, to block them with. Anything. Then she saw it;

the table beside her. She jammed her foot against the table edge and grabbed its nearest leg. She tugged at it with all she had.

'Miss Cooper!?!' Suddenly Dr Dan grabbed her in a bear hug. 'What do you think you're doing!?!'

'I'm breaking off a table leg! What's it look like?' And still she tugged, even with him holding her.

'But that table's not paid for yet.'

She broke off tugging to glare at him. 'Are you serious?'

He backed off timidly.

She resumed tugging, ignoring the sweat pouring down her face.

Landen asked, 'Is there some purpose to this, my dear?'

'You bet there is.' Still she tugged.

'Which is.'

'Like I'm going to tell you.' No way would he have remembered to spray Indestructible Cream inside their throats. It was the last thing you'd think of, especially when you were over confident. But she'd worked with Super-Marcel He Deflects Table Legs Fired From Cannons – With His Teeth, so it was the first thing she'd thought of. When those monstrosities came at her she'd ram the table leg down and out the back of their throats before they could tear her to shreds. It was a long shot but it was the only one she had.

After some thought, Landen said, 'I know what it is. You think that vampires are bullet proof but can be killed by a stake through the heart, so it must work the same with the indestructible. Ha! How moronic. I wish Dr Rama were here. She'd have been a much more worthwhile adversary. But she's far too dangerous. I've had to arrange for her to be kept busy. Well go ahead, my dear. You tear off your little table leg. I'm in no hurry.'

The top of the leg began to crack. It'd only need a

few more tugs. She knew it would. She told the geeks, 'You two.'

'What?'

'Keep him talking.'

'Would you like me to help you, my dear? Landen volunteered, so sure of his victory.

'I don't want anything from you.'

'But the cows?' Dr Steve asked, trying to think of something to say.

'What about them?' Landen asked.

'They've always been good girls. Why would they help you?'

'Everyone has their price. They'll help anyone who can turn them into Power Rangers. Won't you, girls?'

They did something that resembled the Power Rangers salute then fell over, having been designed to stand on four legs not two.

'You can't turn cows into Power Rangers,' she challenged, still tugging.

Finally, the leg came free.

Her momentum took her back a few paces, and she collided with the two doctors. She ignored them and stepped forward a pace, table leg in hands. Now I'm ready, you bastards.

Landen said, 'With this place's genetic machinery I can turn these cows into whatever they like. They'd do it themselves but the equipment's more delicate than that needed to revive me, and they lack the hands to operate it.'

Like she cared.

He glanced at the table leg. 'Are you ready now, my dear?'

'Come and get me,' she sneered, breathing heavy, pulse racing. 'If I'm going, I'm taking you with me.'

And with an insane laugh, George Landen released his velociRamas.

fifty-four

'Hello,' she beamed proudly, 'My name's Teena. And *I'm your mother.*' Rubber plant in hand she stood over her creature, wearing a man's white shirt (sleeves folded neatly up to the elbows) and a close-fitting knee-length skirt (red, with white polka dots). A simple ensemble but bought specially for the occasion. Still holding the plant, she slipped her best shoes on, got her feet comfortable in them, and readied herself to proceed.

Her creature lay on the table, blank-eyed. As expected it made no response to her presence. Its central processing unit was an empty box – one she'd start filling straight away.

She told it, 'As you're not designed to be too bright I'll take this a step at a time. And listen closely, you've a lot of learning to cram into the next five minutes.'

She placed the pot plant on her creature's forehead, stepped back and, with a tug, straightened her shirt. The creation of life; one should look tidy for such an event.

Horticulture being as good a place as any to start an education, she told her creature, 'This is a plant pot. Can *you* say plant pot?'

It took one look at the pot, grabbed it and hit her over the head with it.

fifty-five

It crashed through the ceiling before anyone could react, too fast to be more than a blur, sending dust, plaster and broken timbers flying, flooding the room with a dust that light couldn't penetrate.

And when the dust settled, when everything had calmed down and everyone who mattered had stopped coughing and regained their senses, Sally shouted, 'It's Daisy!'

Delighted she flung the table leg aside. It hit one of the Doctors. He said, 'Ouch!' She didn't know which one it had hit but who cared? She was too busy rushing across to hug the brainless cow which stood, blowing bubbles, atop the now unconscious Landen and his equally out-cold velociRamas. And she didn't care if it did smell, she was never going to stop hugging it.

'Where did that come from?' Dr Steve half-said, half-coughed, behind her.

Still hugging Daisy, eyes full of grit, Sally gazed at the hole in the ceiling. 'Teena covered her in anti gravity cream.'

'Why?' Dr Dan asked.

Sally slackened the hug so she could look back at him. 'Why does Teena do anything? Daisy must have slipped her moorings and floated away. The anti-gravity cream must've worn off just as she passed overhead.'

'But how did a cow landing on Landen and his velociRamas knock them out when even bullets couldn't hurt them?' asked Dr Dan.

'The bullets weren't indestructible. Daisy is. Firing bullets at Landen was like firing plasticine at a brick wall. If you want to knock over a wall, hit it with a wall. If you want to cut diamonds, use diamonds. Daisy's probably the only thing in existence hard enough to have stopped them.'

Hands in trouser pockets Dr Steve leaned back against the wall. He grinned. 'Are we jammy or what?'

The laughing Dr Dan was caked in dust. 'It's almost as though this was part of some bigger scheme, one that was using Landen's masterplan as part of its own mad masterplan.'

'What're you on about?' Dr Steve asked.

'I don't know but it makes you think.'

'It doesn't make me think.' Dr Steve pushed him.

'Nothing makes you think.' Dr Dan pushed him back.

'It wasn't my idea to hire Blind Stan!'

'Exactly! You have no ideas of your own! I have to do all the thinking for you!'

'The important thing,' Dr Steve over-asserted, 'is that everything's sorted out!'

'Except the velociRamas,' Sally warned. Out cold, tongues hanging from of the sides of their mouths, they looked almost cute but, 'When they wake . . .'

Dr Steve chuckled, 'We'll be ready for them. Now we know they can be controlled with tomato sauce, they'll be causing us no more trouble.' He turned his attention to the cows in the corridor. 'As for you girls . . .'

They mooed sheepishly.

'I hope you realize just how naughty you've been. There'll be no Power Rangers for you tonight.'

They mooed a timid protest.

'I'm sorry but that's what happens to girls who try to rule the world. Now off to your rooms, the lot of you. We'll be up with your suppers later.'

'If you're lucky,' Dr Dan warned.

Heads down, the shame-faced cattle trooped off to their rooms, lowing resentfully among themselves but surely realizing they'd got off lightly for trying to destroy the human race. But Sally couldn't help feeling the world hadn't heard the last of Dr Dan and Steve's 'genius' cows.

Hugging and stroking Daisy, she said, 'Now I just need to tie Mr Landen up, take him to Teena's, and this'll all be over.'

fifty-six

'What do you want doing with him?' Teena's thumb easing it open, she shone her pen light into Landen's larger eye. He lay bound, gagged and unconscious on her kitchen table. She wore a man's white shirt (sleeves neatly rolled up to the elbows) and a close-fitting knee-length skirt (red, with white polka dots). It was only her third outfit change of the day.

Stood beside her, Sally checked her watch. 'Get the margarine back in his head, and get it in fast. The Dullness Inspector's here in fifteen minutes.'

Teena released the eye lid then eased open his small eye. She shone the pen light into it, humming the *Odd Couple* theme.

Sally didn't ask about the luggage label dangling from the string dangling from the ring through her nose. Knowing Teena, it was best not to. Instead she glanced across at the pile of twisted metal, cogs, rods and circuit boards in the corner. God alone knew what it had once been.

Teena held Landen's nose between her thumb and fore-finger, tipped his head back and shone her pen light up his nostrils. She gazed up them, looking for who knew what. She said, 'You know what that is?'

Sally assumed she didn't mean Landen's nose. 'It's a pile of junk in the corner.'

'Until twelve minutes ago that "junk" was a bride of Landen.'

'The Bride of Landen? But she was a balloon.'

Teena placed the pen light in her own mouth and gripped it between her front teeth. Like it was a Gladstone bag she yanked Landen's mouth open. She held it there with both hands and, pen light in mouth, stared down his throat. 'Having taken on board your views, and those of a colleague, I decided to create something a little more sophisticated. And, if I say so myself, it was the best robot anyone's ever built in eight minutes. Unfortunately, upon activation, it went berserk.'

'But . . . ?'

'It tried to kill me with a pot plant. Of course if you hadn't made me un-super-evolve that rubber plant she wouldn't have been able to hit me with it. Not that I bear any grudges.'

Plant pot remnants lay scattered among the junk pile.

Teena rolled a sleeve up all the way to her armpit. She placed her hand in Landen's mouth, then her forearm, then her upper arm. Apparently rummaging around in his stomach she said, 'It was as though someone were manipulating the Bride, with a mind control machine, in an attempt to kill me. Though who'd want to kill me I can't imagine.'

'Then . . . ?'

'After a life or death struggle, I de-activated it.'

Sally gazed at the smashed heap. 'You can say that again.'

'I'm a firm advocate of thoroughness.' When she withdrew her hand from Landen's stomach it was holding Sally's gun. The gun's paintwork steamed with corrosion and it dripped stomach juices on the floor. Teena handed it to her. Sally watched it, no idea what to do with a half dissolved gun. She placed it on the table. Teena wiped dry her hand and arm then gave Sally the towel. As Sally dried herself, Teena rolled down her sleeve again. 'During the fight, I took a blow to the cranium, one which would have rendered anyone else useless. Fortunately, being made of sterner stuff, I'm wholly unaffected.' And, pen light between her teeth, she blew the luggage label away from her mouth.

'Teena?'

'Uh huh?'

Sally tossed the towel aside. 'Are you sure you're up to performing surgery?'

'Sally, I can do anything.'

'Even after a blow to the head?'

'Of course. You may know that a couple of years back I had a slight breakdown.'

Sally watched her. 'How "slight"?'

'Total. But even during my period of treatment, I could do surgery. In fact I was encouraged to do so. Gerry, my specialist, felt it'd do my spirits the world of good to keep my hand in, so to speak.'

Sally watched her, incredulous. 'They let you perform surgery while certifiable?'

Teena still held the pen light in her mouth. 'Many surgeons practise while certifiable. Most airline pilots fly while hallucinating. All nuclear technicians work while criminally insane. They have to; we can hardly shut hospitals, airports and reactors while waiting for them to feel better.'

'Then sort him out.'

With her tongue, Teena clicked her pen light off then placed it on the table. Luggage label flapping, she crossed the room. Sally's optimism plunged like a dead chicken. Teena opened a fridge ten times the size of Sally's and leaned into it. After much clattering, rattling and search search searching, she re-emerged, margarine in hand. She back-heeled shut the fridge door, collected her red bucket from under the sink then returned to the table. She placed the bucket and margarine on it. She considered for a moment, index finger pressed against her lips, then crossed to a high cupboard. She opened it. On tip toes, she retrieved a fully stocked surgical instrument tray. She opened a lower cupboard and retrieved two rubber gloves. She placed them on the tray, shut the cupboards and returned to the table. She placed the tray on it.

Like it was a dessert spoon, she picked up a scalpel and breathed on it. She breathed on its other side then wiped it clean on her shirt. 'This Dullness Inspector.' She dropped the scalpel back onto the tray.

'What about him?'

She lifted a small clamp, breathed on it, then wiped it on her shirt. 'Is he really that bad?'

'Bad? They say he's the most miserable man in Yorkshire.'

Teena dropped the clamp onto the tray. 'Sally, that money's as good as yours. A brain transplant in fifteen minutes, what could possibly go wrong?'

That was what Sally was wondering.

Smiling, Teena took a surgical glove from the tray. She slapped it against the table edge, presumably to soften it, then held its wrist against her mouth. She took a breath then blew into it, fully inflating it with one puff. She let the air out, stretched it, then pulled it onto her left hand.

She flexed her fingers.

And her arm dropped off.

fifty-seven

'Oh God! Oh God Oh God Oh God Oh God Oh God Oh God Oh God!' Hands over her mouth, Sally stepped back, mind gripped by horror, and stared at the arm which now lay on the table, filling her vision like it was the only thing on Earth.

'What's up?' Teena asked, smiling.

'Your arm!'

'What about it?'

'It's dropped off!'

'Oh' Teena looked down at it, unperturbed. 'Don't worry about that. It's a little known fact that I have a bionic arm.'

'What!?'

Teena picked it up and studied it. 'I lost the real one in a daring literary experiment several years ago. With my surgical and mechanical skills, it was child's play to create a perfect copy. It's a good job I do have it, otherwise I wouldn't be able to overpower the various products of my experiments. That's how I was able to stop the Bride of Landen, by bludgeoning her to pieces. The repeated impact must have loosened it.' She held it out to Sally. 'Put it back on for me would you?'

Sally watched it, remembering when she was nine and Uncle Al had sat her on his knee to watch that late night horror sequel. A murderer's arm had been cut off by a mad surgeon then went on the rampage around Victorian London. It would leap out at prostitutes and bobbies and strangle them. Even at that age she'd thought it unlikely an arm could leap. But that hadn't stopped her crying, or Cthulha who didn't like the idea of prostitutes being strangled.

'It won't bite.' Teena still held it out for her.

Sally watched it, unconvinced.

Teena said, 'It's an arm, not a Rottweiler.'

Reluctant, Sally stepped forward and took it, between her thumb and forefinger, seeking as little contact with it as possible.

It twitched. Startled she dropped it on the floor.

Teena's expression said, 'Wuss.'

Out to be no one's wuss, she picked it up and tried again, taking hold of Teena's sleeve, almost getting the arm into it before dropping it again.

Teena's expression said, 'Wuss.'

She tried again, this time getting it into the sleeve then manoeuvring it into position against Teena's torso. She tried to press it into place. She jiggled it about but, 'It's no use. I can't get it to fit properly.'

'It needs a good hard bash to click it into place.'

'How hard?'

'Really hard.'

'Hard enough to cause pain?'

'There'll be discomfort, yes.'

So Sally bashed it, hard.
It didn't click into place.
She bashed it harder.
It didn't click into place.
She bashed it *really* hard.
And Teena's head dropped off.

fifty-eight

'Can you believe this?' Eagerly awaiting her meal, Cthulha sat grinning her Bridgetest of Bridget Grins at him.

'Yeah.' Roddy sat studying his replacement menu.

'No you can't.' *Trust him to try and spoil it.*

'Yes I can,' he said.

'You can believe what?' she challenged.

'I don't know.'

'You don't know what you can believe?'

'Who does these days.'

'Then how do you know you can believe "this"?'

'I just do.'

'You're just pretending you can believe it.'

'Why would I?'

'To be contrary.'

'I can believe anything,' he said.

'No one can believe "anything".'

'I can.'

'You can believe in the Loch Ness Monster?' she said.

264

'All the time.'

'You can believe in fairies?'

'I never stop.'

'You can believe in aliens?' she said.

'They abducted me.'

'Who did?'

'Aliens,' he said.

'Bollocks,' she said.

'No. It's how I got here.'

'Roddy, aliens didn't bring you to this restaurant. I did.'

'Not the restaurant – Wyndham.'

'You're sure it wasn't a dream?'

'I never dream.'

'So, how did these "aliens" "abduct" you?'

'One morning I was out sunbathing on my lawn when two of 'em landed beside me. They leapt from their spaceship and, before I could run, grabbed me.'

'Then what'd they do?'

'They shoved a thermometer up my backside, and the big ugly one said, 'Let's see how you lot like it, you little grey jerk.' I never did figure out what that meant.'

She frowned at him. 'And did these "weird" beings have names?'

'Yeah.'

'What?'

'Neil and Buzz.'

'Neil and Buzz?' Her frown deepened. 'What kind of names for aliens are they?'

'Aliens can have any names they like. That's how they keep their presence secret from us.'

'Now you're saying there're aliens among us?'

'I see them everywhere.'

'Sure you do. So – "Neil and Buzz" – what did they do next?'

'Played golf.'

'Then what'd they do?'

'They went for a drive in their golf buggy thing. It was electric, like a milk float. But they just drove round in little circles, so they ended up back where they started.'

'And then?'

'They climbed out again.'

'Without having gone anywhere?'

'That's right. And they had heads that were like switched off TV sets.'

'Congratulations, Roddy.'

'On what?'

'Being the first person ever to have been kidnapped by the Teletubbies.'

'It's not my fault, babe. We can't choose who we get abducted by. When they come for you, you have to go. They threw me in their spaceship, flew me round and round till I got dizzy then dropped me off in Wyndham.'

She squinted at him. 'Roddy?'

'Yeah?' He again studied his menu.

'Where're you from exactly?'

'Leeds.'

'And what's Leeds like?'

'It's all craters and stuff, with mountains that don't look far enough away to be real. And the weird thing is . . .'

'Yeah?'

'It has only one sixth the gravity of anywhere else in England.'

'And that's Leeds?'

'Oui.'

'Only, I'm from Bradford which is like six inches from Leeds. And in Bradford I never heard anything about Leeds having low gravity.'

'It's not something we Leedsers like to talk about.'

'Lovians.'

'Que?'

'People from Leeds are called Lovians. I'd have expected someone from West Yorkshire to know that.'

He just shrugged.

She peered at him, suspicious. 'You know there's something about you I can never put my finger on.'

'That's why chicks find me fascinating, man.' He stuck his fingers in his left ear hole and pulled out a cigarette. He flicked it into the air, let it spin twice, caught it in his mouth then lit it just by blowing down it.

'And how'd you do the trick?'

'What trick?'

'The one where you talk without moving your lips, like you're implanting your thoughts direct into people's heads.'

'It's a Leeds thing.' He shrugged, mouth shut.

She watched him smoke his cigarette and study his menu. Maybe she should voice her suspicions. But no. She'd ask Dr Rama. She'd know about that stuff. She was a scientist. And it'd give Cthulha a chance to introduce herself. Dr Rama'd been here for days. Deprived of her fiancé, she'd be gagging for it by now, and Cthulha knew just the person to supply it. She told Roddy, 'What I was saying I can't believe is that I'm going to be interrogated by the queen of mad moon lesbians.'

He said nothing.

She propped her chin on her palm, elbow on table, and arched an eyebrow at him. 'Jealous?' she said.

'Of what?' He studied his menu, cigarette gently smoking.

'Your chick carrying on with other women.'

'Can I watch?'

She glowered. 'You know, if you were more possessive I might behave better.'

He checked his watch. 'These cows, babe?'

'What about 'em?'

'How long do they take to cook?'

She shrugged. 'It can't be more than twenty minutes or the customers'd get bored and walk out. Mullineks probably has a giant microwave through there and has cows shovelled in *en masse*. She's that type of woman.'

'Are you sure about that?'

'Sure I'm sure. I know Queen Mullineks.'

'But I once read that when you meet your heroes they always let you down.'

'Who says?'

'There was this guy met Sid James. And you know what?'

'What?'

'He was dead.'

'So?'

'He wasn't dead in his movies.'

'Queen Mullineks'd never let me down.'

'Look around you, babe.'

'Why?'

'Just look.'

She did so, taking in the full tasteless glory of it all. She still couldn't believe the place. It was like somewhere from her dreams made real. Failing to see his point, she returned her attention to him. 'I don't see anything.'

'Exactly.'

She watched him, clueless.

He leaned forward, conspiratorially, almond-shaped eyes wide, cigarette in mouth.

She leaned forward accordingly.

His face inches from hers, he looked her in the eyes and said, 'Where are her other customers?'

fifty-nine

'Teena? Are you all right, Teena?'

She didn't answer. Sally hadn't expected her to. Teena lay headless on the floor, stiff as a mannequin, locked in the pose she'd been in when her head had dropped off. The head lay grinning and lifeless on the table. Tentative, Sally prodded it, trying to get a response. It spun slowly from the force of the prod until friction brought it to a gentle halt.

Teena – an android all along? And Sally had never even noticed? But no one had noticed, not her friends, not her relatives, not even her Man Who Does, and he'd seen more of her than anyone.

But what else could have explained her unnatural conceitedness, her lack of empathy with any living being, her belief that insane plans were sensible plans?

Then it hit her, what Teena had said while constructing her Shelleytron; 'Frankenstein's monster and I have much in common.'

She must have been malfunctioning for years. And her

creator was no longer there to fix her. Perhaps he'd died in some lab, like Edward Scissorhands' father. Or perhaps Teena had killed him like she'd killed Mr Landen.

My God! How many people *had* she killed?'

But no. That couldn't be right. Drs Dan and Steve had got DNA from her hair. She must have been real once – or at least her hair had.

Perhaps, bit by bit, she'd replaced her real body parts with machinery. Replacing her hair with rags had been the last part of the process.

Or perhaps she'd just downloaded herself into this machine.

That was it! That explained why a woman clearly rolling in money had chosen a dump like this for a holiday! One last week of boredom before a life time of marital excitement, her eye. She'd come here to visit Uncle Al – her soulmate.

And so . . .

. . . the scientists who'd downloaded her Uncle might be able to repair Teena. However stupid they were they knew about computers. She headed for the door. But from outside came the rumble of a Morris Minor engine being started and, through the window, she saw Steve and Dan's caravan make a quick exit, headed for who knew where.

She checked her watch. The Dullness Inspector was due in twelve minutes.

Perhaps she could reattach the head herself. For the sake of convenience it must have been designed to be reconnectable.

Back at the table, she picked up the head and turned it upside down. It was heavier than she'd expected. It was mostly metal in there. Studying its base, she fingered the spaghetti tangle of wiring which protruded from it. She knew it was hopeless. Even if she could figure out how to

270

reattach it, its wires were burnt out, its fuses melted into each other like cheese.

She let the head drop to the table, pulled out the nearest chair and sat on it. What was she meant to do with a cow brained maniac, a headless scientist, a Dullness Inspector due, and the last dregs of her career vanishing?

But surely Teena wouldn't have had just one head. She'd have had a spare. Even a lunatic like her must have felt she'd need one.

Sally gazed around. A spare head. Where would a girl keep her spare head? On a shelf? By the window? The place was so full of junk, unfinished inventions and abandoned projects, it could be hidden under a pile of anything. She'd keep it somewhere accessible, but out of sight to avoid confusion.

Where, though?

Then she saw it, the closet door in the far corner. The word SPARE had been daubed on it in red paint.

She headed for it. Even if it didn't contain a spare head it at least looked big enough to hide Landen and Teena inside. Sally'd have to hope Dullness Inspectors didn't check cupboards.

At the closet, she rattled the doorknob. It was locked, of course.

She looked around for a tool.

A grubby white tool bag rested by the sink, a crowbar jutting from it. She grabbed the crowbar and jammed it into the gap between door and frame. Jaw set, two-handed, she jemmied.

The lock broke with a loud crack.

She tossed the crowbar aside. It hit the table leg then the floor.

She opened the closet.

And her jaw dropped.

In that cupboard, bound, gagged and hung upside down from a coat hook, was . . .

. . . another Teena?

'. . . And the next thing I knew, I was tied up in the closet.' Didn't she ever shut up? Now stood by the table, Teena rubbed her wrists to restore their circulation as Sally untied her ankles. Teena said, 'It was as though someone had taken control of the Bride of Landen with a mind control machine then got her to knock me out with a pot plant. But who'd want to do such a thing?'

'Want me to get you a phone book?'

'And why was I left in the closet?'

'Who knows?' The final knot was driving Sally mad. It made Spaghetti Junction look like a Roman road. Jaw clenched, she jammed her shoe against Teena's bare foot and gave a sharp tug.

'Do *you mind*?' Teena complained.

'Mind what?' She did it again.

'Your shoe's hurting my foot.'

'Oh excuse me. I'm only the woman trying to save you from killer robots.'

'It's as though I was being stored for future use. But what future use?'

With a huge tug, and just enough foot pressure to inflict the deserved level of pain, Sally yanked the knot free. 'Who cares what some robot did?' She tossed the rope aside then stood up. 'All that matters is we've got eleven minutes. Can you sort out Landen's brain in time?'

Teena turned her attention to the unconscious man on her table. She took the pen light, clicked it on and started

272

checking his big eye. 'Sally, I'm a genius.' She checked his small eye. 'Given eleven minutes, I could swap the brains of every person on Earth.' She shone the light up his nose and peered into it like she could see into his brain cavity.

'I'd rather you restrict your ambitions to people in this room.'

Teena switched off the pen light and placed it on the table. 'Well everything seems in order.'

'Then . . . ?' She was almost afraid to ask.

'Stand back, Sally.' Teena flamboyantly pushed Sally away from her, did all the rubber glove stuff then pulled it onto her hand, with a snap of rubber on flesh. Sally should've complained about the manhandling but was just relieved that Teena's arm hadn't dropped off. Teena pulled the other glove on then flexed her fingers. 'Within ninety seconds, all your troubles will be over.'

Then her head dropped off.

'Teena? Are you all right, Teena?' Of course she wasn't all right. How many times did a woman's head have to fall off before Sally realized she wasn't all right? The second Teena's body lay on the floor, beside the first. The head lay on the table, beside the first, motionless and grinning beside Mr Landen.

Sally pulled out a chair and sat, elbows on table, head in hands, half expecting that to fall off just to make her day complete. Her life was that thing where a monster bursts into your bedroom and, just as it's about to eat you, you wake, relieved to discover it was all a dream. Then a monster bursts in. Then you wake. Then a monster bursts in. Then you wake. Then a monster bursts in. And the whole process repeats itself through eternity.

She looked at the front door, half expecting a third Teena to barge in, bucket in hand, and declare herself here to work miracles, only for her head to drop off before she even got through the door. It didn't happen.

Sally looked across to the open closet. It had room for two bodies at most, no matter how she packed them in. And wasn't that just typical of Teena that everything she owned had to be too big except the one thing she needed to be too big?

She checked her watch. The inspector was due in ten minutes. Not that it mattered. She could hide as many bodies in as many closets as she liked. She was never going to win any safety award. For the first time ever, her uncle had been right about something.

Something flapped in a breeze from under the door.

She ignored it.

It flapped again.

She ignored it.

It flapped again.

So she looked down.

And suddenly she had hope.

That hope was a flapping luggage label tied to a ring through a dead android's nose.

Stood by the kitchen table, Sally told Teena's cell phone, 'I need to talk to someone important.' Holding the first Teena's head, she again checked the luggage label. It said, MY NAME'S TEENA. PLEASE CALL THIS NUMBER IF I GO ON THE RAMPAGE. So she had. It was a slim chance but whoever was behind the original robot must have been a genius, however thick, and a genius was what Sally needed to tell her how to stick the heads back on.

'Hello?' Teena's voice appeared on the phone.

And Sally's heart stopped. 'Teena? You're still alive?' But then she realized, it had the stilted delivery of a pre-recorded message.

'Welcome to the Rama Line. All calls cost forty-nine pence per minute. Forty-five pence goes to charity. If you have the following problem caused by me, and have a touch tone phone, press the following keys . . .

'. . . If you're being dragged around town by a monster brought to life from a comic book, press 1. If your friend wants you to marry a talking rabbit, press 2. If my mother's being a pain in the arse, press 3 . . .'

Come on. Get on with it. Sally prowled back and forth as it ran through a gamut of disasters Teena'd thought herself capable of causing.

At last the list reached, '. . . If your friend now has the wrong brain, press 8-9-6. If I've shrunk you to the size of a germ but your feet are still normal sized, press 8-9-7 . . .'

Hands shaking she pressed 8-9-6.

A beep followed another pause. 'Thank you for calling Rama Line 8-9-6; *My Friend has the Wrong Brain*. You're talking to an interactive computer simulation of Dr Tinashta Ramalalanyrina. All calls are forty-nine pence per minute. Forty-five pence goes to charity. This call should not be viewed as an admission of legal responsibility for the predicament you're in. And remember, all because Dr Ramalalanyrina is cleverer, more beautiful, more charming, more popular and more talented than you, please don't feel in awe of her. View her as your friend and feel free to ask whatever questions you may have, unless they're stupid. Now, what seems to be the problem?'

'Your assistant – Mr Landen – he needs a brain transplant.'

'Do you have both brains to hand?'

She glanced at the table. 'Yes.'

'Do you have Mr Landen to hand?'

'Yes.'

'Do you have a bucket?'

'Yes.'

'Do you have a spade?'

'I'm sorry?' Sally asked.

'A bucket and spade are invaluable tools in brain surgery.'

She glanced around for one but had to conclude that, 'I don't have a spade.'

'Then you'll have to improvise. First remove his upper cranium.'

'How long will this take?' She placed the first android's head on the table. Bending down, she turned the wing nut that locked the top of Landen's head in place.

The Rama Line said, 'One brain transplant? No more than forty seconds.'

'Forty seconds?'

'It's only brain surgery. It's not cookery.'

This was fantastic! When she'd done this she could ask it how to fix the robots. How could she have doubted for a moment that she'd sort out this mess?

She placed the top of his head to one side and, knees still bent, gazed into the brain cavity. It was all cobwebs and dead spiders in there. She flicked aside a Snickers wrapper that blocked her view. 'Now what do I do?'

'Yank out the anomalous brain.'

'Won't that damage it?'

'The human brain's a rubbery substance and, like a superball, may be thrown around without damage.'

276

'Are you sure?'

'Do you have medical qualifications?'

'No.'

'Does Dr Ramalalanyrina?'

'She claimed she did.'

'Then why are you arguing with her?'

Sally propped the phone against one ear, closed her eyes and placed her hands inside his skull. She grabbed the brain, winced at its cold squishiness and, trusting in God, yanked it out.

She kept her eyes shut. It wobbled in her hands like jelly, a cold liquid draining from it and onto her shoes. *Please don't let it be blood.* 'I've removed it. Now what do I do?'

'Drop it into the bucket.'

Eyes still closed, she released it over where she thought the bucket was. It landed on her shoes, with a splat. She opened her eyes. But when she looked down the brain was gone. She looked around for it, spotting no sign of it – anywhere.

The Rama Line said, 'Now upturn the bucket so it covers the brain.'

'I can't do that.' She was still looking for it.

'Sally, if you don't upturn the bucket to trap the brain in then how can you hit it with the spade to stun it so it can't escape?'

'Teena, brains can't escape. They're not wild animals.'

'Where is it now?'

'I-I don't know.' Her heart sank as she looked around. 'It's escaped.'

–sigh– 'Get the replacement.'

She picked up the margarine tub, still looking around. Where the hell was that brain?

The Rama Line said, 'Place it in the subject's skull.'

She did so.

'Put the top of the head back on.'

'Don't I need to connect up nerves or something?'

'I can see you know little of medicine.'

Sally pulled an appropriate face. She took the top of his head, put it in place, aligned it neatly then held it there.

'Now turn the nut that locks it into place.'

She did so.

'Congratulations. You've completed your first brain transplant.'

'That's all there is to it?'

'That's all there is to it.'

She gave a quick laugh. This was unbelievable. Who'd've thought it was so easy to do genius things? An entertainers' assistant? What had she been thinking of? From now on she'd be a brain surgeon. Big money for no work. What was that crap movie Cthulha was always on about? *Doc Hollywood*? That'd be Sally, in Beverly Hills, giving film stars new brains. Now all she had to do was ask about the robots.

And then . . .

. . . she could be a robot scientist!

The Rama Line said, 'Caution. This does not qualify you as a brain surgeon . . .' [Yeah. Right.] '. . . nor legally entitle you to practise professionally within England – though laws are more lax in Beverly Hills. If under sixteen, please seek an adult's permission before attempting any surgery. The service provider accepts no liability for anything that goes wrong as a result of customers not properly following instructions . . .'

Small print. Who cared about that?'

'. . . Under no circumstances attempt to perform this procedure with margarine.'

'What?'

'Under no circumstances attempt to perform this procedure with margarine.'

'But I just have.'

'You have?'

'Yes.'

'Why?'

'Why not?'

An ominous silence followed. It lasted too long. 'Hello?' Sally asked, 'Anyone there?'

No reply. She held the phone at arm's length and watched it, considering bashing it to see if it was broken.

Then the phone spoke.

Hurriedly she pressed it against her ear – in time to hear it say, 'Please press 1-9-2-7: *I've Just Turned My Friend Into a Doomsday Bomb*.'

Her fingers suddenly less nimble than bananas, Sally pressed the appropriate keys on Teena's phone. How the hell could putting margarine in someone's head turn them into a doomsday bomb?

She pressed the phone against her ear. The hissing silence of a line being patched through was followed by, 'Please hold the line, Caller.'

Gnawing at her thumbnail, she waited, too scared of vibrations to start pacing.

Then . . .

Landen started ticking.

Still she waited, a drop of sweat trickling down her forehead then her cheek then her neck. Her heart thumped in her throat. She couldn't breathe, couldn't think. She had to stay calm; not imagine the world being blown up, think of calm things, pleasant things, trees, flowers, birds, streams, birds on fences, birds in trees, birds blown up, reduced to ashes where they stood. She tried to slow her breathing but that just made it faster.

And still the phone said nothing.

Then; 'Thank you for calling line 1-9-2-7; I've Just Turned My Friend into a Doomsday Bomb. All calls cost forty-nine pence per minute. Forty-five pence goes to charity. Now, what seems to be the problem?'

Tick tick tick.

'You've turned your assistant – Mr Landen – into a doomsday bomb,' she gabbled.

'I have no assistant.'

'Your programmer has. And this is ALL HER FAULT!'

'What's this man's current status?'

'Unconscious.'

'How long has he been thus?'

'Thirteen minutes.'

'And how was he rendered unconscious?'

'An indestructible cow fell on him. He's indestructible too.'

'And was that Dr Rama's fault?'

'Yes.'

'She dropped the cow on him?'

'No.'

'She told *you* to drop a cow on him?'

'Look, we don't have time to argue. Just tell me what to do.'

'You have twenty-three minutes to defuse him.'

'Twenty-three?'

'All foodstuffs are volatile under extreme conditions. Though stable in normal usage, when placed inside a human head, most will go nuclear.'

'But he had margarine for a brain before. He didn't go nuclear then.'

'Was the margarine implanted by an expert?'

'He was claimed to be.'

'Food implantation's perfectly safe provided one knows what one's doing.'

'Knows what one's doing? For God's sake, he couldn't spot the difference between it and his brain.'

'Regardless.'

'And he's ticking.'

'He's a time bomb. Upon waking, he'll detonate.'

'But . . . ?'

'Follow all instructions precisely. If you do one thing – one thing – you're told not to, you'll take the world with you. And while you may feel the world deserves such a fate for its treatment of minorities, as a person of ethnicity, Dr Rama would point out that other worlds may well have such skeletons in their–'

'Never mind that bollocks. What do I do?'

'Remove his upper cranium.'

Leaning forward she unscrewed the wing nut. As it came loose, her trembling fingers dropped it. It hit the floor with a clink.

Landen didn't explode.

She sighed with relief.

Carefully she removed his upper cranium.

She placed it to one side.

She looked into his skull. It looked innocuous enough in there. But still there was the ticking, louder now the top of his head was off. 'Now what do I do?'

'Bend forward.'

'I am.'

'Brace yourself.'

'Okay.'

'Take your little finger . . .'
'Yes?'
'Crook it.'
'Okay.'
'Take a deep breath.'
She took a deep breath.
'Take another deep breath.'
She took another deep breath.
'Take another deep breath.'
She took another deep breath.
'Take another deep breath.'
'Can we get on with this please!?!'
'Steady your finger.'
She steadied it as best she could, though it was still shaking all over the place.
'Move that finger forward.'
She moved that finger forward.
'And to defuse him . . .'
'Yes?'
'Simply . . .'
'Yes?'
'Simply . . .'
'Yes?'
'Place that finger in his beep.'
'Place it in his what?'
'Beep.'
'In his beep?' she complained. 'What do you mean in his beep? What the hell's his beep?'
'This service has terminated. Beep.'
'What?'
'Dr Ramalalanyrina went on holiday before completing this program. Beep. Please hang on until her return. Beep. Her hiatus will last a further twelve hours. In the meantime, please enjoy this random selection of easy listening.'

'But she's dead,' she complained as syrupy violins played Nirvana's Lithium, 'Both of her.'

The phone said, 'If you need to talk to her urgently, please contact; The Manager, Uncle Al's Magical Land of Caravans, Wyndham, Yorkshire, England.'

'But that's me, you stupid bitch!'

'Would you like me to send you a letter to her?'

sixty

She'd called the army, the police, the Ministry of Defence, the air force, the navy, the fire brigade, the coast guards, MI5 and MI6, the Pentagon and the Kremlin. For some reason, their numbers were stored on Teena's mobile phone. She'd even tried *Jim'll Fix It*, except they'd said they didn't make it anymore – and no, she didn't want Carol bloody Smillie. The moment she'd told each of them about the human doomsday bomb and the need for them to send someone round quick to defuse him, they all hung up. For God's sake, what do we pay our taxes for? And the BBC, what a waste of a license fee money that'd turned out to be. So much for public service broadcasting.

So that was it, the end of the world, caused by her, Sally Cooper, everyone on the planet wiped out; Cthulha, Mr Bushy, Davey Farrel, Charlie Dunnett, Drs Dan and Steve, everyone she'd known at school, everyone she'd known through work, even Jimmy Lawson, the postman who she'd always hoped would ask her out but never had because he seemed scared of her. And yes, she did realize there were more people on the planet than just those people but she didn't know them.

So she sat on Teena's front steps, elbows on knees, chin on knuckles, awaiting the big bang, Mr Bushy scampering around on her head. She should have been crying but she couldn't. Killing so many people over the last three years had worn out her tear ducts. And Uncle Al – poor Uncle Al who must have loved her really to have put up with her all this time, he was supposed to be immortal and she'd even killed *him*.

But there was one death she was glad about; that bastard Man Who Does. If not for him and his marriage proposals, Teena'd never have gone on holiday and we'd all have been fine. What was it with him? He couldn't have found someone safer to stick his big fat knob in?

Footsteps approached. So what?

The feet stopped just in front of her, wearing dull brown shoes. A voice attached to them said, 'Miss Smith?'

'Sod off.'

'Miss Smith?'

'Sod off.'

'I'm Archie Drizzle, the Dullness Inspector.' He extended a hand for her to shake.

She ignored it, so he withdrew it. 'Miss Smith?'

'What?'

'Is there a problem?'

Without moving, she looked up at him. He stood before her, clipboard in hand, an overweight, middle-aged man with a brown suit, a doctor's bag and a Bobby Charlton combover.

Half hearted, she made her thumb gesture for him to look over her shoulder.

He did so, peering in through Teena's open front door. After a few moments he said, 'What am I looking for?'

'What's on the table?'

'A man,' he said.

'No,' she said.

'No?' He looked at her.

'It's a human doomsday bomb primed to explode within minutes. I created it. That's how safe this place is. So why don't you run along to Bruce Wayne's caravan park and give him the award? That's assuming you can get there before we all go up in smoke.'

He put down his doctor's bag. He took a pen from his inside breast pocket, removed the cap then stuck it on the other end. 'Young lady, do I look like a man who believes in wasting his time?'

She shrugged, not caring.

He grabbed her arm and yanked her to her feet and, as she stared moodily at the ground, said, 'I've travelled a long way to inspect this camp, and that's precisely what I intend to do. As for doomsday bombs, I'll be the judge of how dangerous they are.'

sixty-one

'That's it! I've had enough!' Cthulha flung down the paper napkin she'd spent the last five minutes trying to bend into a pecking bird with flapping wings. Origami, who needed it? It hit the table, a crumpled mess. She pushed her chair backward and stood up. 'I'm going to see what's taking so long with my cow.'

Looking up from his menu, Roddy asked, 'Whatcha gonna do, babe?'

She looked at the black, round windowed door that connected the dining area to the kitchen. 'I'm going to march into that kitchen and demand my cow. And if she doesn't produce one there and then, you know what I'm going to do?'

'Cry?'

'I'm going to lie on her table and stay there till she comes up with the goods. I'd like to see her try cooking with *me* on her preparation table!'

The round windowed door swung back and forth behind her till it creaked to a halt, and Roddy sat awaiting the return of that chick whose name he could never remember. When she didn't return, he put down his menu. He reached across, took her screwed up napkin-monster thing, unfolded it and smoothed it flat on the table. He considered it for a moment then tilted his head to the right. He slapped the left side of his head and his marker pen fell out of his right ear hole. He caught it in one hand. He removed its cap, placed the cap on the pen's blunt end, pulled the napkin nearer to him, hung his tongue out the side of his mouth, hoping no one'd stand on it, and began to draw.

Before any of us was born, Roddy's contemporary, Pablo Picasso, attended Sheffield's world peace conference. While there he stopped in at a local cafe. As payment for his meal, he drew a dove of peace on a paper napkin and donated it to the cafe's delighted owner. It has hung on the wall ever since, framed, in pride of place.

Roddy drew a dinosaur on his napkin, a dinosaur like those he'd seen being taken for a walk on the Common, but larger, much larger, big enough to squash mountains. Once it was done, he'd donate it to that other chick, the one who ran the restaurant. Then, like Picasso's dove of peace, his mountain squashing dinosaur would hang in pride of place forever.

To his right, a guy dressed as Sally Bowles emerged from behind a pair of crushed velvet curtains, violin in hand. But Roddy had reached the drawing's tricky part – the feet. Any artist could tell you feet are difficult. Great artists can never remember whether it's toes that feet have, or fingers. So he gave them twenty of each to be on the safe side.

Sally Bowles coughed into the side of his hand then introduced himself. 'Ladies and gentlemen, my name's Charles Dunnett. Some of you may already know me from my recent arrest on the Common. I can assure you I was merely gathering daffodils for my employer, Mr Bracewell, and any newspaper reports to the contrary are highly speculative.'

Roddy gave the dinosaur's left foot another fifteen fingers. Dinosaurs were big, their feet had more room for fingers. And he gave its right foot a pub, in case it got thirsty.

Undeterred by the lack of audience, Mr Dunnett said, 'By the auspices of the owner, I'll be your host for the evening. Now, to celebrate our grand opening we've a full range of entertainments lined up for you. I hope you'll enjoy them. First we have an act all the way from Tijuana, Mexico. Ladies and gentlemen,' his voice raised to whip up excitement, 'we present the crazy jazz sounds of Senor Lopez and his singing violin.'

Crazy jazz? Did he say crazy jazz? Suddenly Roddy was listening.

With a wave of the hand, Mr Dunnett stepped aside. The velvet curtains swished open to reveal an unlit stage. A spotlight settled on a microphone stand.

Mr Dunnett called across, 'Senor Lopez, if you please?'

The big bunny sitting at the table, far corner, broke off from hypnotizing spoons. He got up and crossed to the stage. At the stage, Mr Dunnett handed him the violin then got out of the way, behind the curtains, though you could still see his tap shoes sticking out from under them.

The bunny climbed on stage. He moved centre stage. He turned to face his audience. He took position behind the microphone. He adjusted the microphone stand. He held the violin ready.

And he placed it on his head.

'What the hell *is* this?' Cthulha stood transfixed with horror, just inside the kitchen doorway.

In the centre of the room, Dr Rama lay face down, out cold on the table, a silly grin on her face. Mullineks stood over her, smiling, Paxo box in hand, ready to climb onto the table and administer it. She said, 'This? This is your meal.'

'I ordered a cow!' said Cthulha.

'This is a cow.'

'No it's not.'

'Yes it is.'

Cthulha strode across to the table. 'It's a scientist. It's not even a good scientist. Sally says all its experiments go wrong and it doesn't even notice. Look at it.' She flicked its head rags. 'It's got no udders. It's got no horns. It doesn't even moo. How does it qualify as cattle?'

'It's on my table.'

'So?'

'Tuesday's Cow Night. If it's on my table, it's cattle.'

'And if I were on your table?'

'You'd be cattle.'

'And if you were on that table?'

'I'd be cattle.'

'And you'd stuff yourself?'

'Of course.' With little grace, Mullineks climbed onto the table. Paxo box in hand, she sat astride the doctor, who still wore the silly grin. Mullineks said, 'All meals must be stuffed.'

'For your information . . .' Cthulha snatched the Paxo box from her and slammed it on the table, '. . . you don't stuff cows.'

'You don't?'

'No.'

Disheartened, Mullineks considered this, watching the doctor as though that might provide inspiration. At last she found some. 'But you do stuff them,' she smirked. 'You stuff them if they've been naughty.'

'And has she been naughty?' Cthulha challenged.

'She's been very naughty.'

'How's she been naughty?'

'My mind control machine didn't work on her, so I couldn't get her to lie on my table. I had to go to the trouble of using it to get her android to knock her out and bring her here. But don't worry, little cow.' She kissed the side of Dr Rama's head. 'I forgive you.'

Cthulha fumed. 'Ordinarily, I'd pay good money to watch this but right now I WANT MY COW!'

'*This* is it.'

'No it's *not*!'

'It's near enough for the likes of you.'

'And what's that supposed to mean?'

'Oh I know your type; loose girls who sleep around before they're married instead of saving themselves for their future husbands like I did. Believe me, if you save yourself you enjoy it so much more.'

'Excuse me!?! You're Queen Mullineks. You can't lecture on sexual morality. And you can't have a husband!'

'Why not?'

'You're queen of the lesbians.'

'And a queen can do whatever she wishes.'

'Show me your license.'

'I need no license to be a lesbian.'

'I meant your license to cook cows.'

'I need no license to cook cows.'

'Everyone needs a license to cook cows. It's the law.'

'Then this shall be my license.' From nowhere, she produced the world's biggest meat cleaver, raised it above her head, like a battle axe, and prepared to bring it down on Dr Rama's neck.

Cthulha punched the side of her head and sent her sprawling.

But this couldn't be right. In *Mad Moon Lesbians Go Cowgirl*, Mullineks had killed a Hell's Angel leader with one punch then challenged the rest of his chapter to a fight. Terrified, they'd climbed on their bikes and rode off while she stood laughing, taunting them for being 'Little Men'. Cthulha shouldn't have been able to send her sprawling; no one should. Married? Punchable? Moral? It was like it had all been make-believe and she was just some woman.

Mullineks was on the floor, on her backside, wiping blood from her lip with the back of her hand. She was twelve feet away from Cthulha. Cthulha closed in on her. Her knuckles felt half broken but so what? She wasn't facing some growth hormone swollen friesian now. She was facing a woman. Women she could beat.

'You hit me,' Mullineks complained from the floor, watching the blood on her hand. Now she looked around for something. She found it. She grabbed it, and Cthulha suddenly realized why starting this fight had been a bad idea.

Meat cleaver in hand, Mullineks launched herself at Cthulha.

sixty-two

Why was she even bothering? In Teena's mobile home, Sally and the Dullness Inspector stood over two dead androids as Landen ticked away on the table.

Clipboard in hand, Mr Drizzle made notes as Sally said, 'This is two androids I killed. I don't know how but it's a safe bet it was my fault. You've probably noticed they had dangerously high beauty levels.'

He simply scribbled more notes.

'Is there really any point going on with this?' Sally asked.

He scribbled more notes and she felt like ramming that stupid clip board down his throat. He said, 'I need to see the whole camp, Miss Cooper.'

So they stood outside by the bins, her looking round to see if anyone was watching. They weren't. She raised the lid of the bin nearest, told him, 'These are our bins,' and gestured for him to take a look.

Before he could, a Terry Thomas voice echoed from within. 'I say, has anyone got a body I could borrow?'

Mr Drizzle looked at Sally.

Sally looked at Mr Drizzle.

They leaned forward and peered into the bin. Eyeballs on stalks, a brain sat at the bin bottom, surrounded by broken glass. Where the hell had *that* come from? It didn't look like the one that had escaped during her brain swap attempt.

And Mr Drizzle scribbled more notes.

'That Rottweiler, if you remove its Easter bonnet, it tears your throat out. And believe me you don't want to go into this restaurant.' Sally's dispiriting tour of the camp finished where it had started, outside Bab's Steakhouse. The mooseheads were going full tilt. Fortunately they'd already discharged their antlers for the evening.

Mr Drizzle scribbled more notes.

She'd have thought it impossible to feel embarrassed when you knew the world was about to end, but showing him round this place had proven her wrong. This had to have been the most humiliating experience of even her life. But at least she'd soon be dead. She said, 'As you can see from the ring I've painted round it, the restaurant isn't technically a part of the caravan park but you'll probably want to count it as such.' Her left foot pointed out the line. The ground outside it was foam rubber. The ground inside was grass.

He scribbled more notes.

She said, 'Its manager cooks people.'

He scribbled more notes. He had to be the most unfazeable man she'd ever met.

She tested him further. 'My uncle says the manager has three eyes and claims to be from outer space. That's ridiculous. I have it on good authority that no one's from outer space.'

He scribbled more notes. Was he for real?

He popped the top back on his pen then placed it in his jacket. He straightened his lapel and then his tie.

And this was it. This is where she got the lecture about how in all his years as Wyndham's safety officer he'd never once met such a disgrace as her.

Maybe at a time like this she should be thinking of bigger issues. But she wasn't.

Clipboard under one arm, he opened his doctor's bag and rummaged around inside, setting various objects rattling. Perhaps he was going to pull a gun and shoot her.

Instead he produced a shapeless lump of tin.

She frowned at it. 'What's that supposed to be?'

He snapped shut his case. 'This, Miss Cooper, is the Dullness Award.'

She watched it. 'Are you going to hit me with it?'

'No.'

'Then . . . ?'

'I'm going to award it to you.'

'You think this place is *safe*?' Sally studied her surroundings, amazed.

Across the way, Mr Bushy launched himself from a caravan roof. Having forgotten to first attach the elastic to his tail, he hit the ground, head first, with a stunned squeak. Then he scampered back up the side of the caravan, and did it again.

Mr Drizzle stood before Sally, award in hand. 'It's clearly a well run camp where all risk has been scrupulously minimized.'

'Where's my cow, you bitch!?!' Broken glass went flying as Bridget Fonda and a mad moon lesbian crashed out through the restaurant window. Fighting to the death, they rolled around on the ground between Sally and Mr Drizzle, first Fonda on top, then the lesbian, then Fonda. They punched, kicked and scratched. Now Mullineks was on top, waving her cleaver. Now Fonda was on top, strangling Mullineks.

Mr Drizzle watched them impassively

It occurred to Sally that she should help Cthulha, her being her 'mother' but, as she was going to die anyway, there didn't seem much point. 'And is *that* safe?' she asked, pointing to the fight.

Lightly gripping her arm, he guided her away from the fight and to a place of safety some five yards away. Once there, he said, 'Mere youthful high jinks. We in the safety profession must always remember not to be killjoys.'

'But that woman's got a meat cleaver.'

'I've seen more dangerous fights.'

'When have you seen more dangerous fights?'

'Godzilla versus Megalon. I really thought Godzilla was done for in that one.'

'Godzilla versus Megalon wasn't real.'

He looked across at the fight. Cthulha was banging Mullineks' head on the ground. As the ground was covered with foam rubber, it wasn't doing the hoped-for damage.

Mr Drizzle said, 'Perhaps it wasn't real, but the costumes were better.'

'Give me that!' Sally snatched the clip board from him and rifled through its pages. What was this? DOOMSDAY BOMB; SAFE? DEAD ANDROIDS; SAFE? DISCARDED

296

BRAIN IN DANGER OF GLASS IMPALEMENT; SAFE? Every single thing she'd shown him, he'd ticked off as safe!?!. 'What's going on here?' she demanded.

'Going on?' He tried to look innocent.

She shoved the clip board back at him. 'You're supposed to be the meanest man in Yorkshire.'

'I am the meanest man in Yorkshire. That's why I appreciate the value of money.'

'You mean . . . ?'

One eyebrow raised, he tapped the side of his nose and gave a half nod. 'Your uncle and I have an understanding.'

She stared at him, incredulous. 'You take bribes?'

'How do you think Wyndham came to have such a terrible safety record when it has a full time safety officer? How do you think the likes of Dynamite Pete, Madam Tallulah and Magic Keith got performance licenses when they were clearly idiots?'

She stared at him, incredulous. 'They all bribed you?'

'Every single one of them. No way should they have been allowed to perform.'

'Then . . . then . . : it's *your* fault they died – not mine.'

'I suppose it is. Still, never mind.'

'Never mind!?! I've gone through hell because of you; guilt, torture, sleepless nights, psychotherapy. If not for you, I wouldn't have this job and I wouldn't be in this mess! And those people who got eaten last year . . . ?'

'Someone may have encouraged me to be a little lax in checking the meat consignment dockets, yes.'

She clenched her right fist, ready to give him the hiding he deserved. 'And haven't you missed something?'

He smirked. 'I don't think so.'

'How're you going to spend Uncle Al's bribe after you've been blown up?'

'Unlike many, I happen to know you can take it with you.'

By the restaurant, the panting Cthulha now sat astride the exhausted Mullineks. Cthulha drew back her arm and, with one great swing, landed the knockout blow. Teeth went flying.

Drizzle ignored the fight's climax (and the fact that Sally was about to start a new one). He adopted an officious stance, cleared his throat, and held the Dullness Award before him. 'Miss Cooper, it gives me great pleasure to declare Uncle Al's Magical Land of Caravans to be the safest caravan park in Wyndham.'

Then an asteroid hit him.

sixty-three

'♪Spooder Yo-Yo. Spooder Yo-Yo. ♪'
  'Can you stop doing that?'
  'Doing what?'
  'Singing, ♪Spooder Yo-Yo. ♪'
  'You're just jealous.'
  'Of what?'
  'My husband.'
  'What husband?'
  'Roddy.'
  'Who's Roddy?'
  'My husband.'
  'What husband?'
'Of course, he doesn't actually know he's my husband; I haven't told him yet. But he'll go along with it – he knows what's good for him. He bought me this the other day.' Cthulha held it up to show her. For the last five minutes, she'd been sat beside Sally, driving a pink toy sports car up and down her shins,

singing some useless jingle everyone else had forgotten decades ago.

But who could believe it? Cthulha was a heroine. That was what the police had said upon learning that her mindless act of violence had rescued the best bit of talent in town and captured the woman responsible for that scandal last year. Like Sally couldn't have caught her – if it had occurred to her.

Now Cthulha waved her toy around: 'Roddy said that as neither of us would ever be able to afford to replace the real car I lost with my job, I should have this instead. It's the only nice thing anyone's ever done for me.'

'What, apart from me giving you all that money over the years – and that time you crashed a car into a lamp-post and I told the police *I'd* been driving, because you were off your head on God knows what?'

'♪Spooder Yo-Yo.♪' She resumed driving the car up and down her leg.

And Sally gave up on her.

Bang bang bash.

They were sat on Teena's front steps, waiting for the 'genius' to sort things out like she'd said she would once she'd got her head together.

Bang bang bang. Slam slam bang bang bash.

Sally winced then gazed over her shoulder at the open door through which the banging emanated. 'What's Teena doing in there?'

'Hitting that short bloke's head on the table.'

'Why?'

'To wear out his indestructibility.'

Slam slam bash.

'She's banging it a lot,' Sally said.

'There's a lot of indestructibility to wear out.'

An agonized scream came from within.

'I think it's worn off,' Cthulha said.

Slam bang bash.

'Dr Rama?' Cthulha called, still playing with the car. 'I think you can stop banging his head now.'

Slam slam bam.

Sally asked Cthulha, 'Why's she so angry with him if she's just put his original brain back in? It was the margarine brain that locked her out.'

Cthulha put the toy car down then hitched up her little black dress to reveal a black suspender. Tucked between it and her thigh was a folded sheet of paper. She took the sheet, unfolded it and, with the heel of her palm, ironed it flat against her lap. 'See this?'

Sally leaned across to see it.

Cthulha said, 'Mr Landen's brain told her he'd design the ideal woman.'

'And?'

'This is it.'

Sally studied the drawing. It showed a smiling girl reclining naked in the style of *The Venus of Urbino* by Titian. 'So?' She shrugged. 'He drew a woman with no clothes on. What did she expect?'

'Sally, have you no eyes? This isn't a woman.'

'It's not?' She studied it closer. It still looked like a woman to her.

Cthulha said, 'It's a love goddess. The only way in which this doesn't match Dr Rama is Dr Rama's got the nose.'

'What nose?'

'How useless are you? It's *the* nose. No one's got a nose as perfectly curved as hers. Whichever angel gave her that nose, I hope she says a prayer of thanks to it every night. She owes it big time.'

'And what does this have to do with the drawing?'

'You know who this is?'

301

'Obviously not.'

'It's her sister.'

Bang slam bash.

'Spurred on by this slight,' Cthulha said, 'Dr Rama decided the short bloke should have wanted her. So she made a copy of herself for him. But it knocked her out with a pot plant. Having got her out of the way, it acted like she would and made a copy of itself. The second copy then aped the first and knocked it out, hiding it in the closet. I'm amazed you didn't figure all this out at the time.'

'Then what was that pile of junk in the corner?'

'A pile of junk.'

'Cthulha?'

'Yeah?'

'How do you know all this?'

'Because, while you were stood gaping at asteroids, feeling sorry for yourself, I was reviving and talking to the good doctor . . .'

Bang slam bash.

'. . . and clearly she's a woman to hold a grudge.' Cthulha refolded the paper, hitched up her dress and popped the paper back in her suspender belt for 'future use'. She released the suspender with a Carry On twang then resumed running the toy car up and down her shin. 'Spooder Yo-Yo .'

Sally studied her Dullness Award and sighed.

'What's up?' asked Cthulha.

'I feel like a fraud.'

'Yeah. Right. You've won six hundred grand and an award. I've never won an award in my life.'

'But I only won it because Uncle Al bribed the inspector. And I killed him.'

'Wyndham's in a cosmic flight path. Every twenty years

302

or so someone gets hit by an asteroid. You can't blame yourself for that. Even Lizzie Henthorpe wouldn't have blamed you for that – and she blamed everyone for everything. Anyway, he was asking for it – all those people he got eaten. Ugh!'

'Ugh? Excuse me, but when it was announced on the radio as to where that meat had come from, halfway through us eating it, I threw up on the floor and you grabbed my plate, saying, "Does that mean you won't be eating this?" before polishing the lot off, gravy and all.'

'No! Excuse me! Not all of us grew up in a fancy house and due to inherit a caravan park fortune. Where I grew up we were encouraged to eat what was on the table and be grateful for it.'

'My god, I didn't dare turn my back on you for a month afterwards, in case you tried chewing on me.'

'Yeah, as if a pasty-faced wreck like you'd be worth eating. Now, that Dr Rama, she'd be a meal.'

'I think I'm going to chuck.'

'And you've a tape of that Dullness Inspector confessing he was to blame for all those other deaths. So now you can apply for jobs as an entertainers' assistant, with proof you're not dangerous.'

'Cthulha, I don't have a taped confession. And I was the only witness.'

'Then what's that over there?' She nodded towards the restaurant, and the security camera above its door. 'The entire thing's on videotape. All you have to do is hire a lip reader.'

'Sally?' Behind her, Teena emerged from indoors.

Sally stood, and turned to face her. Before Teena could speak, Sally snapped, 'And I hope you've learned your lesson.'

'Which is?' Stood at the top of the steps, Teena removed her surgical gloves.

'To be more choosy where you let men stick things.'

'I take it you mean my fiancé?'

'If not for your desperation for a good knobbing . . .'

'Why thank you, Sally, that certainly was a valuable lesson.' And she pointedly dropped the rubber gloves onto the mobile home's steps, knowing it was Sally's job to clear up anything dropped outside a residence. Teena said, 'On a more important note, you'll be pleased to hear Mr Landen's no longer indestructible, nor explosive. And he has his original brain back – if you regard that as an improvement.'

'And how is he?'

'He's currently . . .' she gazed around evasively, '. . ."resting".'

'And the Dullness Inspector?'

'What about him?'

'When do you bring him back to life?'

'I don't.'

'But the Shelleytron–'

'Is for reviving people *I've* killed.'

'But . . .'

'I can't revive others. If I revived one corpse, I'd have to revive them all. Then where would we be in a town full of living corpses?'

Cthulha said, 'Mabelthorpe.'

Sally said, 'But . . .'

Teena said, 'Sally, look at him.'

So she turned to watch the smoking, hissing, caravan-sized asteroid ten yards away. Mr Drizzle lay somewhere beneath it. 'What about him?'

'He's been squashed flat. I don't think he'd want to live squashed flat, do you?'

'Can't you pump him up?'

'Pardon?' Teena sounded non plussed.

'Can't you pump him up?' Sally turned to face her. 'With air?'

Teena watched her, stone faced. 'Sally, this isn't a cartoon.'

'But I thought you could do anything.'

'I can't do Tom and Jerry things.'

'Oh.' Now she felt stupid.

Teena said, 'I believe there's a couple of "scientists" I need a word with about unauthorized cloning. While I'm there I'll put the sentient margarine in the brainless cow. I suspect margarine would be happier as a cow than a brain scientist. Then everything'll be sorted out, I can return home for my wedding, and EVERYONE WILL BE HAPPY.'

Cthulha stood up, turned towards Teena, paused to run the rule over her, then straightened her dress with a two handed tug and tried to look her best despite the bruised cheek, grazed chin and black eye. 'Dr Rama?' She did her Bridget grin.

Teena looked at her. 'Capgras Syndrome.'

'What is?'

'Your belief that your boyfriend's been replaced by an alien.'

'Never mind that. I prefer him that way. Being small makes him easier to push around. But, Dr Rama, I've been thinking.'

'Call me Teena.'

'I'd rather imagine you as a doctor, with a cold stethoscope and warm fingers.'

'Can I be of help?'

'You may have noticed I'm an attractive woman without the need for unsightly aerobics.'

Teena looked her up and down. 'I suppose you are,

though, for some reason, when I look at you, I can't help thinking of glove puppets. Have you ever been a children's entertainer?'

Cthulha's eyes narrowed to angry slits, a slighted tension gripped her smile. 'I was thinking.'

'Uh huh?'

'Would you say I saved your life?'

'I suppose you did. Thank you. Though I'm sure I'd have escaped anyway.'

'While unconscious?'

'That's right.'

'Face down on a table?'

'That's right.'

'Mouth open, tongue hanging out, dribbling like an idiot?'

'Is there a point to this?'

'Too right there is.'

'Which is?'

'Round here, we have a law.'

'Just one?'

'We're not very good at laws. The one we have relates to this being a coastal town . . .'

Sally groaned, knowing what was coming next.

Cthulha continued, '. . . and also a big gay resort. It involves coast guards and flat-stomached sailor boys; the pick of the ship's crew.'

Teena said, 'Keep going.'

Cthulha told Teena's chest. 'Round here, if someone saves your life . . .'

'Yes?'

'You have to be their rumpy pumpy boing boing toy for sixty-six and a half days.'

Teena frowned at her. '"Rumpy pumpy boing boing toy"?'

Cthulha looked her up and down, suggestively. 'I reckon you could do "boing boing toy".'

Teena looked at Sally. 'Is this true?'

Sally shrugged, embarrassed. 'Well, sort of. It's based on the belief that all sailors and most coast guards are gay. The man who thought it up also built all Wyndham's tower blocks. That was before anyone'd noticed the whole council were morons.'

Teena said, 'That'd explain why there's an impenetrable line of tower blocks between the beach and sea.'

'The council thought it'd look continental,' Cthulha told Teena's chest. 'So; should I apply the ice cube before or after the blindfold?'

'Before.'

'You . . . you mean it?' Cthulha stared at her, gaze flickering over Teena's face, clearly amazed by her luck. In fifteen years of trying, she'd not managed to pull one woman, due to her having no understanding at all of the way the female mind works.

'No,' Teena stated bluntly. 'I don't mean it. Frankly, I'd rather be decapitated.'

Cthulha pushed her. Teena pushed *her*. Cthulha pushed her back. Teena pushed *her* back. Cthulha's attempts at female seduction always ended in a shoving match. Sally had tried to tell her, frequently, 'Cthulha, women aren't like men. They won't let you seduce them if you push them.' But she'd never listen.

As their quarrel continued, Sally claimed a seat on the bottom step and studied her Dullness Award. And maybe it was the ugliest thing she'd ever seen. Maybe it was only tin. But Cthulha was right; it was hers and she should be proud of that. Now all she had to do was decide where to put it. Maybe on her mantelpiece, beside her art deco woman whose upper half Cthulha had once snapped off then superglued back on the wrong way round, swearing it'd double the value. Then she'd snapped the head off and stuck it on the right way round, saying it'd triple the value. Then she'd snapped a leg off and glued it to the head, claiming it'd quadruple the value. Then it'd turned out she hadn't known the difference between art deco and Salvador Dali.

But one thing still bothered Sally. 'Excuse me,' she interrupted Teena and Cthulha's over-heated debate on the enforceability of laws passed by morons.

They stopped arguing, and looked at her.

Sally said, 'Isn't there still a brain missing?'

Like a collie dog, the escaped brain scampered across the lawns of Uncle Al's mansion, barging aside whatever strolling herons got in his way. He went back and knocked over some more, then more, till they were all gone. He scampered on.

His goal came in sight, the gleaming Spooder Yo-Yo parked at the end of Bracewell's drive. Oh yes, he'd planned this well. Always leave yourself an escape route. And he'd left himself the best.

Reaching the car, he hopped on board and landed on the front seat, ready to grab the wheel and drive. Thanks to Roddy McDoddy's alien technology, it could do six hundred miles an hour and a thousand miles to the pint. Nothing would be able to catch him, nothing. Then, when he'd had time to regroup and recover, to get a new body and set up base, he'd begin anew his plans for world repopulation.

He jumped onto the steering wheel, put the key in the

ignition and turned it. The engine roared to life. Through the steering column, he felt the rumble of immeasurable power.

Now no one could stop him.

He looked down.

. . . All he had to do was work out how to reach the pedals.

FLERTIE THE DYNASORE GATHERS
DAISIES IN THE HIMMERLAYERS.

R. McDottly
2006